MB

W9-CBG-937

EVERYTHING
I NEVER TOLD YOU

This Large Print Book carries the
Seal of Approval of N.A.V.H.

EVERYTHING
I NEVER TOLD YOU

CELESTE NG

THORNDIKE PRESS

A part of Gale, Cengage Learning

GALE
CENGAGE Learning®

Farmington Hills, Mich • San Francisco • New York • Waterville, Maine
Meriden, Conn • Mason, Ohio • Chicago

LIBRARY OF CONGRESS CATALOGING-IN-PUBLICATION DATA

Ng, Celeste.
    Everything I never told you / by Celeste Ng. — Large print edition.
        pages ; cm. — (Thorndike Press large print reviewers' choice)
    ISBN 978-1-4104-7245-8 (hardcover) — ISBN 1-4104-7245-0 (hardcover)
    1. Large type books. 2. Daughter—Death—Fiction. 3. Drowning—Fiction.
4. Grief—Fiction. I. Title.
PS3614.G83E94 2014b
813'.6—dc23   2014021142

Published in 2014 by arrangement with The Penguin Press, a member of Penguin Group (USA) LLC, a Penguin Random House Company

Printed in Mexico
1 2 3 4 5 6 7 18 17 16 15 14

for my family

ONE

Lydia is dead. But they don't know this yet. 1977, May 3, six thirty in the morning, no one knows anything but this innocuous fact: Lydia is late for breakfast. As always, next to her cereal bowl, her mother has placed a sharpened pencil and Lydia's physics homework, six problems flagged with small ticks. Driving to work, Lydia's father nudges the dial toward WXKP, Northwest Ohio's Best News Source, vexed by the crackles of static. On the stairs, Lydia's brother yawns, still twined in the tail end of his dream. And in her chair in the corner of the kitchen, Lydia's sister hunches moon-eyed over her cornflakes, sucking them to pieces one by one, waiting for Lydia to appear. It's she who says, at last, "Lydia's taking a long time today."

Upstairs, Marilyn opens her daughter's door and sees the bed unslept in: neat hospital corners still pleated beneath the comforter, pillow still fluffed and convex. Nothing seems out of place. Mustard-colored corduroys tangled on the floor, a single rainbow-striped sock. A row of science fair ribbons on the wall, a postcard of Einstein. Lydia's duffel bag crumpled on the floor of the closet. Lydia's green bookbag slouched against her desk. Lydia's bottle of Baby Soft atop the dresser, a sweet, powdery, loved-baby scent still in the air. But no Lydia.

Marilyn closes her eyes. Maybe, when she opens them, Lydia will be there, covers pulled over her head as usual, wisps of hair trailing from beneath. A grumpy lump bundled under the bedspread that she'd somehow missed before. *I was in the bathroom, Mom. I went downstairs for some water. I was lying right here all the time.* Of course, when she looks, nothing has changed. The closed curtains glow like a blank television screen.

Downstairs, she stops in the doorway of the kitchen, a hand on each side of the frame. Her silence says everything. "I'll check outside," she says at last. "Maybe for some reason —" She keeps her gaze trained on the floor as she heads for the front door, as if Lydia's footprints might be crushed into the hall runner.

8

Nath says to Hannah, "She was in her room last night. I heard her radio playing. At eleven thirty." He stops, remembering that he had not said goodnight.

"Can you be kidnapped if you're sixteen?" Hannah asks.

Nath prods at his bowl with a spoon. Cornflakes wilt and sink into clouded milk.

Their mother steps back into the kitchen, and for one glorious fraction of a second Nath sighs with relief: there she is, Lydia, safe and sound. It happens sometimes — their faces are so alike you'd see one in the corner of your eye and mistake her for the other: the same elfish chin and high cheekbones and left-cheek dimple, the same thin-shouldered build. Only the hair color is different, Lydia's ink-black instead of their mother's honey-blond. He and Hannah take after their father — once a woman stopped the two of them in the grocery store and asked, "Chinese?" and when they said yes, not wanting to get into halves and wholes, she'd nodded sagely. "I knew it," she said. "By the eyes." She'd tugged the corner of each eye outward with a fingertip. But Lydia, defying genetics, somehow has her mother's blue eyes, and they know this is one more reason she is their mother's favorite. And their father's, too.

Then Lydia raises one hand to her brow and becomes his mother again.

"The car's still here," she says, but Nath had known it would be. Lydia can't drive; she doesn't even have a learner's permit yet. Last week she'd surprised them all by failing the exam, and their father wouldn't even let her sit in the driver's seat without it. Nath stirs his cereal, which has turned to sludge at the bottom of his bowl. The clock in the front hall ticks, then strikes seven thirty. No one moves.

"Are we still going to school today?" Hannah asks.

Marilyn hesitates. Then she goes to her purse and takes out her keychain with a show of efficiency. "You've both missed the bus. Nath, take my car and drop Hannah off on your way." Then: "Don't worry. We'll find out what's going on." She doesn't look at either of them. Neither looks at her.

When the children have gone, she takes a mug from the cupboard, trying to keep her hands still. Long ago, when Lydia was a baby, Marilyn had once left her in the living room, playing on a quilt, and went into the kitchen for a cup of tea. She had been only eleven months old. Marilyn took the kettle off the stove and turned to find Lydia standing in the doorway. She had started and set

10

her hand down on the hot burner. A red, spiral welt rose on her palm, and she touched it to her lips and looked at her daughter through watering eyes. Standing there, Lydia was strangely alert, as if she were taking in the kitchen for the first time. Marilyn didn't think about missing those first steps, or how grown up her daughter had become. The thought that flashed through her mind wasn't *How did I miss it?* but *What else have you been hiding?* Nath had pulled up and wobbled and tipped over and toddled right in front of her, but she didn't remember Lydia even beginning to stand. Yet she seemed so steady on her bare feet, tiny fingers just peeking from the ruffled sleeve of her romper. Marilyn often had her back turned, opening the refrigerator or turning over the laundry. Lydia could have begun walking weeks ago, while she was bent over a pot, and she would not have known.

She had scooped Lydia up and smoothed her hair and told her how clever she was, how proud her father would be when he came home. But she'd felt as if she'd found a locked door in a familiar room: Lydia, still small enough to cradle, had secrets. Marilyn might feed her and bathe her and coax her legs into pajama pants, but already parts of her life were curtained off. She kissed Lydia's cheek and pulled her close, trying to warm herself against her daughter's small body.

Now Marilyn sips tea and remembers that surprise.

The high school's number is pinned to the corkboard beside the refrigerator, and Marilyn pulls the card down and dials, twisting the cord around her finger while the phone rings.

"Middlewood High," the secretary says on the fourth ring. "This is Dottie."

She recalls Dottie: a woman built like a sofa cushion, who still wore her fading red hair in a beehive. "Good morning," she begins, and falters. "Is my daughter in class this morning?"

Dottie makes a polite cluck of impatience. "To whom am I speaking, please?"

It takes her a moment to remember her own name. "Marilyn. Marilyn Lee. My daughter is Lydia Lee. Tenth grade."

"Let me look up her schedule. First period —" A pause. "Eleventh-grade physics?"

"Yes, that's right. With Mr. Kelly."

"I'll have someone run down to that classroom and check." There's a thud as the secretary sets the receiver down on the desk.

Marilyn studies her mug, the pool of water

it has made on the counter. A few years ago, a little girl had crawled into a storage shed and suffocated. After that the police department sent a flyer to every house: *If your child is missing, look for him right away. Check washing machines and clothes dryers, automobile trunks, toolsheds, any places he might have crawled to hide. Call police immediately if your child cannot be found.*

"Mrs. Lee?" the secretary says. "Your daughter was not in her first-period class. Are you calling to excuse her absence?"

Marilyn hangs up without replying. She replaces the phone number on the board, her damp fingers smudging the ink so that the digits blur as if in a strong wind, or underwater.

She checks every room, opening every closet. She peeks into the empty garage: nothing but an oil spot on the concrete and the faint, heady smell of gasoline. She's not sure what she's looking for: Incriminating footprints? A trail of breadcrumbs? When she was twelve, an older girl from her school had disappeared and turned up dead. Ginny Barron. She'd worn saddle shoes that Marilyn had desperately coveted. She'd gone to the store to buy cigarettes for her father, and two days later they found her body by the side of the road, halfway to Charlottesville, strangled and naked.

Now Marilyn's mind begins to churn. The summer of Son of Sam has just begun — though the papers have only recently begun to call him by that name — and, even in Ohio, headlines blare the latest shooting. In a few months, the police will catch David Berkowitz, and the country will focus again on other things: the death of Elvis, the new Atari, Fonzie soaring over a shark. At this moment, though, when dark-haired New Yorkers are buying blond wigs, the world seems to Marilyn a terrifying and random place. Things like that don't happen here, she reminds herself. Not in Middlewood, which calls itself a city but is really just a tiny college town of three thousand, where driving an hour gets you only to Toledo, where a Saturday night out means the roller rink or the bowling alley or the drive-in, where even Middlewood Lake, at the center of town, is really just a glorified pond. (She is wrong about this last one: it is a thousand feet across, and it is deep.) Still, the small of her back prickles, like beetles marching down her spine.

Inside, Marilyn pulls back the shower curtain, rings screeching against rod, and stares at the white curve of the bathtub. She searches all the cabinets in the kitchen. She looks inside the pantry, the coat closet, the oven. Then she opens the refrigerator and peers inside. Olives. Milk. A pink foam package of chicken, a head of iceberg, a cluster of jade-colored grapes. She touches the cool glass of the peanut butter jar and closes the door, shaking her head. As if Lydia would somehow be inside.

Morning sun fills the house, creamy as lemon chiffon, lighting the insides of cupboards and empty closets and clean, bare floors. Marilyn looks down at her hands, empty too and almost aglow in the sunlight. She lifts the phone and dials her husband's number.

For James, in his office, it is still just another Tuesday, and he clicks his pen against his teeth. A line of smudgy typing teeters slightly uphill: *Serbia was one of the most powerful of the Baltic nations.* He crosses out *Baltic,* writes *Balkan,* turns the page. *Archduke France Ferdinand was assassinated by members of Black Ann.* Franz, he thinks. Black *Hand.* Had these students ever opened their books? He pictures himself at the front of the lecture hall, pointer in hand, the map of Europe unfurled behind him. It's an intro class, "America and the World Wars"; he doesn't expect depth of knowledge or critical insight. Just a basic understanding of the facts, and one student who can spell *Czechoslovakia* correctly.

He closes the paper and writes the score on the front page — sixty-five out of one hundred — and circles it. Every year as summer approaches, the students shuffle and rustle; sparks of resentment sizzle up like flares, then sputter out against the windowless walls of the lecture hall. Their papers grow halfhearted, paragraphs trailing off, sometimes midsentence, as if the students could not hold a thought that long. Was it a waste, he wonders. All the lecture notes he's honed, all the color slides of MacArthur and Truman and the maps of Guadalcanal. Nothing more than funny names to giggle at, the whole course just one more requirement to check off the list before they graduated. What else could he expect from this place? He stacks the paper with the others and drops the pen on top. Through the window he can see the small green quad and three kids in blue jeans tossing a Frisbee.

When he was younger, still junior faculty, James was often mistaken for a student himself. That hasn't happened in years. He'll be forty-six next spring; he's tenured, a few silver hairs now mixed in among the black. Sometimes, though, he's still mistaken for other things. Once, a receptionist at the provost's office thought he was a visiting diplomat from Japan and asked him about his flight from Tokyo. He enjoys the surprise on people's faces when he tells them he's a professor of American history. "Well, I *am* American," he says when people blink, a barb of defensiveness in his tone.

Someone knocks: his teaching assistant, Louisa, with a stack of papers.

"Professor Lee. I didn't mean to bother you, but your door was open." She sets the essays on his desk and pauses. "These weren't very good."

"No. My half weren't either. I was hoping you had all the As in your stack."

Louisa laughs. When he'd first seen her, in his graduate seminar last term, she'd surprised him. From the back she could have been his daughter: they had almost the same hair, hanging dark and glossy down to the shoulder blades, the same way of sitting with elbows pulled in close to the body. When she turned around, though, her face was completely her own, narrow where Lydia's was wide, her eyes brown and steady. "Professor Lee?" she had said, holding out her hand. "I'm Louisa Chen." Eighteen years at Middlewood College, he'd thought, and here was the first Oriental student he'd ever had. Without realizing it, he had found himself smiling.

Then, a week later, she came to his office. "Is that your family?" she'd asked, tilting the photo on his desk toward her. There was a pause as she studied it. Everyone did the same thing, and that was why he kept the photo on display. He watched her eyes move from his photographic face to his wife's, then his children's, then back again. "Oh," she said after a moment, and he could tell she was trying to hide her confusion. "Your wife's — not Chinese?"

It was what everyone said. But from her he had expected something different.

"No," he said, and straightened the frame so that it faced her a little more squarely, a perfect forty-five-degree angle to the front of the desk. "No, she isn't."

Still, at the end of the fall semester, he'd asked her to act as a grader for his under-graduate lecture. And in April, he'd asked her to be the teaching assistant for his summer course.

"I hope the summer students will be better," Louisa says now. "A few people insisted that the Cape-to-Cairo Railroad was in Europe. For college students, they have surprising trouble with geography."

"Well, this isn't Harvard, that's for sure," James says. He pushes the two piles of essays into one and evens them, like a deck of cards, against the desktop. "Sometimes I wonder if it's all a waste."

"You can't blame yourself if the students don't try. And they're not all so bad. A few got As." Louisa blinks at him, her eyes suddenly serious. "Your life is not a waste."

James had meant only the intro course, teaching these students who, year after year, didn't care to learn even the basic timeline. She's twenty-three, he thinks; she knows nothing about life, wasted or otherwise. But it's a nice thing to hear.

"Stay still," he says. "There's something in your hair." Her hair is cool and a little damp, not quite dry from her morning shower. Louisa holds quite still, her eyes open and fixed on his face. It's not a flower petal, as he'd first thought. It's a lady-bug, and as he picks it out, it tiptoes, on thread-like yellow legs, to hang upside down from his fingernail.

"Damn things are everywhere this time of year," says a voice from the doorway, and James looks up to see Stanley Hewitt leaning through. He doesn't like Stan — a florid ham hock of a man who talks to him loudly and slowly, as if he's hard of hearing, who

19

makes stupid jokes that start *George Wash-ington, Buffalo Bill, and Spiro Agnew walk into a bar . . .*

"Did you want something, Stan?" James asks. He's acutely conscious of his hand, index finger and thumb outstretched as if pointing a popgun at Louisa's shoulder, and pulls it back.

"Just wanted to ask a question about the dean's latest memo," Stanley says, holding up a mimeographed sheet. "Didn't mean to interrupt anything."

"I have to get going anyway," Louisa says. "Have a nice morning, Professor Lee. I'll see you tomorrow. You too, Professor Hewitt." As she slides past Stanley into the hallway, James sees that she's blushing, and his own face grows hot. When she is gone, Stanley seats himself on the corner of James's desk.

"Good-looking girl," he says. "She'll be your assistant this summer too, no?"

"Yes." James unfolds his hand as the ladybug moves onto his fingertip, walking the path of his fingerprint, around and around in whorls and loops. He wants to smash his fist into the middle of Stanley's grin, to feel Stanley's slightly crooked front tooth slice his knuckles. Instead he smashes the ladybug with his thumb. The shell snaps between his fingers, like a popcorn hull, and the insect crumbles to sulfur-colored powder. Stanley keeps running his finger along the spines of James's books. Later James will long for the ignorant calm of this moment, for that last second when Stan's leer was the worst problem on his mind. But for now, when the phone rings, he is so relieved at the interruption that at first he doesn't hear the anxiety in Marilyn's voice.

"James?" she says. "Could you come home?"

The police tell them lots of teenagers leave home with no warning. Lots of times, they say, the girls are mad at their parents and the parents don't even know. Nath watches them circulate in his sister's room. He expects talcum powder and feather dusters, sniffing dogs, magnifying glasses. Instead the policemen just *look:* at the posters thumbtacked above her desk, the shoes on the floor, the half-opened bookbag. Then the younger one places his palm on the rounded pink lid of Lydia's perfume bottle, as if cupping a child's head in his hand.

Most missing-girl cases, the older policeman tells them, resolve themselves within twenty-four hours. The girls come home by themselves.

"What does that mean?" Nath says. "*Most?* What does that mean?"

The policeman peers over the top of his bifocals. "In the vast majority of cases," he says.

"Eighty percent?" Nath says. "Ninety? Ninety-five?"

"Nathan," James says. "That's enough. Let Officer Fiske do his work."

The younger officer jots down the particulars in his notebook: Lydia Elizabeth Lee, sixteen, last seen Monday May 2, flowered halter-neck dress, parents James and Marilyn Lee. At this Officer Fiske studies James closely, a memory surfacing in his mind.

"Now, your wife also went missing once?" he says. "I remember the case. In sixty-six, wasn't it?"

Warmth spreads along the back of James's neck, like sweat dripping behind his ears. He is glad, now, that Marilyn is waiting by the phone downstairs. "That was a misunderstanding," he says stiffly. "A miscommunication between my wife and myself. A family matter."

"I see." The older officer pulls out his own pad and makes a note, and James raps his knuckle against the corner of Lydia's desk.

"Anything else?"

In the kitchen, the policemen flip through

the family albums looking for a clear head shot. "This one," Hannah says, pointing. It's a snapshot from last Christmas. Lydia had been sullen, and Nath had tried to cheer her up, to blackmail a smile out of her through the camera. It hadn't worked. She sits next to the tree, back against the wall, alone in the shot. Her face is a dare. The directness of her stare, straight out of the page with not even a hint of profile, says *What are you looking at?* In the picture, Nath can't distinguish the blue of her irises from the black of her pupils, her eyes like dark holes in the shiny paper. When he'd picked up the photos at the drugstore, he had regretted capturing this moment, the hard look on his sister's face. But now, he admits, looking at the photograph in Hannah's hand, this looks like her — at least, the way she looked when he had seen her last.

"Not that one," James says. "Not with Lydia making a face like that. People will think she looks like that all the time. Pick a nice one." He flips a few pages and pries out the last snapshot. "This one's better."

At her sixteenth birthday, the week before, Lydia sits at the table with a lipsticked smile. Though her face is turned toward the camera, her eyes are looking at something outside the photo's white border. What's so funny? Nath wonders. He can't remember if it was him, or something their father said, or if Lydia was laughing to herself about something none of the rest of them knew. She looks like a model in a magazine ad, lips dark and sharp, a plate of perfectly frosted cake poised on a delicate hand, having an improbably good time.

James pushes the birthday photo across the table toward the policemen, and the younger one slides it into a manila folder and stands up.

"This will be just fine," he says. "We'll make up a flyer in case she doesn't turn up by tomorrow. Don't worry. I'm sure she will." He leaves a fleck of spit on the photo album page and Hannah wipes it away with her finger.

"She wouldn't just leave," Marilyn says. "What if it's some crazy? Some psycho kidnapping girls?" Her hand drifts to that morning's newspaper, still lying in the center of the table.

"Try not to worry, ma'am," Officer Fiske says. "Things like that, they hardly ever happen. In the vast majority of cases —" He glances at Nath, then clears his throat. "The girls almost always come home."

When the policemen have gone, Marilyn

24

and James sit down with a piece of scratch paper. The police have suggested they call all of Lydia's friends, anyone who might know where she's gone. Together they construct a list: Pam Saunders. Jenn Pittman. Shelley Brierley. Nath doesn't correct them, but these girls have never been Lydia's friends. Lydia has been in school with them since kindergarten, and now and then they call, giggly and shrill, and Lydia shouts through the line, "I got it." Some evenings she sits for hours on the window seat on the landing, the phone base cradled in her lap, receiver wedged between ear and shoulder. When their parents walk by, she lowers her voice to a confidential murmur, twirling the cord around her little finger until they go away. This, Nath knows, is why his parents write their names on the list with such confidence.

But Nath's seen Lydia at school, how in the cafeteria she sits silent while the others chatter; how, when they've finished copying her homework, she quietly slides her notebook back into her bookbag. After school, she walks to the bus alone and settles into the seat beside him in silence. Once, he had stayed on the phone line after Lydia picked up and heard not gossip, but his sister's voice duly rattling off assignments — *read*

Act I of Othello, *do the odd-numbered prob-lems in Section 5* — then quiet after the hang-up click. The next day, while Lydia was curled on the window seat, phone pressed to her ear, he'd picked up the extension in the kitchen and heard only the low drone of the dial tone. Lydia has never really had friends, but their parents have never known. If their father says, "Lydia, how's Pam doing?" Lydia says, "Oh, she's great, she just made the pep squad," and Nath doesn't contradict her. He's amazed at the stillness in her face, the way she can lie without even a raised eyebrow to give her away.

Except he can't tell his parents that now. He watches his mother scribble names on the back of an old receipt, and when she says to him and Hannah, "Anyone else you can think of?" he thinks of Jack and says no.

All spring, Lydia has been hanging around Jack — or the other way around. Every afternoon, practically, driving around in that Beetle of his, coming home just in time for dinner, when she pretended she'd been at school all the time. It had emerged sud-denly, this friendship — Nath refused to use any other word. Jack and his mother have lived on the corner since the first grade, and once Nath thought they could be friends. It hadn't turned out that way. Jack had humiliated him in front of the other kids, had laughed when Nath's mother was gone, when Nath had thought she might never come back. As if, Nath thinks now, as if Jack had any right to be talking, when he had no father. All the neighbors had whispered about it when the Wolffs had moved in, how Janet Wolff was *divorced*, how Jack ran wild while she worked late shifts at the hospital. That summer, they'd whispered about Nath's parents, too — but Nath's mother had come back. Jack's mother was still divorced. And Jack still ran wild.

And now? Just last week, driving home from an errand, he'd seen Jack out walking that dog of his. He had come around the lake, about to turn onto their little dead-end street, when he saw Jack on the path by the bank, tall and lanky, the dog loping just ahead of him toward a tree. Jack was wearing an old, faded T-shirt and his sandy curls stood up, unbrushed. As Nath drove past, Jack looked up and gave the merest nod of the head, a cigarette clenched in the corner of his mouth. The gesture, Nath had thought, was less one of greeting than of recognition. Beside Jack, the dog had stared him in the eye and casually lifted its leg.

And Lydia had spent all spring with him.

If he says anything now, Nath thinks, they'll say, *Why didn't we know about this before?* He'll have to explain that all those afternoons when he'd said, "Lydia's studying with a friend," or "Lydia's staying after to work on math," he had really meant, *She's with Jack* or *She's riding in Jack's car* or *She's out with him god knows where.* More than that: saying Jack's name would mean admitting something he doesn't want to. That Jack was a part of Lydia's life at all, that he'd been part of her life for months.

Across the table, Marilyn looks up the numbers in the phone book and reads them out; James does the calling, carefully and slowly, clicking the dial around with one finger. With each call his voice becomes more confused. *No? She didn't mention anything to you, any plans? Oh. I see. Well. Thank you anyway.* Nath studies the grain of the kitchen table, the open album in front of him. The missing photo leaves a gap in the page, a clear plastic window showing the blank white lining of the cover. Their mother runs her hand down the column of the phone book, staining her fingertip gray. Under cover of the tablecloth, Hannah stretches her legs and touches one toe to Nath's. A toe of comfort. But he doesn't look up. Instead he closes the album, and across the table, his mother crosses another name off the list.

When they've called the last number, James puts the telephone down. He takes the slip of paper from Marilyn and crosses out *Karen Adler,* bisecting the K into two neat Vs. Under the line he can still see the name. Karen Adler. Marilyn never let Lydia go out on weekends until she'd finished all her schoolwork — and by then, it was usually Sunday afternoon. Sometimes, those Sunday afternoons, Lydia met her friends at the mall, wheedling a ride: "A couple of us are going to the movies. *Annie Hall.* Karen is *dying* to see it." He'd pull a ten from his wallet and push it across the table to her, meaning: *All right, now go and have some fun.* He realizes now that he had never seen a ticket stub, that for as long as he can remember, Lydia had been alone on the curb when he came to take her home. Dozens of evenings he'd paused at the foot of the stairs and smiled, listening to Lydia's half of a conversation float down from the landing above: "Oh my god, I *know,* right? So then what did she say?" But now, he knows, she hasn't called Karen or Pam or Jenn in years. He thinks now of those long afternoons, when they'd thought she was staying after school to study. Yawning gaps of time when she could have been anywhere, doing anything. In a moment, James realizes he's obliterated Karen Adler's name under a crosshatch of black ink.

He lifts the phone again and dials. "Officer Fiske, please. Yes, this is James Lee. We've called all of Lydia's —" He hesitates. "Everyone she knows from school. No, nothing. All right, thank you. Yes, we will."

"They're sending an officer out to look for her," he says, setting the receiver back on the hook. "They said to keep the phone line open in case she calls."

Dinnertime comes and goes, but none of them can imagine eating. It seems like something only people in films do, something lovely and decorative, that whole act of raising a fork to your mouth. Some kind of purposeless ceremony. The phone does not ring. At midnight, James sends the children to bed and, though they don't argue, stands at the foot of the stairs until they've gone up. "Twenty bucks says Lydia calls before morning," he says, a little too heartily. No one laughs. The phone still does not ring.

Upstairs, Nath shuts the door to his room and hesitates. What he wants is to find Jack — who, he's sure, knows where Lydia is.

But he cannot sneak out with his parents still awake. His mother is already on edge, startling every time the refrigerator motor kicks on or off. In any case, from the window he can see that the Wolffs' house is dark. The driveway, where Jack's steel-gray VW usually sits, is empty. As usual, Jack's mother has forgotten to leave the front-door light on.

He tries to think: had Lydia seemed strange the night before? He had been away four whole days, by himself for the first time in his life, visiting Harvard — Harvard! — where he would be headed in the fall. In those last days of class before reading period — "Two weeks to cram and party before exams," his host student, Andy, had explained — the campus had had a restless, almost festive air. All weekend he'd wandered awestruck, trying to take it all in: the fluted pillars of the enormous library, the red brick of the buildings against the bright green of the lawns, the sweet chalk smell that lingered in each lecture hall. The purposeful stride he saw in everyone's walk, as if they knew they were destined for greatness. Friday he had spent the night in a sleeping bag on Andy's floor and woke up at one when Andy's roommate, Wes, came in with his girlfriend. The light had flicked on and Nath froze in place, blinking at the doorway, where a tall, bearded boy and the girl holding his hand slowly emerged from the blinding haze. She had long, red hair, loose in waves around her face. "Sorry," Wes had said and flipped the lights off, and Nath heard their careful footsteps as they made their way across the common room to Wes's bedroom. He had kept his eyes open, letting them readjust to the dark, thinking, *So this is what college is like.*

Now he thinks back to last night, when he had arrived home just before dinner. Lydia had been holed up in her room, and when they sat down at the table, he'd asked her how the past few days had been. She'd shrugged and barely glanced up from her plate, and he had assumed this meant *nothing new.* Now he can't remember if she'd even said hello.

In her room, up in the attic, Hannah leans over the edge of her bed and fishes her book from beneath the dust ruffle. It's Lydia's book, actually: *The Sound and the Fury.* Advanced English. Not meant for fifth graders. She'd filched it from Lydia's room a few weeks ago, and Lydia hadn't even noticed. Over the past two weeks she's worked her way through it, a little each night, savoring the words like a cherry Life

32

Saver tucked inside her cheek. Tonight, somehow, the book seems different. Only when she flips back, to where she stopped the day before, does she understand. Throughout, Lydia has underlined words here and there, occasionally scribbling a note from class lectures. *Order vs. chaos. Corruption of Southern aristocratic values.* After this page, the book is untouched. Hannah flips through the rest: no notes, no doodles, no blue to break up the black. She's reached the point where Lydia stopped reading, she realizes, and she doesn't feel like reading any more.

Last night, lying awake, she had watched the moon drift across the sky like a slow balloon. She couldn't see it moving, but if she looked away, then back through the window, she could see that it had. In a little while, she had thought, it would impale itself on the shadow of the big spruce in the backyard. It took a long time. She was almost asleep when she heard a soft thud, and for a moment she thought that the moon had actually hit the tree. But when she looked outside, the moon was gone, almost hidden behind a cloud. Her glow-in-the-dark clock said it was two A.M.

She lay quiet, not even wiggling her toes, and listened. The noise had sounded like the front door closing. It was sticky: you had to push it with your hip to get it to latch. *Burglars!* she thought. Through the window, she saw a single figure crossing the front lawn. Not a burglar, just a thin silhouette against darker night, moving away. Lydia? A vision of life without her sister in it had flashed across her mind. She would have the good chair at the table, looking out the window at the lilac bushes in the yard, the big bedroom downstairs near everyone else. At dinnertime, they would pass her the potatoes first. She would get her father's jokes, her brother's secrets, her mother's best smiles. Then the figure reached the street and disappeared, and she wondered if she had seen it at all.

Now, in her room, she looks down at the tangle of text. It was Lydia, she's sure of it now. Should she tell? Her mother would be upset that Hannah had let Lydia, her favorite, just walk away. And Nath? She thinks of the way Nath's eyebrows have been drawn together all evening, the way he has bitten his lip so hard, without realizing, that it has begun to crack and bleed. He'd be angry, too. He'd say, *Why didn't you run out and catch her?* But I didn't know where she was going, Hannah whispers into the dark. I didn't know she was really going anywhere.

Wednesday morning James calls the police again. Were there any leads? They were checking all possibilities. Could the officer tell them anything, anything at all? They still expected Lydia would come home on her own. They were following up and would, of course, keep the family informed.

James listens to all this and nods, though he knows Officer Fiske can't see him. He hangs up and sits back down at the table without looking at Marilyn or Nath or Hannah. He doesn't need to explain anything: they can tell by the look on his face that there's no news.

It doesn't seem right to do anything but wait. The children stay home from school. Television, magazines, radio: everything feels frivolous in the face of their fear. Outside, it's sunny, the air crisp and cool, but no one suggests that they move to the porch or the yard. Even housekeeping seems wrong: some clue might be sucked into the vacuum, some hint obliterated by lifting the dropped book and placing it, upright, on the shelf. So the family waits. They cluster at the table, afraid to meet each other's eyes, staring at the wood grain of the tabletop as if it's a giant fingerprint, or a map locating what they seek.

It's not until Wednesday afternoon that a passerby notices the rowboat out on the lake, adrift in the windless day. Years ago, the lake had been Middlewood's reservoir, before the water tower was built. Now, edged with grass, it's a swimming hole in summer; kids dive off the wooden dock, and for birthday parties and picnics, a park employee unties the rowboat kept there. No one thinks much of it: a slipped mooring, a harmless prank. It is not a priority. A note is made for an officer to check it; a note is made for the commissioner of parks. It's not until late Wednesday, almost midnight, that a lieutenant, going over loose ends from the day shift, makes the connection and calls the Lees to ask if Lydia ever played with the boat on the lake.

"Of course not," James says. Lydia had refused, *refused,* to take swim classes at the Y. He'd been a swimmer as a teenager himself; he'd taught Nath to swim at age three. With Lydia he'd started too late, and she was already five when he took her to the pool for the first time and waded into the shallow end, water barely to his waist, and waited. Lydia would not even come near the water. She'd laid down in her swimsuit by the side of the pool and cried, and James finally hoisted himself out, swim trunks dripping but top half dry, and promised he would not make her jump. Even now, though the lake is so close, Lydia goes in just ankle-deep in summer, to wash the dirt from her feet.

"Of course not," James says again. "Lydia doesn't know how to swim." It's not until he says these words into the telephone that he understands why the police are asking. As he speaks, the entire family catches a chill, as if they know exactly what the police will find.

It's not until early Thursday morning, just after dawn, that the police drag the lake and find her.

Two

How had it begun? Like everything: with mothers and fathers. Because of Lydia's mother and father, because of her mother's and father's mothers and fathers. Because long ago, her mother had gone missing, and her father had brought her home. Because more than anything, her mother had wanted to stand out; because more than anything, her father had wanted to blend in. Because those things had been impossible.

In her first year at Radcliffe, 1955, Marilyn had enrolled in introductory physics, and her advisor glanced at her course schedule and paused. He was a plump man with a tweed suit and a crimson bowtie, a dark gray hat brim-down on the table beside him. "Why do you want to take physics?" he asked, and she explained shyly that she was hoping to become a doctor. "Not a nurse?" he'd said, with a chuckle. From a folder he pulled her high-school transcript and studied it. "Well," he said. "I see you received very good grades in your high-school physics course." She'd had the highest grade in her class, had set the curve on every test; she had loved physics. But he couldn't know that. On the transcript, it said only "A." She held her breath, waiting, afraid he would tell her that science was too hard, that she'd better try something like English or history instead. In her mind she prepared her retort. Instead he said, "All right, then, why don't you try chemistry — if you think you can handle it," and signed her course slip and handed it over, just like that.

When she arrived at the laboratory, though, she found herself the only girl in a room of fifteen men. The instructor tut-tutted and said, "Miss Walker, you'd better tie up those golden locks." "Can I light the burner for you?" someone else would say. "Let me open that jar for you." When she broke a beaker, the second day of class, three men rushed to her side. "Careful," they said. "Better let us help." Everything, she soon realized, started with *better*: "Better let me pour that acid for you." "Better stand back — this will make a pop." By the third day of class, she decided to show them. She said no, thank you, when people offered to make her pipettes, then hid a grin as they watched her melt glass tubes over the Bunsen burner and stretch them, like taffy, into perfectly tapered droppers. While her classmates sometimes splashed their lab coats, burning holes all the way down through their suits, she measured acids with steady hands. Her solutions never bubbled onto the counter like baking-soda volcanoes. Her results were the most accurate; her lab reports the most complete. By midterm, she set the curve for every exam, and the instructor had stopped smirking.

She had always liked surprising people that way. In high school, she had approached her principal with a request: to take shop instead of home ec. It was 1952, and in Boston, researchers were just beginning to develop a pill that would change women's lives forever — but girls still wore skirts to school, and in Virginia, her request had been radical. Home economics was required for every sophomore girl, and Marilyn's mother, Doris Walker, was the only home ec teacher at Patrick Henry Senior High. Marilyn had asked to switch into shop with the sophomore boys. It was the same class period, she pointed out. Her schedule wouldn't be disrupted. Mr. Tolliver, the principal, knew her well; she had been at the top of her class — girls and boys — since the sixth grade, and her mother had taught at the school for years. So he nodded and smiled as she made her case. Then he shook his head.

"I'm sorry," he said. "We can't make an exception for anyone, or everyone will expect it." At the look on Marilyn's face, he reached across the desk and patted her hand. "Some of the equipment in the shop would be difficult for you to use," he told her. "And to be honest, Miss Walker, having a girl like you in the classroom would be very distracting to the boys in the class." He meant it as a compliment, she knew. But she also knew that it wasn't. She smiled and thanked him for his time. It wasn't a true smile, and her dimples didn't show.

So she had slouched in the back row of the home ec classroom, waiting out the first-day welcome speech her mother had given for a dozen years, drumming her fingers as her mother promised to teach them everything a *young lady* needed to keep a house. As if, Marilyn thought, it might run away when you weren't looking. She studied the other girls in her class, noting who bit her nails, whose sweater was pilled, who smelled faintly of a cigarette snuck over lunch. Across the hall, she could see Mr. Landis, the shop teacher, demonstrating the correct way to hold a hammer.

Keeping house, she had thought. Each day she watched her classmates, clumsy in thimbled fingers, sucking the ends of thread, squinting for the needle's eye. She thought of her mother's insistence on changing clothes before dinner, though there was no longer a husband to impress with her fresh face and crisp housedress. It was after her father left that her mother had begun to teach. Marilyn had been three. Her clearest memory of her father was a feel and a smell: the bristle of his cheek against hers as he lifted her up, and the tingle of Old Spice in her nostrils. She didn't remember his leaving but knew it had happened. Everyone did. And now, everyone had more or less forgotten it. Newcomers to the school district assumed Mrs. Walker was a widow. Her mother herself never mentioned it. She still powdered her nose after cooking and before eating; she still put on lipstick before coming downstairs to make breakfast. So they called it *keeping house* for a reason, Marilyn thought. Sometimes it did run away. And in English class, on a test, she wrote, *Irony: a contradictory outcome of events as if in mockery of the promise and fitness of things,* and received an A.

She began tangling the thread on her sewing machine. She snipped patterns without unfolding them, making paper-cut lace of the layers beneath. Her zippers ripped out of their dresses. She stirred eggshell fragments into the pancake batter; she switched salt and sugar in the sponge cake. One day she left her iron facedown on the board, causing not only a blackened burn in the cover but enough smoke to set off the fire sprinklers. That evening, at dinner, her mother finished her last bite of potato and set her knife and fork down, crossed neatly, on the plate.

"I know what you're trying to prove," she said. "But believe me, I will fail you if you keep this up." Then she gathered the dishes and carried them to the sink.

Marilyn did not move to help as she usually did. She watched her mother tie a ruffled apron around her waist, fingers knotting the strings in one quick motion. After the last dish was washed, her mother rinsed her hands and applied a dab of lotion from the bottle on the counter. Then she came to the table, brushed Marilyn's hair from her face, and kissed her forehead. Her hands smelled like lemons. Her lips were dry and warm.

For the rest of her life, this would be what

Marilyn thought of first when she thought of her mother. Her mother, who had never left her hometown eighty miles from Charlottesville, who always wore gloves outside the house, and who never, in all the years Marilyn could remember, sent her to school without a hot breakfast. Who never mentioned Marilyn's father after he left, but raised her alone. Who, when Marilyn earned a scholarship to Radcliffe, hugged her for a long time and whispered, "How proud I am of you. You have no idea." And then, when she loosened her arms, looked into Marilyn's face and tucked her hair behind her ears and said, "You know, you'll meet a lot of wonderful Harvard men."

It would bother Marilyn, for the rest of her life, that her mother had been right. She worked her way through chemistry, majored in physics, ticked the requirements for medical school off her list. Late at night, bent over her textbooks while her roommate wound curlers into her hair and patted cold cream onto her cheeks and went to bed, Marilyn sipped double-strength tea and kept awake by picturing herself in a white doctor's coat, laying a cool hand against a feverish forehead, touching a stethoscope to a patient's chest. It was the furthest thing she could imagine from her mother's life, where sewing a neat hem was a laudable accomplishment and removing beet stains from a blouse was cause for celebration. Instead she would blunt pain and stanch bleeding and set bones. She would save lives. Yet in the end it happened just as her mother predicted: she met a man.

It was September 1957, her junior year, at the back of a crowded lecture hall. Cambridge was still sweltering and sticky, and everyone was waiting for the crisp cool of fall to sweep the city clean. The course was new that year — "The Cowboy in American Culture" — and everyone wanted to take it: rumor had it that their homework would be watching *The Lone Ranger* and *Gunsmoke* on television. Marilyn took a piece of looseleaf from her folder and, while her head was bent, quiet fell over the room like snow. She glanced up at the professor approaching the podium, and then she understood why everyone had gone silent.

The course catalog had listed the instructor as *James P. Lee.* He was a fourth-year graduate student and no one knew anything about him. To Marilyn, who had spent all her years in Virginia, *Lee* conjured a certain kind of man: a Richard Henry, a Robert E. Now she realized that she — that everyone — had expected someone in a sand-colored

45

blazer, someone with a slight drawl and a Southern pedigree. The man setting his papers on the lectern was youngish and thin, but that was as close as he came to what they all had pictured. *An Oriental,* she thought. She had never seen one in person before. He was dressed like an undertaker: black suit, black tie knotted tight, shirt so white it glowed. His hair was slicked back and parted in a perfect pale line, but one wisp stood straight up in back, like an Indian chief's feather. As he started to speak, he reached up with one hand to smooth down the cowlick, and someone snickered.

If Professor Lee heard, he didn't show it. "Good afternoon," he said. Marilyn found herself holding her breath as he wrote his name on the board. She could see him through her classmates' eyes, and she knew what they were thinking. This was their professor? This little man, five foot nine at most and not even *American,* was going to teach them about cowboys? But when she studied him again, she noticed how slender his neck was, how smooth his cheeks. He looked like a little boy playing dress-up, and she closed her eyes and prayed for the class to go well. The silence stretched, taut as the surface of a bubble, ready to be popped.

Someone shoved a sheaf of mimeographed syllabi over her shoulder, and she jumped.

By the time she had taken the top copy and passed the rest on, Professor Lee had begun to speak again.

"The image of the cowboy," he said, "has existed longer than we might imagine." There was no trace of an accent in his voice, and she slowly let out her breath. Where had he come from, she wondered. He sounded nothing like what she'd been told Chinamen sounded like: *so solly, no washee.* Had he grown up in America? Ten minutes in, the room began to rustle and murmur. Marilyn glanced at the notes she'd jotted down: phrases like "undergone multiple evolutions in each era of American history" and "apparent dichotomy between social rebel and embodiment of quintessential American values." She scanned the syllabus. Ten required books, a midterm exam, three essays. This wasn't what her classmates had had in mind. A girl at the side of the room tucked her book beneath her arm and slipped out the door. Two girls from the next row followed. After that it was a slow but steady trickle. Every minute or two another few students left. One boy from the first row stood up and cut right in front of the podium on his way out. The last to leave were three boys from the back. They whispered and sniggered as they edged past just-emptied seats, their thighs bumping each armrest with a soft thump, thump, thump. As the door closed behind them, Marilyn heard one shout "Yippee-ki-yay-ay!" so loud that he drowned out the lecture. Only nine other students still remained, all studiously bent over notebooks, but they were all reddening in the cheeks and at the edges of their ears. Her own face was hot and she didn't dare look at Professor Lee. Instead she turned her face to her notes and put her hand to her forehead, as if shielding her eyes from the sun.

When she finally peeked up at the podium again, Professor Lee gazed out over the room as if nothing were amiss. He didn't seem to notice that his voice now echoed in the nearly empty hall. He finished his lecture with five minutes remaining in the period and said, "I'll hold office hours until three o'clock." For just a few seconds, he stared straight ahead, toward a distant horizon, and she squirmed in her seat as if he were staring directly at her.

It was that last moment, the tingle at the back of her neck as he stacked his notes and left the room, that brought her to his office after the lecture. The history department had the peaceful quiet of a library, the air still and cool and slightly dusty. She found him at his desk, head propped against the wall, reading that morning's *Crimson.* The part in his hair had blurred, and the cowlick stuck up again.

"Professor Lee? I'm Marilyn Walker. I was in your lecture just now?" Though she hadn't meant it to, the end of her voice swerved up into a question, and she thought, *I must sound like a teenage girl, a stupid, silly, shallow teenage girl.*

"Yes?" He did not look up, and Marilyn fiddled with the top button of her sweater.

"I just wanted to check," she said, "if you thought I'd be able to keep up with the work."

He still didn't look up. "Are you a history major?"

"No. Physics."

"A senior?"

"No. A junior. I'm going to medical school. So history — it's not my field."

"Well," he said, "to be honest, I don't think you'll have any problems. If you choose to stay in the course, that is." He half-folded the newspaper, revealing a mug of coffee, took a sip, then fanned out the paper again. Marilyn pursed her lips. She understood that her audience was now over, that she was expected to turn around and walk back into the hallway and leave him alone. Still, she'd come here for something, though she wasn't sure what, and she jutted out her jaw and pulled a chair up to his desk.

"Was history your favorite subject in school?"

"Miss Walker," he said, looking up at last, "why are you here?" When she saw his face up close, just a table-width away, she saw again how young he was. Maybe only a few years older than she was, not even thirty, she thought. His hands were broad, the fingers long. No rings.

"I just wanted to apologize for those boys," she said suddenly, and realized this was really why she'd come. He paused, eyebrows slightly raised, and she heard what he'd just heard: "boys," a trivializing word. *Boys will be boys.*

"Friends of yours?"

"No," Marilyn said, stung. "No. Just idiots."

At that he laughed, and she did, too. She watched tiny crinkles form around the corners of his eyes, and when they unfolded, his face was different, softer, a real person's face now. From here, she saw that his eyes were brown, not black, as they'd seemed in the lecture hall. How skinny he was, she thought, how wide his shoulders were, like a swimmer's, his skin the color of tea, of fall leaves toasted by the sun. She had never seen anyone like him.

"I guess that sort of thing must happen all the time," she said softly.

"I wouldn't know. That was my first lecture. The department let me take this class as a trial."

"I'm sorry."

"It's all right," he said. "You stayed until the end." They both looked down — he at his now-empty mug, she at the typewriter and neat sheaf of carbon paper perched at the end of his desk.

"Paleontology," he said after a moment.

"What?"

"Paleontology," he repeated. "My favorite subject. It was paleontology. I wanted to dig up fossils."

"That's a kind of history, though," she said.

"I guess it is." He grinned into his coffee cup, and Marilyn leaned across the desk and kissed him.

On Thursday, at the next lecture, Marilyn sat off to the side. When Professor Lee came into the room, she didn't look up. Instead she wrote the date carefully in the corner of her notes, looping a demure *S* in September, crossing the *t* in a perfectly horizontal line. As he began to speak, her cheeks went hot, as if she'd stepped into summer sun. She was positive she was bright red, blazing like a lighthouse, but when she finally looked around, out of the corners of her eyes, everyone was focused on the lecture. There were a handful of other students in the room, but they were scribbling in their notebooks or facing the podium up front. No one noticed her at all.

When she'd kissed him, she had surprised herself. It had been such an impulse — the way she sometimes reached out to catch a stray leaf on the wind, or jumped a puddle on a rainy day — something done without thinking or resisting, something pointless and harmless. She had never done anything like that before and never would again, and looking back on it, she would forever be surprised at herself, and a little shocked. But at that moment she had known, with a certainty she would never feel about anything else in her life, that it was right, that she wanted this man in her life. Something inside her said, *He understands. What it's like to be different.*

The touch of his lips on hers had startled her. He had tasted like coffee, warm and slightly bitter, and he had kissed back. That had startled her, too. As if he were ready for it, as if it were as much his idea as hers. After they finally drew apart, she'd been too embarrassed to meet his eyes. Instead she looked down into her lap, studying the soft plaid flannel of her skirt. Sweat bunched her slip to her thighs. In a moment she grew braver and peeked at him through the curtain of her hair. He looked shyly up at her then, through his lashes, and she saw that he wasn't angry, that his cheeks were pink. "Perhaps we'd better go somewhere else," he said, and she'd nodded and picked up her bag.

They'd walked down along the river, passing the redbrick dorms in silence. The crew team had been practicing, the oarsmen bending and unbending over their oars in perfect unison, the boat sliding across the water without sound. Marilyn knew these men: they asked her to mixers, to movies, to football games; they all looked alike, the same blend of sandy hair and ruddy skin she'd seen all through high school, all her life — as familiar as boiled potatoes. When she turned them down to finish a paper or catch up on her reading, they moved on to woo other girls down the hall. From where she stood on the riverbank, the distance made them anonymous, expressionless as

53

dolls. Then she and James — as she did not even dare, yet, to think of him — had reached the footbridge, and she stopped and turned to face him. He hadn't looked like a professor, but like a teenage boy, bashful and eager, reaching out to take her hand.

And James? What had he thought of her? He would never tell her this, would never admit it to himself: he had not noticed her at all, that first lecture. He had looked right at her, over and over, as he held forth on Roy Rogers and Gene Autry and John Wayne, but when she came to his office he had not even recognized her. Hers had been just one of the pale, pretty faces, indistinguishable from the next, and though he would never fully realize it, this was the first reason he came to love her: because she had blended in so perfectly, because she had seemed so completely and utterly at home.

All through the second lecture, Marilyn remembered the smell of his skin — clean and sharp, like the air after a rainstorm — and the feel of his hands at her waist, and even her palms grew warm. Through her fingers, she watched him: the tip of his ballpoint tapping the top of the podium, the deliberate flick as he turned over another page of his notes. He looked everywhere but toward her, she realized. At the end of the hour, she dawdled in her seat, slowly slipping her papers into her folder, tucking her pencil into the pocket. Her classmates, hurrying to other courses, squeezed past her into the aisle, jostling her with their bags. At the podium, James sorted his notes, dusted his hands, replaced the chalk on the blackboard ledge. He didn't look up when she stacked her books, or when she tucked them in the curve of her arm and headed toward the door. Then, just as her hand touched the knob, he called, "A moment, Miss Walker," and something inside her jumped.

The classroom was empty now, and she leaned against the wall, trembling, while he closed his briefcase and descended the steps of the platform. She curled her fingers around the doorknob behind her to hold herself in place. But when he reached her, he wasn't smiling. "Miss Walker," he said again, taking a deep breath, and she found that she wasn't smiling either.

He was her teacher, he reminded her. She was his student. As her teacher, he would feel he was taking advantage of his position if they were — he looked down, fiddling with the handle of his briefcase — if they were to develop any kind of relationship. He wasn't looking at Marilyn, but she didn't know. She was looking down at her feet, at the scuffed toes of her shoes.

Marilyn tried to swallow and couldn't. She concentrated on the gray scratches against the black leather and steeled herself by thinking of her mother, all those hints about meeting a *Harvard man. You weren't here to find a man,* she told herself. *You were here for something better.* But instead of the anger she hoped for, a hot ache swelled at the base of her throat.

"I understand," she said, looking up at last.

The next day, Marilyn came to his office hours to tell him that she'd dropped the class. Within a week they were lovers.

They spent all autumn together. James had a seriousness, a reserve, unlike anyone she had met before. He seemed to look at things more closely, to think more carefully, to hold himself a half step apart. Only when they came together, in his tiny Cambridge apartment, did that reserve drop, with a fierceness that made her catch her breath. Afterward, curled up on his bed, Marilyn ruffled his hair, spiky with sweat. For those afternoon hours, he seemed at ease with himself, and she loved that she was the only thing that made him feel that way. They would lie together, dozing and dreaming, until six o'clock. Then Marilyn slipped her dress back over her head, and James buttoned his shirt and combed his hair again. His cowlick would stand up at the back, but she never told him, loving that little reminder of the side only she got to see. She simply kissed him and hurried back for evening sign-in at the dormitory. James himself began to forget about the cowlick; after Marilyn left, he seldom remembered to look in the mirror. Every time she kissed him, every time he opened his arms and she crawled into them, felt like a miracle. Coming to her made him feel perfectly welcomed, perfectly at home, as he had never in his life felt before.

He had never felt he belonged here, even though he'd been born on American soil, even though he had never set foot anywhere else. His father had come to California under a false name, pretending to be the son of a neighbor who had emigrated there some years earlier. America was a melting pot, but Congress, terrified that the molten mixture was becoming a shade too yellow, had banned all immigrants from China. Only the children of those already in the States could enter. So James's father had taken the name of his neighbor's son, who had drowned in the river the year before, and come to join his "father" in San Francisco. It was the story of nearly every Chinese immigrant from the time of Chester A. Arthur to the end of the Second World War. While the Irish and the Germans and the Swedes crowded onto steamship decks, waving as the pale green torch of the Statue of Liberty came into view, the *coolies* had to find other means to reach the land where all men were created equal. Those who made it would visit their wives in China and return each time celebrating the birth of a son. Those at home in the villages who longed to make their fortunes would adopt the names of those mythical sons and make the long journey across the sea. While the Norwegians and the Italians and the Russian Jews ferried from Ellis Island to Manhattan, fanning out by road and railway to Kansas and Nebraska and Minnesota, the Chinese who bluffed their way to California mostly stayed put. In Chinatowns, the lives of all those *paper sons* were fragile and easily torn. Everyone's name was false. Everyone hoped not to be found out and sent back. Everyone clustered together so they wouldn't stand out.

James's parents, however, had not stayed put. In 1938, when James was six, his father received a letter from a paper brother who had gone east looking for work when the

Depression began. He had found a place at a small boarding school in Iowa, the "brother" wrote, doing groundswork and maintenance. Now his (real, nonpaper) mother was ill and he was returning to China, and his employers wondered if he had any reliable friends who might do as good a job. They like the Chinese, the letter said; they feel we are quiet and hardworking and clean. It was a good position, a very exclusive school. There might be a job for his wife in the school kitchens. Would he be interested?

James could not read Chinese but all his life he held the memory of the letter's last paragraph, a scrawl of fountain-pen calligraphy, which caught his parents' attention. There was a special policy, said the brother, for children of employees. If they could pass an entrance exam, they could attend the school for free.

Jobs were scarce and everyone was hungry, but it was because of this paragraph that the Lees sold their furniture and moved across the country with two suitcases between them. It took five Greyhound rides and four days. When they reached Iowa, James's "uncle" took them to his apartment. James remembered only the man's teeth, more crooked even than his father's, one tooth turned sideways, like a sliver of rice waiting to be toothpicked out. The next day, his father put on his best shirt, buttoned up to the collar, and went with his friend to Lloyd Academy. By afternoon it was settled: he would start the following week. The morning after that his mother put on her best dress and went with his father to the school. That evening, each brought home a navy-blue uniform stitched with a new English name: *Henry. Wendy.*

A few weeks later, James's parents brought him to Lloyd for the entrance exam. A man with a large white mustache like cotton brought him into an empty classroom and gave him a booklet and a yellow pencil. Looking back, James realized what a brilliant idea it was: what six-year-old would be able to read, let alone pass, such an exam? A teacher's son, perhaps, if she had studied with him. Surely not a janitor's son, or a cafeteria lady's son, or a groundskeeper's son. *If a square playing field is forty feet on a side, how long is the fence that goes around it? When was America discovered? Which of these words is a noun? Here is a sequence of shapes; which shape completes the pattern?* We're sorry, the principal could say. Your son didn't pass the test. He isn't up to Lloyd academic standards. And no tuition would be necessary.

James, though, had known all the answers. He had read every newspaper he could get his hands on; he had read all the books his father had bought, a nickel a bag, at library book sales. *One hundred sixty feet,* he wrote. *1492. Automobile. The circle.* He finished the test and set the pencil in the slot at the top of the desk. The man with the mustache didn't look up until twenty minutes later. "Finished already?" he said. "You were so quiet, sonny." He took away the booklet and the pencil and brought James back to the kitchens, where his mother was working. "I'll grade the test and let you know the results next week," he told them, but James already knew he had passed.

When the term began in September, he rode in to school with his father in the Ford truck the school had lent him for his maintenance work. "You're the first Oriental boy to attend Lloyd," his father reminded him. "Set a good example." That first morning, James slid into his seat and the girl next to him asked, "What's wrong with your eyes?" It wasn't until he heard the horror in the teacher's voice — "Shirley Byron!" — that he realized he was supposed to be embarrassed; the next time it happened, he had learned his lesson and turned red right away. In every class, every day that first week, the other students studied him: where had he come from, this boy? He had a book-bag, a Lloyd uniform. Yet he didn't live at the school like the rest of them; he looked like no one they'd ever seen. Now and then, his father would be called in to loosen a squeaky window, replace a lightbulb, mop up a spill. James, scrunched in the back row, saw his classmates glance from his father to him and knew that they suspected. He would bend his head over his book, so close that his nose nearly touched the page, until his father left the room. By the second month, he asked his parents for permission to walk to and from school by himself. Alone, he could pretend to be just another student. He could pretend that, in the uniform, he looked just like everyone else.

He spent twelve years at Lloyd and never felt at home. At Lloyd, everyone seemed to be descended from a Pilgrim or a senator or a Rockefeller, but when they did family tree projects in class, he pretended to forget the assignment rather than draw his own complicated diagram. *Don't ask any questions,* he prayed silently as the teacher marked a small red zero beside his name. He set himself a curriculum of studying American culture — listening to the radio, reading comics, saving his pocket money for double features, learning the rules of the new board games — in case anyone ever said, *Hey, didya hear Red Skelton yesterday?* or *Wanna play Monopoly?* though no one ever did. As he got older, he did not attend the dances, or the pep rallies, or the junior or senior proms. At best, girls smiled silently at him in the hallways; at worst, they stared as he passed, and he heard their snickers as he turned the corner. At graduation, the yearbook ran one photo of him besides the obligatory senior portrait: a shot of him at an assembly to greet President Truman, his head visible over the shoulder of the class treasurer and a girl who would go on to marry a Belgian prince. His ears, blushing pink in real life, were a deep and unnatural gray in the photograph, his mouth slightly open, as if he had been caught trespassing. At college, he hoped things would be different. Yet after seven years at Harvard — four as an undergrad, three and counting as a graduate student — nothing had changed. Without realizing why, he studied the most quintessentially American subject he could find — cowboys — but he never spoke of his parents, or his family. He still had few acquaintances and no friends. He still found himself shifting in his seat, as if at any moment someone might notice him and ask him to leave.

So that fall of 1957, when Marilyn had leaned over his desk and kissed him, this beautiful honey-haired girl, when she came into his arms and then into his bed, James could not quite believe it. The first afternoon they'd spent together, in his tiny white-washed studio apartment, he marveled at how her body fit so perfectly against his: her nose nestled exactly into the hollow between his collarbones; her cheek curved to match the side of his neck. As if they were two halves of a mold. He had studied her with the air of a sculptor, tracing the contours of her hips and calves, his fingertips grazing her skin. When they made love, her hair came alive. It darkened from golden-wheat to amber. It kinked and curled like a fiddlehead fern. It amazed him that he could have such an effect on anyone. As she dozed in his arms, her hair slowly relaxed, and when she woke, it had stretched back to its usual waves. Then her easy laugh sparkled in that white, bare room; as she chattered, breathless, her hands fluttered until he caught them in his and they lay warm and still, like resting birds, and then she pulled him to her again. It was as if America herself was taking him in. It was

64

too much luck. He feared the day the universe would notice he wasn't supposed to have her and take her away. Or that she might suddenly realize her mistake and disappear from his life as suddenly as she had entered. After a while, the fear became a habit, too.

He began to make small changes he thought she might like: he trimmed his hair; he bought a blue-striped Oxford shirt after she admired one on a passerby. (The cowlick, persistent, still stood up; years later, Nath and Hannah would inherit it, too.) One Saturday, at Marilyn's suggestion, he bought two gallons of pale yellow paint, pushed the furniture to the middle of the apartment, and spread drop cloths across the parquet. As they brushed one section, then another, the room brightened like panes of sunlight stretching across the walls. When everything was painted, they opened all the windows and curled up on the bed in the center of the room. The apartment was so small that nothing was more than a few feet from the wall, but surrounded by his desk and chairs, the armchair and the dresser pressed close, he felt as if they were on an island, or afloat in the sea. With Marilyn tucked in the curve of his shoulder, he kissed her and her arms circled his neck, her body rose to meet his. Another tiny miracle, every time.

Later that afternoon, waking in the fading light, he noticed a tiny yellow blotch on the tip of Marilyn's toe. After a moment of searching, he found a smudge on the wall near the end of the bed, where her foot had touched it as they made love: a dime-sized spot where the paint was blotted away. He said nothing to Marilyn, and when they pushed the furniture back into place that evening, the dresser concealed the smudge. Every time he looked at that dresser he was pleased, as if he could see through the pine drawers and his folded clothing straight to it, that mark her body had left in his space.

At Thanksgiving, Marilyn decided not to go home to Virginia. She told herself, and James, that it was too far for such a short holiday, but in reality she knew her mother would ask her, again, if she had any *prospects,* and this time she did not know how to respond. Instead, in James's tiny kitchen, she roasted a chicken, cubed potatoes, peeled yams into a casserole dish the size of a steno pad: Thanksgiving dinner in miniature. James, who had never cooked himself a meal, who subsisted on burgers from Charlie's Kitchen and English muffins from the Hayes-Bickford, watched in awe. After

Marilyn basted the chicken, she looked up defiantly, closed the oven, and peeled the oven mitts from her hands.

"My mother is a home economics teacher," she said. "Betty Crocker is her personal goddess." It was the first thing she had told him about her mother. The way she said it, it sounded like a secret, something she had kept hidden and now deliberately, trustingly, revealed.

James felt he should return this privilege, this private gift. He had mentioned once, in passing, that his parents had worked at a school, leaving it at that, hoping she'd think *teacher.* But he had never told her how the school kitchen had been like the land of the giants, everything economy-sized: rolls of tinfoil half a mile long, jars of mayonnaise big enough to hold his head. His mother was in charge of bringing the world down to scale, chopping melons into dice-sized cubes, portioning pats of butter onto saucers to accompany each roll. He had never told anyone how the other kitchen ladies snickered at his mother for wrapping up the leftover food instead of throwing it away; how at home they'd reheat it in the oven while his parents quizzed him: What did you do in geography? What did you do in math? And he'd recite: *Montgomery is the capital of*

Alabama. Prime numbers have only two factors. They didn't understand his answers, but they'd nodded, pleased that James was learning things they did not know. As they spoke, he would crumble crackers into a cup of celery soup, or peel waxed paper from a wedge of cheese sandwich, and pause, confused, certain he'd done this before, uncertain whether he was reviewing his studies or the whole schoolday. In the fifth grade, he had stopped speaking Chinese to his parents, afraid of tinting his English with an accent; long before that, he had stopped speaking to his parents at school at all. He was afraid to tell Marilyn these things, afraid that once he admitted them, she would see him as he had always seen himself: a scrawny outcast, feeding on scraps, reciting his lines and trying to pass. An imposter. He was afraid she would never see him any other way.

"My parents are both dead," he said. "They died just after I started college."

His mother had died his second year, a tumor blossoming in her brain. His father had gone six months later. Complications of pneumonia, the doctors had said, but James had known the truth: his father simply hadn't wanted to live alone.

Marilyn didn't say anything, but she

reached out and cupped his face in her hands, and James felt the leftover heat from the oven in her soft palms. They were there only a moment before the timer buzzed and she turned back to the stove, but they warmed him through. He remembered his mother's hands — scarred from steam burns, callused from scouring pots — and wanted to press his lips to the tender hollow where Marilyn's life line and love line crossed. He promised himself he would never let those hands harden. As Marilyn took the chicken, burnished and bronze, from the oven, he was mesmerized by her deftness. It was beautiful, the way broth thickened to gravy under her guidance, how potatoes fluffed like cotton beneath her fork. This was the closest thing he'd seen to magic. A few months later, when they married, they would make a pact: to let the past drift away, to stop asking questions, to look forward from then on, never back.

That spring, Marilyn was making plans for her senior year; James was finishing his Ph.D. and waiting, still, to see if he would be taken on in the history department. There was an opening and he had applied, and Professor Carlson, the department head, had hinted he was by far the most accomplished in his class. Now and then, he would interview for positions elsewhere — in New Haven, in Providence — just in case. Deep inside, though, he was certain that he would be hired at Harvard. "Carlson as good as told me I'm in," he said to Marilyn whenever the subject came up. Marilyn nodded and kissed him and refused to think about what would happen when she graduated the next year, when she headed off to medical school who knew where. Harvard, she thought, ticking off her fingers. Columbia. Johns Hopkins. Stanford. Each digit a step farther away.

Then, in April, two things neither of them expected: Professor Carlson informed James that he was very, very sorry to disappoint him, but they had decided to take his classmate William McPherson instead, and of course they knew James would find many other opportunities elsewhere. "Did they say why?" Marilyn asked, and James replied, "I wasn't the right *fit* for the department, they said," and she did not raise the subject again. Four days later, an even bigger surprise: Marilyn was pregnant.

So instead of Harvard, an offer at last from humble Middlewood College, accepted with relief. Instead of Boston, small-town Ohio. Instead of medical school, a wedding. Nothing quite as planned.

"A baby," Marilyn said to James, over and over. "Our baby. So much better." By the time they were married, Marilyn would be only three months along, and it wouldn't show. To herself, she said, *You can come back and finish that last year, when the baby is older.* It would be almost eight years before school would seem real and possible and tangible again, but Marilyn didn't know that. As she left the dean's office, an indefinite leave secured, she was certain that everything she had dreamed for herself — medical school, doctorhood, that new and important life — sat poised for her return, like a well-trained dog awaiting its master. Still, when Marilyn sat down at the telephone table in the dorm lobby and gave the long-distance operator her mother's number, her voice shook with each digit. As her mother's voice finally came over the line, she forgot to say hello. Instead she blurted out, "I'm getting married. In June."

Her mother paused. "Who is he?"

"His name is James Lee."

"A student?"

Marilyn's face warmed. "He's just finishing his Ph.D. In American history." She hesitated and decided on a half-truth. "Harvard was thinking of hiring him, in the fall."

"So he's a professor." A sudden alertness

tinted her mother's voice. "Sweetheart, I'm so happy for you. I can't wait to meet him."

Relief flooded Marilyn. Her mother wasn't upset about her leaving school early; why would she mind? Hadn't she done just what her mother had hoped: met a wonderful Harvard man? She read off the information from a slip of paper: Friday, June 13, eleven thirty, with the justice of the peace; lunch afterward at the Parker House. "It won't be a big party. Just us, and you, and a few of our friends. James's parents are both dead."

"Lee," her mother mused. "Is he connected to anyone we know?"

Marilyn realized, suddenly, what her mother was imagining. It was 1958; in Virginia, in half the country, their wedding would break the law. Even in Boston, she sometimes saw disapproval in the eyes of the passersby. Her hair was no longer the white-blond of her childhood, but it was still light enough to catch attention when bent toward James's inky black head in movie theaters, on a park bench, at the counter at the Waldorf Cafeteria. A gaggle of Radcliffe girls came down the stairs, one hovering nearby to wait for the phone, the others crowding around the hall mirror to apply powder to their noses. One of them, just a week before, had heard about Marilyn's marriage and came by her room "to see if it was really true."

Marilyn squeezed the receiver and pressed one palm to her belly and kept her voice sweet. "I don't know, Mother," she said. "Why don't you ask him when you meet him?"

So her mother came in from Virginia, the first time she'd ever left the state. Standing at the station with James hours after his graduation, waiting for her mother's train, Marilyn told herself: she would have come anyway, even if I'd told her. Her mother stepped onto the platform and spotted Marilyn and a smile flashed across her face — spontaneous, proud — and for that instant, Marilyn believed it completely. *Of course she would have.* Then the smile flickered just for a moment, like a flash of static. Her gaze darted back and forth between the stout blond woman standing on her daughter's left and the skinny Oriental man on her right, looking for the advertised James, not finding him. Finally understanding. A few seconds passed before she shook James's hand, told him she was very, very happy to meet him, and allowed him to take her bag.

Marilyn and her mother had dinner alone that night, and her mother did not mention

James until dessert. She knew what her mother would ask — *Why do you love him?* — and steeled herself for the question. But her mother didn't ask this at all, didn't mention the word *love*. Instead she swallowed a bite of cake and studied her daughter from across the table. "You're sure," she said, "that he doesn't just want a green card?"

Marilyn couldn't look at her. Instead she stared at her mother's hands, spotted despite the gloves and the lemon-scented lotion, at the fork pinched between the fingers, at the crumb clinging to the tines. A tiny wrinkle creased her mother's eyebrows, as if someone had nicked her forehead with a knife. Years later, Hannah would spy this same mark of deep worry on her mother's face, though she would not know its source, and Marilyn would never have admitted the resemblance. "He was born in California, Mother," she said, and her mother looked away and dabbed at her mouth with her napkin, leaving two red smears on the linen.

The morning of the wedding, as they waited in the courthouse, Marilyn's mother kept fiddling with the clasp of her purse. They'd gotten there almost an hour early, worried about traffic, about parking, about missing their spot with the justice of the peace. James had put on a new suit and kept

74

patting the breast pocket, checking for the rings through the navy-blue wool. Such a timid and nervous gesture made Marilyn want to kiss him right there in front of everyone. In twenty-five minutes she would be his wife. And then her mother stepped closer and took Marilyn's elbow in a grip that felt like a clamp.

"Let's touch up your lipstick," she said, nudging Marilyn toward the ladies' room.

She should have known it was coming. All morning her mother had been dissatisfied with everything. Marilyn's dress wasn't white but cream. It didn't look like a wedding dress; it was too plain, like something a *nurse* would wear. She didn't know why Marilyn wouldn't get married in a church. There were plenty nearby. She didn't like the weather in Boston; why was it so gray in June? Daisies weren't a wedding flower; why not roses instead? And why was she in such a *hurry,* why get married now, why not wait awhile?

It would have been easier if her mother had used a slur. It would have been easier if she had insulted James outright, if she had said he was too short or too poor or not accomplished enough. But all her mother said, over and over, was, "It's not right, Marilyn. It's not right." Leaving *it* unnamed, hanging in the air between them.

Marilyn pretended not to hear and took her lipstick from her purse.

"You'll change your mind," her mother said. "You'll regret it later."

Marilyn swiveled up the tube and bent close to the mirror, and her mother grabbed her by both shoulders suddenly, desperately. The look in her eyes was fear, as if Marilyn were running along the edge of a cliff.

"Think about your children," she said. "Where will you live? You won't fit in anywhere. You'll be sorry for the rest of your life."

"Stop it," Marilyn shouted, slamming her fist against the edge of the sink. "This is my life, Mother. Mine." She jerked herself free and the lipstick went flying, then skittered to a stop on the floor tiles. Somehow she had made a long red streak down her mother's sleeve. Without another word, she pushed the door of the bathroom open, leaving her mother alone.

Outside, James glanced anxiously at his wife-to-be. "What's wrong?" he murmured, leaning close. She shook her head and whispered quickly, laughingly: "Oh, my mother just thinks I should marry someone more like me." Then she took his lapel in her fist, pulled his face to hers, and kissed him. Ridiculous, she thought. So obvious that she didn't even need to say it.

Just days before, hundreds of miles away, another couple had married, too — a white man, a black woman, who would share a most appropriate name: Loving. In four months they would be arrested in Virginia, the law reminding them that Almighty God had never intended white, black, yellow, and red to mix, that there should be no *mongrel citizens,* no *obliteration of racial pride.* It would be four years before they protested, and four years more before the court concurred, but many more years before the people around them would, too. Some, like Marilyn's mother, never would.

When Marilyn and James separated, her mother had returned from the ladies' room and stood silently watching them from a distance. She had blotted her sleeve again and again on the roller towel, but the red mark still showed beneath the damp spot, like an old bloodstain. Marilyn wiped a smudge of lipstick from James's upper lip and grinned, and he patted his breast pocket again, checking the rings. To her mother it looked as if James were congratulating himself.

Afterward, the wedding reduced to a slideshow in Marilyn's memory: the thin white line, like a hair, in the justice's bifocals; the knots of baby's breath in her bouquet; the fog of moisture on the wineglass her old roommate, Sandra, raised to toast. Under the table, James's hand in hers, the strange new band of gold cool against her skin. And across the table, her mother's carefully curled hair, her powdered face, her lips kept closed to cover the crooked incisor.

That was the last time Marilyn saw her mother.

THREE

Until the day of the funeral, Marilyn has never thought about the last time she would see her daughter. She would have imagined a touching bedside scene, like in the movies: herself white-haired and elderly and content, in a satin bed jacket, ready to say her good-byes; Lydia a grown woman, confident and poised, holding her mother's hands in hers, a doctor by then, unfazed by the great cycle of life and death. And Lydia, though Marilyn does not admit it, is the face she would want to see last — not Nath or Hannah or even James, but the daughter she thinks of first and always. Now her last glimpse of Lydia has already passed: James, to her bewilderment, has insisted on a closed-casket funeral. She will not even get to see her daughter's face one last time, and for the past three days, she has told James this over and over, sometimes furious, sometimes through tears. James, for his part, cannot find the words to tell her what he discovered on going to identify Lydia's body: there is only half a face left, barely preserved by the cold water of the lake; the other half had already been eaten away. He ignores his wife and keeps his eyes trained on the rearview mirror as he backs into the street.

The cemetery is only a fifteen-minute walk from their house, but they drive anyway. As they turn onto the main road that circles the lake, Marilyn looks sharply to the left, as if she's spotted something on the shoulder of her husband's jacket. She doesn't want to see the pier, the rowboat now remoored, the lake itself stretching out into the distance. James has the car windows rolled up tight, but the breeze shakes the leaves of the trees on the banks and corrugates the surface of the water. It will be there forever, the lake: every time they leave their house, they will see it. In the backseat, Nath and Hannah wonder in unison if their mother will turn her head away for the rest of her life, every time she passes by. The lake glints in the sun like a shiny tin roof, and Nath's eyes begin to water. It seems inappropriate for the light to be so bright, for the sky to be so blue, and he's relieved when a cloud drifts over the sun and the water turns from silver to gray.

At the cemetery, they pull into the parking lot. Middlewood is proud of its garden cemetery, a sort of graveyard and botanical garden in one, with winding paths and small brass signs to identify the flora. Nath remembers middle-school science trips with sketch pads and field guides; once the teacher had promised ten extra-credit points to the person who could gather the most kinds of leaves. There had been a funeral that day, too, and Tommy Reed had tiptoed between rows of folding chairs to the sassafras tree, right in the middle of the eulogy, and plucked a leaf from a low-hanging branch. Mr. Rexford hadn't noticed and had complimented Tommy on being the only one to find *Sassafras albidum,* and the whole class had stifled giggles and high-fived Tommy on the bus ride home. Now, as they walk single file toward the cluster of chairs set up in the distance, Nath wants to go back in time and punch Tommy Reed.

In Lydia's honor, the school has closed for the day, and Lydia's classmates come, lots of them. Looking at them, James and Marilyn realize just how long it has been since they've seen these girls: years. For a moment they don't recognize Karen Adler with her hair grown long, or Pam Saunders without her braces. James, thinking of the crossed-out list of names, finds himself staring and turns away. Slowly the chairs fill with some of Nath's classmates, with juniors and freshmen he finds vaguely familiar but doesn't really know. Even the neighbors, as they file in, feel like strangers. His parents never go out or entertain; they have no dinner parties, no bridge group, no hunting buddies or luncheon pals. Like Lydia, no real friends. Hannah and Nath recognize a few professors from the university, their father's teaching assistant, but most of the faces in the chairs are strangers. Why are they even here, Nath wonders, and when the service starts and they all crane their necks toward the coffin at the front, under the sassafras tree, he understands. They are drawn by the spectacle of sudden death. For the past week, ever since the police dragged the lake, the headlines in the Middlewood *Monitor* have all been about Lydia. *Oriental Girl Found Drowned in Pond.*

The minister looks like President Ford, flat-browed, white-toothed, clean-cut, and solid. The Lees do not attend church, but the funeral home had recommended him, and James had accepted without asking any questions. Now James sits up straight, pressing the chair's back into his shoulder blades, and tries to listen to the service. The minister reads the Twenty-third Psalm, but in the revised text: *I have everything I need* instead of *I shall not want; Even if I walk through a very dark valley* instead of *Yea, though I walk through the valley of the shadow of death.* It feels disrespectful, a corner cut. Like burying his daughter in a plywood box. *What else could you expect from this town,* he thinks. On his right, the scent of the lilies on the casket hits Marilyn like a warm, wet fog, and she nearly retches. For the first time, she wishes she were the sort of woman, like her mother, who carried a handkerchief. She would have pressed it to her face and let it filter the air, and when she lowered it the cloth would be dirty pink, the color of old bricks. Beside her, Hannah knits her fingers. She would like to worm her hand onto her mother's lap, but she doesn't dare. Nor does she dare look at the coffin. Lydia is not inside, she reminds herself, taking a deep breath, only her body — but then where is Lydia herself? Everyone is so still that to the birds floating overhead, she thinks, they must look like a cluster of statues.

Out of the corner of his eye, Nath spots Jack sitting at the edge of the crowd beside his mother. He imagines grabbing Jack by the shirt collar to find out what he knows. For the past week, his father has called the police every morning asking for new information, but Officer Fiske says only, over and over, that they are still investigating. If only the police were here now, Nath thinks. Should he tell his father? Jack stares at the ground in front of him, as if he is too ashamed to look up. And then, when Nath himself glances back to the front, the coffin has already been lowered into the ground. The polished wood, the white lilies fastened to its top — vanished, just like that: nothing but the blank space where it had once stood. He's missed it all. His sister is gone.

Something wet touches his neck. He reaches up to wipe it away and discovers that his whole face is wet, that he's been crying silently. On the other side of the crowd, Jack's blue eyes are suddenly fixed on him, and Nath blots his cheek in the crook of his arm.

The mourners begin to leave, a thin line of backs filing toward the parking area and the street. A few of Nath's classmates, like Miles Fuller, give him a sympathetic glance, but most — embarrassed by his tears — decide not to speak to him, and turn away. They won't have another chance; in light of Nath's high grades and the tragic situation, the principal will exempt him from the last three weeks of school, and Nath himself will decide not to attend commencement. Some of the neighbors circle the Lees, squeezing their arms and murmuring condolences; a few of them pat Hannah on the head, as if she's a tiny child, or a dog. Except for Janet Wolff, her usual white doctor's coat replaced by a trim black suit, James and Marilyn don't recognize most of them. By the time Janet reaches her, Marilyn's palms feel grimy, her whole body dirty, like a rag passed from hand to soiled hand, and she can barely stand Janet's touch on her elbow.

On the other side of the grave, Jack stands off to the side, waiting for his mother, half-hidden in the shadow of a big elm. Nath weaves his way over, cornering him against the tree trunk, and Hannah, trapped at her parents' side by a thicket of adults, watches her brother nervously.

"What are you doing here?" Nath demands. Up close, he can see that Jack's shirt is dark blue, not black, that though he's wearing dress pants he still has on his old black-and-white tennis shoes with the hole in the toe.

"Hey," Jack says, eyes still on the ground. "Nath. How are you?"

"How do you think I am?" Nath's voice

cracks, and he hates himself for it.

"I gotta go," Jack says. "My mom's waiting." A pause. "I'm really sorry about your sister." He turns away, and Nath catches him by the arm.

"Are you?" He's never grabbed anyone before, and he feels tough doing it, like a detective in a movie. "You know, the police want to talk to you." People are beginning to stare — James and Marilyn hear their son's raised voice and look around — but he doesn't care. He leans in closer, almost to Jack's nose. "Look, I know she was with you that Monday."

For the first time Jack looks Nath in the face: a flash of startled blue eyes. "She told you?"

Nath lurches forward so that he and Jack are chest to chest. Blood throbs in his right temple. "She didn't have to tell me. Do you think I'm stupid?"

"Look, Nath," Jack mumbles. "If Lydia told you that I —"

He breaks off suddenly, as Nath's parents and Dr. Wolff come within earshot. Nath stumbles backward a few steps, glaring at Jack, at his father for interrupting, at the elm tree itself for not being farther away.

"Jack," Dr. Wolff says sharply. "Everything all right?"

"Fine." Jack glances at Nath, then at the adults. "Mr. Lee, Mrs. Lee, I'm very sorry for your loss."

"Thank you for coming," says James. He waits until the Wolffs have started down the curving path out of the cemetery before grabbing Nath by the shoulder. "What's the matter with you?" he hisses. "Picking a fight at your sister's funeral."

Behind his mother, Jack gives a quick backward glance, and when his gaze meets Nath's, there's no doubt: he is frightened. Then he turns the curve and is gone.

Nath lets out his breath. "That bastard knows something about Lydia."

"You don't go around making trouble. You let the police do their work."

"James," Marilyn says, "don't shout." She touches her fingers to her temple, as if she has a headache, and closes her eyes. To Nath's horror, a dark drop of blood runs down the side of her face — no, it's only a tear, stained black by mascara, leaving a dirty gray trail on her cheek. Hannah, her small heart awash in pity, reaches up to take her hand, but her mother doesn't notice. In a moment Hannah contents herself by clasping her own fingers behind her back.

James fishes in his jacket pocket for his keys. "I'm taking your mother and sister home. When you've cooled off, you can walk." As the words leave his mouth, he winces. Deep inside, he wants more than anything to calm Nath, to put a comforting and weighty hand on his shoulder, to fold him into his arms, on this day of all days. But already it takes all his strength to keep his own face from crumpling, to stop his own knees from buckling and spilling him to the ground. He turns away and grabs Hannah's arm. Hannah, at least, always does what she's told.

Nath sinks down on the roots of the elm and watches his parents head back toward the car, Hannah trailing after them with one wistful backward glance. His father doesn't know what Jack is like. Jack has lived down the street from them for eleven years, since he and Nath were in the first grade, and to Nath's parents he is just a neighbor boy, the scruffy one with the dog and that old secondhand car. In school, though, everyone knows. Every few weeks a different girl. Every girl the same story. Jack doesn't date; there are no dinners out, no flowers, no boxes of chocolates in cellophane wrap. He simply drives the girl out to the Point or the drive-in or a parking lot somewhere and spreads a blanket across the backseat of his car. A week or two later, he stops calling and moves on. He's known to make a specialty of deflowering virgins. At school, the girls are proud of it, like they've joined an exclusive club; clustered at their lockers, they whisper a giggling, salacious play-by-play. Jack himself talks to no one. It's common knowledge that he's alone most of the time: his mother works night shifts at the hospital, six nights a week. He does not eat in the school cafeteria; he does not go to the dances. In class, he sits in the back row, picking the next girl he'll ask for a ride. This spring he had picked Lydia.

Nath huddles in the cemetery an hour, two hours, three, watching the cemetery workers stack the folding chairs, gather the flowers, pluck balled-up papers and tissues from the grass. In his mind, he dredges up every single thing he's ever heard about Jack, every fact, every rumor. The two begin to blur, and by the time he is ready to head home, he is bubbling with a terrible fury. He tries to imagine Lydia with Jack, tries desperately not to picture them together. Had Jack hurt her somehow? He doesn't know. He knows only that Jack is at the heart of everything, and he promises himself he will find out how. Only when the gravediggers lift their shovels and approach the open grave does Nath clamber to his feet and turn away.

As he skirts the edge of the lake and turns onto their street, he spots a police car parked outside Jack's house. *About goddamn time,* Nath thinks. He sidles closer to the house, slouching below the line of windows. Behind the screen, the front door stands open, and he climbs the porch stairs on his toes, sticking to the edges of the worn boards, making sure they don't squeak. It's his sister they're talking about, he tells himself with each step; he has every right. At the top, he leans toward the screen door. He can't see anything except the entryway, but he can hear Jack in the living room, explaining slowly, loudly, as if it's the second or third time.

"She had skipped ahead into physics. Her mom wanted her in with the juniors."

"*You* were in that class. Aren't you a senior?"

"I told you," Jack says, impatient. "I had to take it over. I failed."

Dr. Wolff's voice, now: "He has a B-plus in the class this term. I told you you'd do fine if you would just do the work, Jack."

Outside, Nath blinks. Jack? A B-plus?

A rustle, as if the policeman has turned the page of a notebook. Then: "What was the nature of your relationship with Lydia?"

90

The sound of his sister's name in the policeman's voice, so crisp and official, as if it were nothing more than a label, startles Nath. It seems to startle Jack, too: there's a sharpness to his tone that wasn't there before.

"We were friends. That's all."

"Several people said they saw the two of you together after school in your car."

"I was teaching her to drive." Nath wishes he could see Jack's face. Didn't they know he must be lying? But the policeman seems to accept this.

"When was the last time you saw Lydia?" the policeman asks now.

"Monday afternoon. Before she disappeared."

"What were you doing?"

"We were sitting in my car and smoking."

A pause as the policeman makes a note of this. "And you were at the hospital, Mrs. Wolff?"

"Doctor."

The policeman coughs gently. "Pardon me. Dr. Wolff. You were at work?"

"I usually take the evening shift. Every day except Sundays."

"Did Lydia seem upset on Monday?"

Another pause before Jack responds. "Lydia was always upset."

91

Because of you, Nath thinks. His throat is so tight the words can't squeeze through. The edges of the door waver and blur, like a heat mirage. He digs his fingernail into his palm, hard, until the doorway sharpens again.

"Upset about what?"

"Upset about everything." Jack's voice is lower now, almost a sigh. "About her grades. About her parents. About her brother leaving for college. Lots of things." He sighs then for real, and when he speaks again, his voice is brittle, ready to snap. "How should I know?"

Nath backs away from the door and creeps down the stairs. He doesn't need to hear any more. At home, not wanting to see anyone, he slips upstairs to his room to ruminate over what he's heard.

There's no one for him to see anyway. While Nath fretted under the elm tree, his family has dispersed. During the car ride, Marilyn doesn't look at James once, focusing instead on her knuckles, picking at her cuticles, fiddling with the strap of her handbag. As soon as they come inside, Marilyn says she wants to lie down, and Hannah too vanishes into her room without a word. For a moment James considers joining Marilyn in their bedroom. He's filled with a deep longing to burrow against her, to feel her weight and warmth surrounding him, shielding him from everything else. To cling to her and feel her cling to him and let their bodies comfort each other. But something scratches and scratches at the edge of James's mind, and at last he lifts his keys from the table again. There is something he must do at the office, urgently. It cannot wait another minute.

When the police had asked if he wanted a copy of the autopsy, he had given them his office address. Then yesterday, a thick manila envelope appeared in his mail cubby, and he decided he'd made a mistake: he didn't want to see it, ever. At the same time, he could not bring himself to throw it away. Instead he slipped it into the bottom drawer of his desk and locked it. It would be there, he thought, if he ever changed his mind. He had never expected to.

It is lunchtime, and the office is almost empty; only Myrna, the department secretary, still sits at her desk, changing the ribbon of her typewriter. All the other office doors are shut, their frosted-glass windows dim. Now James unlocks the drawer, takes a deep breath, and slits the envelope open with his finger.

He has never seen an autopsy report

before and expects charts and diagrams, but it opens like a teacher's progress report: *The subject is a well-developed, well-nourished Oriental female.* It tells him things he already knows: that she was sixteen years old, sixty-five inches tall; that her hair was black, that her eyes were blue. It tells him things he hadn't known: the circumference of her head, the length of each limb, that a small crescent moon scarred her left knee. It tells him that there were no intoxicants in her blood, that there were no signs of foul play or sexual trauma, but that suicide, homicide, or accident could not yet be determined. The cause of death was *asphyxia by drowning.*

And then it begins in earnest: *The chest is opened using a Y-shaped incision.*

He learns the color and size of each of her organs, the weight of her brain. That a white foam had bubbled up through her trachea and covered her nostrils and mouth like a lace handkerchief. That her alveoli held a thin layer of silt as fine as sugar. That her lungs had marbled dark red and yellow-gray as they starved for air; that like dough, they took the impression of a fingertip; that when they were sectioned with a scalpel, water flowed out. That in her stomach were snippets of lake-bottom weeds, sand, and six ounces of lake water she'd swallowed as she sank. That the right side of her heart had swollen, as if it had had too much to hold. That from floating head down in the water, the skin of her head and neck had reddened to her shoulders. That due to the low temperature of the water, she had not yet decomposed, but that the skin of her fingertips was just beginning to peel off, like a glove.

The office air-conditioning clicks on and a cool breeze floats up from the floor. His whole body trembles, as if he's caught a sudden, lasting chill. With his toe, he closes the vent, but he can't keep his hands from shaking. He balls them into fists and clenches his jaw to stop his teeth from chattering. In his lap, the autopsy report quivers like something alive.

He can't imagine telling Marilyn that these things could happen to a body they loved. He doesn't ever want her to know. Better to leave it as the police summed it up: drowning. No details to catch in the crevices of her mind. The air-conditioning shuts off, silence ballooning to fill the room, then the whole department. The weight of everything he's read settles on him, crushing him to his chair. It is too heavy. He cannot even lift his head.

"Professor Lee?"

It's Louisa, at the door, still wearing the black dress she'd worn at the funeral that morning.

"Oh," she says. "I'm so sorry. I didn't think you'd come in after —" She stops.

"It's okay." His voice crackles at the edges, like old leather.

Louisa slips into the room, leaving the door ajar. "Are you all right?" She takes in his red-rimmed eyes, the slouch of his shoulders, the manila envelope in his lap. Then she comes to stand beside him and gently takes the papers from his hands. "You shouldn't be here," she says, setting them on his desk.

James shakes his head. With one hand he holds out the report.

Louisa looks down at the sheaf of papers and hesitates.

Read, James says — or tries to say. No sound emerges, but to him it seems Louisa hears anyway. She nods, leans against the edge of the desk, and bends her head over the pages. Her face doesn't change as she reads, but she grows stiller and stiller, until, at the end of the report, she rises and takes James's hand.

"You shouldn't be here," Louisa says again. It's not a question. With her other hand, she touches the small of his back, and he can feel her warmth through his shirt. Then she says, "Why don't you come to my apartment. I'll cook you some lunch." And he nods.

Her apartment is a third-floor walk-up, only six blocks from campus. Outside apartment 3A Louisa hesitates, just for a moment. Then she unlocks the door and lets them in and leads him straight to the bedroom.

Everything about her is different: the flex of her limbs, the texture of her skin. Even her taste is different, slightly tangy, like citrus, as he touches his tongue to hers. When she kneels over him to undo the buttons of his shirt, her hair curtains her face. James closes his eyes then, lets out a long, shuddering sigh. Afterward he falls asleep with Louisa still atop him. Since Lydia was *found* — the only word he can bear to use for it — the little sleep he's had has been restless. In his dreams, no one but him remembers what has happened to Lydia; he alone is acutely aware, and over and over he must persuade Marilyn, Nath, complete strangers that his daughter is dead. *I saw her body. One of her blue eyes was gone.* Now, still slicked to Louisa with sweat, he sleeps soundly for the first time in days, a

97

dreamless sleep: his mind, for the moment, gone blissfully blank.

At home, in their bedroom, Marilyn too wills her mind to go blank, but nothing happens. For hours, trying to sleep, she has been counting the flowers on her pillowcase: not the big red poppies that sprawl across the cotton, but the blue forget-me-nots of the background pattern, the chorus dancers behind the divas. She keeps losing track, moving from eighty-nine back down to eighty, crossing a fold in the fabric and forgetting which are accounted for, which have yet to be numbered. By the time she reaches two hundred, she knows that sleep is impossible. She can't keep her eyes closed; even blinking makes her jittery. Whenever she tries to lie still, her mind whirrs to life like an overwound toy. Upstairs, there is no sound from Hannah; downstairs, no sign of Nath. At last, just as James sinks into sleep across town, she rises and goes where her thoughts have been all this time: Lydia's room.

It still smells like Lydia. Not just the powdery flowers of her perfume, or the clean scent of shampoo on her pillowcase, or the trace of cigarette smoke — *Karen smokes,* Lydia had explained when Marilyn sniffed suspiciously one day. *It gets all on my clothes and books and everything.* No, when Marilyn breathes in deep, she can smell Lydia herself under all those surface layers, the sour-sweet smell of her skin. She could spend hours here, drawing the air up and holding it against her palate like the bouquet of a fine wine. Drinking her in.

In this room a deep ache suffuses her, as if her bones are bruised. Yet it feels good, too. Everything here reminds her of what Lydia could have been. Prints of Leonardo's Vitruvian Man, of Marie Curie holding up a vial — every poster she'd given to Lydia since she was a child — still hung proudly on the wall. Since childhood, Lydia had wanted to be a doctor, just as her mother once had. Last summer she had even taken a biology course at the college so that she could skip ahead into physics. On the bulletin board hang blue ribbons from years of science fairs, an illustrated periodic table, a real stethoscope that Marilyn had special-ordered for her thirteenth birthday. The bookshelf is so full of books that some are crammed in sideways at the top: *A Brief History of Medicine,* she reads upside down. *Rosalind Franklin and DNA.* All the books Marilyn had given her over the years to inspire her, to show her what she could accomplish. Everywhere, evidence of her daughter's talent and ambition. A fine layer of dust has already begun to coat everything. For a long time, Lydia had shooed her out when she came to vacuum and dust and tidy. "I'm *busy,* Mom," she had said, tapping the tip of her pen against her textbook, and Marilyn would nod and kiss her on the head and shut the door behind her. Now there is no one to turn her away, but she looks at Lydia's boot, tipped on its side on the carpet, thinks of her daughter kicking it off, and lets it lie.

Somewhere in this room, she is sure, is the answer to what happened. And there, on the bottom shelf of the bookcase, she sees the neat row of diaries lined up by year. Marilyn had given Lydia her first diary the Christmas she was five, a flowered one with gilt edges and a key lighter than a paper clip. Her daughter had unwrapped it and turned it over and over in her hands, touching the tiny keyhole, as if she didn't know what it was for. "For writing down your secrets," Marilyn had said with a smile, and Lydia had smiled back up at her and said, "But Mom, I don't have any secrets."

At the time, Marilyn had laughed. What secrets could a daughter keep from her mother, anyway? Still, every year, she gave Lydia another diary. Now she thinks of all those crossed-out phone numbers, that long list of girls who said they barely knew Lydia at all. Of boys from school. Of strange men who might lurch out of the shadows. With one finger, she tugs out the last diary: 1977. It will tell her, she thinks. Everything Lydia no longer can. Who she had been seeing. Why she had lied to them. Why she went down to the lake.

The key is missing, but Marilyn jams the tip of a ballpoint into the catch and forces the flimsy lock open. The first page she sees, April 10, is blank. She checks May 2, the night Lydia disappeared. Nothing. Nothing for May 1, or anything in April, or anything in March. Every page is blank. She takes down 1976. 1975. 1974. Page after page of visible, obstinate silence. She leafs backward all the way to the very first diary, 1966: not one word. All those years of her daughter's life unmarked. Nothing to explain anything.

Across town, James wakes in a blurry haze. It's almost evening, and Louisa's apartment has grown dim. "I have to go," he says, dizzy with the thought of what he has done, and Louisa wraps herself in the sheet and watches him dress. Under her gaze, his fingers grow clumsy: he mis-buttons his shirt not once but twice, and even when he gets it on properly it doesn't feel right. It hangs strangely, pinching him under the arms, bulging at his belly. How did you say good-bye, after something like this?

"Goodnight," he says finally, lifting his bag, and Louisa says simply, "Goodnight." As if they're leaving the office, as if nothing has happened. Only in the car, when his stomach begins to rumble, does he realize there'd been no lunch at Louisa's apartment, that he had never actually expected there to be.

And while James clicks on his headlights and eases the car into motion, stunned at how much has happened in one day, his son peers through his bedroom window in the growing dimness, staring out at Jack's house, where the porch light has just turned on, where the police car has long since pulled away. Up in the attic, Hannah curls up in her bed, sifting through each detail of the day: the white spot on each of her father's knuckles as he grasped the steering wheel; the tiny beads of sweat that clung to the minister's upper lip, like dew; the soft thump the coffin made as it touched the bottom of the grave. The small figure of her brother — spied through the west-facing window of her room — rising slowly from Jack's front steps and trudging home, head bowed. And the faint questioning creak of her mother's bedroom door opening, answered by the quiet click of Lydia's door latching shut. She has been in there for hours. Hannah wraps her arms around herself and squeezes, imagines comforting her mother, her mother's arms comforting her in return.

Marilyn, unaware that her youngest is listening so closely, so longingly, blots her eyes and replaces the diaries on the shelf and makes herself a promise. She will figure out what happened to Lydia. She will find out who is responsible. She will find out what went wrong.

FOUR

Just before Marilyn had given Lydia that first diary, the university had held its annual Christmas party. Marilyn had not wanted to go. All fall she'd been wrestling a vague discontentment. Nath had just started the first grade, Lydia had just started nursery school, Hannah had not yet even been imagined. For the first time since she'd been married, Marilyn found herself unoccupied. She was twenty-nine years old, still young, still slender. Still smart, she thought. She could go back to school now, at last, and finish her degree. Do everything she'd planned before the children came along. Only now she couldn't remember how to write a paper, how to take notes; it seemed as vague and hazy as something she had done in a dream. How could she study when dinner needed cooking, when Nath needed to be tucked in, when Lydia wanted to play? She leafed through the Help Wanted ads in the paper, but they were all for waitresses, accountants, copywriters. Nothing she knew how to do. She thought of her mother, the life her mother had wanted for her, the life her mother had hoped to lead herself: husband, children, house, her sole job to keep it all in order. Without meaning to, she'd acquired it. There was nothing more her mother could have wished her. The thought did not put her in a festive mood.

James, however, had insisted that they *put in an appearance* at the Christmas party; he was up for tenure in the spring, and *appearances* mattered. So they had asked Vivian Allen from across the street to babysit Nath and Lydia, and Marilyn put on a peach cocktail dress and her pearls and they headed to the crepe-papered gymnasium, where a Christmas tree had been erected on the midcourt line. Then, after the obligatory round of hellos and how-are-yous, she retreated to the corner, nursing a cup of rum punch. That was where she ran into Tom Lawson.

Tom brought her a slice of fruitcake and introduced himself — he was a professor in the chemistry department; he and James had worked together on the thesis committee of a double-majoring student who'd written about chemical warfare in World War I. Marilyn tensed against the inevitable questions — *And what do you do, Marilyn?* — but instead they exchanged the usual benign civilities: how old the children were, how nice this year's Christmas tree looked. And when he began to tell her about the research he was doing — something to do with the pancreas and artificial insulin — she interrupted to ask if he needed a research assistant, and he stared at her over his plate of pigs in blankets. Marilyn, afraid of seeming unqualified, offered a flood of explanations: she had been a chemistry major at Radcliffe and she'd been planning on medical school and she hadn't quite finished her degree — yet — but now that the children were a bit older —

In fact, Tom Lawson had been surprised at the tone of her request: it had the murmured, breathless quality of a proposition. Marilyn looked up at him and smiled, and her deep dimples gave her the earnestness of a little girl.

"Please," she said, putting her hand on his elbow. "I'd really enjoy doing some more academic work again."

Tom Lawson grinned. "I guess I could use some help," he said. "If your husband doesn't mind, that is. Maybe we could meet and talk about it after New Year's, when term starts." And Marilyn said yes, yes, that would be wonderful.

James was less enthusiastic. He knew what people would say: *He couldn't make enough — his wife had to hire herself out.* Years had passed, but he still remembered his mother rising early each morning and donning her uniform, how one winter, when she'd been home from work with the flu for two weeks, they'd had to turn off the heat and bundle in double blankets. He remembered how at night, his mother would massage oil into her calloused hands, trying to soften them, and his father would leave the room, ashamed. "No," he told Marilyn. "When I get tenure, we'll have all the money we need." He took her hand, uncurled her fingers, kissed her soft palm. "Tell me you won't worry about working anymore," he said, and at last she had agreed. But she kept Tom Lawson's phone number.

Then, in the spring, while James — newly tenured — was at work and the children were at school and Marilyn, at home, folded her second load of laundry, the phone rang. A nurse from St. Catherine's Hospital, in Virginia, telling her that her mother had died. A stroke. It was April 1, 1966, and the first thing Marilyn thought was: what a terrible, tasteless joke.

By then she had not spoken to her mother in almost eight years, since her wedding day. In all that time, her mother had not written once. When Nath had been born, then Lydia, Marilyn had not informed her mother, had not even sent a photograph. What was there to say? She and James had never discussed what her mother had said about their marriage that last day: *it's not right.* She had not ever wanted to think of it again. So when James came home that night, she said simply, "My mother died." Then she turned back to the stove and added, "And the lawn needs mowing," and he understood: they would not talk about it. At dinner, when she told the children that their grandmother had died, Lydia cocked her head and asked, "Are you sad?"

Marilyn glanced at her husband. "Yes," she said. "Yes, I am."

There were things to be taken care of: papers to be signed, burial arrangements to be made. So Marilyn left the children with James and drove to Virginia — she'd long since stopped thinking of it as *home* — to sort out her mother's things. As mile after mile of Ohio, then West Virginia, streamed past, her daughter's question echoed in her mind. She could not answer for sure.

Was she sad? She was more surprised than anything: surprised at how familiar her mother's house still felt. Even after eight years, she still remembered exactly how to wiggle the key — down and to the left — to get the lock to open; she still remembered the screen door that slowly closed itself with a hiss. The light in the foyer had burned out and the heavy curtains in the living room were closed, but her feet moved by instinct despite the dark: years of rehearsal had taught her the dance step around the arm-chair and the ottoman to the table beside the sofa. Her fingers caught the ribbed switch of the lamp on the first try. It could have been her house.

When the light came on, she saw the same shabby furniture she'd grown up with, the same pale lilac wallpaper with a grain, like silk. The same china cabinet full of her mother's dolls, whose unblinking eyes gave her the same cold tingle on the back of her neck. On the mantel, the same photographs of her as a child. All the things that she needed to clear away. Was she sad? No, after the daylong drive, only tired. "Many people find this job overwhelming," the undertaker told her the next morning. He gave her the number of a cleaning company that special-ized in making houses ready to sell. *Ghouls,*

Marilyn thought. What a job, clearing the homes of the dead, piling whole lives into garbage bins and lugging them to the curb.

"Thank you," she said, lifting her chin. "I'd rather take care of it myself."

But when she tried to sort her mother's things, she could find nothing she wanted to keep. Her mother's gold ring, her twelve settings of china, the pearl bracelet from Marilyn's father: mementos of an ill-fated wedding day. Her demure sweater sets and pencil skirts, the gloves and hat-boxed hats: relics of a corseted existence that Marilyn had always pitied. Her mother had loved her doll collection, but their faces were blank as chalk, white china masks under horsehair wigs. Little strangers with cold stares. Marilyn leafed through photo albums for a picture of herself with her mother and couldn't find one. Only Marilyn in kindergarten pigtails; Marilyn in third grade with a missing front tooth; Marilyn at a school party, a paper crown on her head. Marilyn in high school in front of the Christmas tree in a precious Kodachrome. Three photo albums of Marilyn and not a single shot of her mother. As if her mother had never been there.

Was she sad? How could she miss her mother when her mother was nowhere to be found?

And then, in the kitchen, she discovered her mother's Betty Crocker cookbook, the spine cracking and mended, twice, with Scotch tape. On the first page of the cookie section, a deliberate line in the margin of the introduction, the kind she herself had made in college to mark an important passage. It was no recipe. *Always cookies in the cookie jar!* the paragraph read. *Is there a happier symbol of a friendly house?* That was all. Her mother had felt the need to highlight this. Marilyn glanced at the cow-shaped cookie jar on the counter and tried to picture the bottom. The more she thought about it, the less sure she was that she had ever seen it.

She flipped through the other chapters, looking for more pencil lines. In "Pies," she found another: *If you care about pleasing a man — bake a pie. But make sure it's a perfect pie. Pity the man who has never come home to a pumpkin or custard pie.* Under "Basic Eggs": *The man you marry will know the way he likes his eggs. And chances are he'll be fussy about them. So it behooves a good wife to know how to make an egg behave in six basic ways.* She imagined her mother touching the pencil tip to her tongue, then drawing a careful dark mark down the margin so that she would remember.

You'll find your skill with a salad makes its own contribution to the quality of life in your house.

Does anything make you feel so pleased with yourself as baking bread?

Betty's pickles! Aunt Alice's peach conserve! Mary's mint relish! Is there anything that gives you a deeper sense of satisfaction than a row of shining jars and glasses standing on your shelf?

Marilyn looked at Betty Crocker's portrait on the back cover of the cookbook, the faint streaks of gray at her temples, the hair that curled back from her forehead, as if pushed back by the arch of her eyebrow. For a second, it resembled her mother. *Is there anything that gives you a deeper sense of satisfaction?* Certainly her mother would have said no, no, no. She thought with sharp and painful pity of her mother, who had planned on a golden, vanilla-scented life but ended up alone, trapped like a fly in this small and sad and empty house, this small and sad and empty life, her daughter gone, no trace of herself left except these pencil-marked dreams. Was she sad? She was angry. Furious at the smallness of her mother's life. *This,* she thought fiercely, touching the cookbook's cover. *This is all I need to remember about her. This is all I want to keep.*

The next morning, she called the house-cleaning company the undertaker had recommended. The two men who arrived at her door wore blue uniforms, like janitors. They were clean-shaven and courteous; they looked at her with sympathy but said nothing about "your loss." With the efficiency of movers they packed dolls and dishes and clothes into cartons. They swaddled furniture in quilted pads and trundled it to the truck. Where did it go, Marilyn wondered, cradling the cookbook — the mattresses, the photographs, the emptied-out book-shelves? The same place people went when they died, where everything went: on, away, out of your life.

By dinnertime, the men had emptied the entire house. One of them tipped his hat to Marilyn; the other gave her a polite little nod. Then they stepped out onto the stoop, and the truck's engine started outside. She moved from room to room, the cookbook tucked under her arm, checking that nothing had been left behind, but the men had been thorough. Her old room was hardly recognizable with the pictures peeled from its walls. The only signs of her time there were the thumbtack holes in the wallpaper, invisible unless you knew where to look. It could have been a stranger's house. Through the open curtains she could see nothing, only panes of dusk and her face faintly reflected back to her in the glow of the ceiling light. On her way out, she paused in the living room, where the carpet was pockmarked with the ghosts of chair feet, and studied the mantel, now a clean line under a stretch of bare wall.

As she pulled onto the highway, heading toward Ohio and home, those empty rooms kept rising in her mind. She swallowed uneasily, pushing the thought aside, and pressed the gas pedal harder.

Outside Charlottesville, flecks of rain appeared on the windows. Halfway across West Virginia the rain grew heavy, sheeting the windshield. Marilyn pulled to the roadside and turned off the car, and the wipers stopped midsweep, two slashes across the glass. It was past one o'clock in the morning and no one else was on the road: no taillights on the horizon, no headlights in the rearview, only farmland stretching out on either side. She snapped off her own lights and leaned back against the headrest. How good the rain would feel, like crying all over her body.

She thought again of the empty house, a lifetime of possessions now bound for the thrift shop, or the garbage dump. Her mother's clothes on some stranger's body, her ring circling some stranger's finger. Only the cookbook, beside her at the other end of the front seat, had survived. That was the only thing worth keeping, Marilyn reminded herself, the only place in the house there was any trace of her.

It struck her then, as if someone had said it aloud: her mother was dead, and the only thing worth remembering about her, in the end, was that she had cooked. Marilyn thought uneasily of her own life, of hours spent making breakfasts, serving dinners, packing lunches into neat paper bags. How was it possible to spend so many hours spreading peanut butter across bread? How was it possible to spend so many hours cooking eggs? Sunny-side up for James. Hard-boiled for Nath. Scrambled for Lydia. *It behooves a good wife to know how to make an egg behave in six basic ways.* Was she sad? Yes. She was sad. About the eggs. About everything.

She unlocked the door and stepped out onto the asphalt.

The noise outside the car was deafening:

a million marbles hitting a million tin roofs, a million radios all crackling on the same non-station. By the time she shut the door she was drenched. She lifted her hair and bowed her head and let the rain soak the curls beneath. The drops smarted against her bare skin. She leaned back on the cooling hood of the car and spread her arms wide, letting the rain needle her all over.

Never, she promised herself. *I will never end up like that.*

Under her head she could hear water thrumming on the steel. Now it sounded like tiny patters of applause, a million hands clapping. She opened her mouth and let rain drip into it, opened her eyes and tried to look straight up into the falling rain.

Back in the car, she peeled off her blouse and skirt and stockings and shoes. At the far end of the passenger seat they made a sad little heap beside the cookbook, like a melting scoop of ice cream. The rain slowed, and the gas pedal was stiff under her bare foot as she coaxed the car into motion. In the rearview mirror she caught a glimpse of her reflection, and instead of being embarrassed to see herself stripped so naked and vulnerable, she admired the pale gleam of her own skin against the white of her bra.

Never, she thought again. *I will never end*

up like that.

She drove on into the night, homeward, her hair weeping tiny slow streams down her back.

At home, James did not know how to make eggs behave in any way. Each morning, he served the children cereal for breakfast and sent them to school with thirty cents apiece for the lunch line. "When is Mom coming home?" Nath asked every night, crimping the foil tray of his TV dinner. His mother had been gone for nearly a week, and he longed for hard-boiled eggs again. "Soon," James answered. Marilyn had not left the number at her mother's, and anyway, that line would soon be disconnected. "Any day now. What shall we do this weekend, hmm?"

What they did was head to the Y to learn the breaststroke. Lydia hadn't yet learned to swim, so James left her across the street with Mrs. Allen for the afternoon. All week he had looked forward to some father-son time. He had even planned out how he would begin: *Keep your arms underwater. Whip your legs out. Like this.* Although James himself had been a swimmer in high school, he had never won a trophy; he had gone home alone while the others piled into someone's car for celebratory hamburgers and milkshakes. Now he suspected that Nath had the makings of a swimmer, too: he was short, but he was wiry and strong. In last summer's swim class, he had learned the front crawl and the dead-man's float; already he could swim underwater all the way across the pool. In high school, James imagined, Nath would be the star of the team, the collector of trophies, the anchorman in the relay. He would be the one driving everyone to the diner — or wherever kids would go in the far-off 1970s — after meets.

That Saturday, when they got to the pool, the shallow end was full of children playing Marco Polo; in the deep end, a pair of elderly men glided in laps. No space for breaststroke lessons yet. James nudged his son. "Go in and play with the others until the pool empties out."

"Do I have to?" Nath asked, pleating the edge of his towel. The only other kid he recognized was Jack, who by then had been living on their street for a month. Although Nath had not yet come to hate him, he already sensed that they would not be friends. At seven Jack was tall and lanky, freckled and bold, afraid of nothing. James, not attuned to the sensitivities of the playground, was suddenly annoyed at his son's shyness, his reluctance. The confident young man in his imagination dwindled to a nervous little boy: skinny, small, hunched so deeply that his chest was concave. And though he would not admit it, Nath — legs twisted, stacking the toes of one foot atop the other — reminded him of himself at that age.

"We came here to swim," James said. "Mrs. Allen is watching your sister just so *you* could learn the breaststroke, Nathan. Don't waste everyone's time." He tugged the towel from his son's grasp and steered him firmly toward the water, hovering over him until he slid in. Then he sat down on the vacant poolside bench, nudging aside discarded flippers and goggles. It's good for him, James thought. He needs to learn how to make friends.

Nath circled the girl who was *It* with the other children, bouncing on his toes to keep his head above water. It took James a few minutes to recognize Jack, and when he did, it was with a twinge of admiration. Jack was a good swimmer, cocky and confident in the water, weaving around the others, shining and breathless. He must have walked over by himself, James decided; all spring, Vivian Allen had been whispering about Janet Wolff, how she left Jack alone while

119

she worked at the hospital. *Maybe we can give him a ride home,* he thought. *He could stay to play at our house until his mother finishes her shift.* He would be a nice friend for Nath, a good role model. He imagined Nath and Jack inseparable, rigging a tire swing in the backyard, biking through the neighborhood. In his own schooldays, he'd been embarrassed to ask classmates to his house, afraid that they'd recognize his mother from the lunch line, or his father from mopping the hallway. They hadn't had a yard, anyway. Maybe they would play pirates, Jack as the captain and Nath as the first mate. Sheriff and deputy. Batman and Robin.

By the time James focused his attention back on the pool, Nath was *It.* But something was wrong. The other children glided away. Silently, stifling giggles, they hoisted themselves out of the water and onto the tile surround. Eyes closed, Nath drifted all alone in the middle of the pool, wading in small circles, feeling his way through the water with his hands. James could hear him: *Marco. Marco.*

Polo, the others called back. They circled the shallow end, splashing the water with their hands, and Nath moved from one side to the other, following the sounds of motion. *Marco. Marco.* A plaintive note in his voice now.

It wasn't personal, James told himself. They'd been playing for who knows how long; they were just tired of the game. They were just messing around. Nothing to do with Nath.

Then an older girl — maybe ten or eleven — shouted, "Chink can't find China!" and the other children laughed. A rock formed and sank in James's belly. In the pool, Nath paused, arms outstretched on the surface of the water, uncertain how to proceed. One hand opened and closed in silence.

On the sidelines, his father, too, was uncertain. Could he make the children get back in the pool? Saying anything would draw attention to the trick. He could call his son. *It's time to go home,* he might say. Then Nath would open his eyes and see nothing but water all around him. The smell of chlorine began to bite at James's nostrils. Then, on the far side of the pool, he saw the blur of a body sliding silently into the water. A figure glided toward Nath, a sandy head broke the surface: Jack.

"Polo," Jack shouted. The sound echoed off the tiled walls: *Polo. Polo. Polo.* Giddy with relief, Nath lunged, and Jack held still, treading water, waiting, until Nath caught his shoulder. For a moment, James saw sheer joy on his son's face, the dark furrow of frustration wiped away.

Then Nath opened his eyes, and the glow vanished. He saw the other kids squatting around the pool, laughing now, the pool empty except for Jack in front of him. Jack himself turned to Nath and grinned. To Nath, it was a taunt: *Joke's on you.* He shoved Jack aside and ducked underwater, and when he reemerged at the edge, he climbed straight out without shaking himself. He didn't even wipe the water from his eyes, just let it stream over his face as he stalked toward the door, and because of this James could not tell if he was crying.

In the locker room, Nath refused to say a word. He refused to put his clothes or even his shoes on, and when James held out his slacks for the third time, Nath kicked the locker so hard he left a dent in the door. James glanced back over his shoulder and saw Jack peeking through the door from the pool area. He wondered if Jack was about to speak, maybe apologize, but instead he stood silent and staring. Nath, who hadn't spotted Jack at all, marched out into the lobby, and James bundled up their things and let the door swing shut behind them.

Part of him wanted to gather his son into

his arms, to tell him that he understood. Even after almost thirty years, he still remembered P.E. class at Lloyd, how once he'd gotten tangled up in his shirt and emerged to find his pants missing from the bench. Everyone else had already dressed and was stuffing gym uniforms into lockers and lacing shoes. He had tiptoed back into the gym, hiding his bare thighs and calves behind his knapsack, looking for Mr. Childs, the P.E. teacher. By then the bell had rung and the locker room had emptied. After ten minutes of searching, mortified at being in his undershorts in front of Mr. Childs, his pants were revealed under a sink, legs tied around the U-bend, dust bunnies caught in the cuffs. "Probably just got mixed up in someone else's things," Mr. Childs had said. "Hurry along to class now, Lee. You're tardy." James had known it was no accident. After that, he had developed a system: pants first, then shirt. He had never told anyone about it, but the memory clung.

So part of him wanted to tell Nath that he knew: what it was like to be teased, what it was like to never fit in. The other part of him wanted to shake his son, to slap him. To shape him into something different. Later, when Nath was too slight for the football team, too short for the basketball team, too clumsy for the baseball team, when he seemed to prefer reading and poring over his atlas and peering through his telescope to making friends, James would think back to this day in the swimming pool, this first disappointment in his son, this first and most painful puncture in his fatherly dreams.

That afternoon, though, he let Nath run up to his room and slam the door. At dinnertime, when he knocked to offer a Salisbury steak, Nath did not respond, and downstairs, James allowed Lydia to nestle against him on the couch and watch *The Jackie Gleason Show.* What could he say to comfort his son? *It will get better?* He could not bring himself to lie. Better just to forget the whole thing. When Marilyn arrived home early Sunday morning, Nath sat sullen and silent at the breakfast table, and James said merely, with a wave of the hand, "Some kids teased him at the pool yesterday. He needs to learn to take a joke."

Nath bristled and glared at his father, but James, cringing at the memory of all he had left out — *Chink can't find China* — didn't notice, and neither did his mother, who, preoccupied, set bowls and the box of cornflakes in front of them. At this last outrage, finally, Nath broke his silence. "I want a *hard-boiled egg,"* he insisted. Marilyn, to everyone's surprise, burst into tears, and in the end, subdued and unprotesting, they all ate cereal anyway.

It was clear to the entire family, however, that something had changed in their mother. For the rest of the day, her mood was sulky and stormy. At dinner, though they all anticipated a roast chicken, or a meat loaf, or a pot roast — a real meal at last, after so many Swanson's dinners warmed in the oven — Marilyn opened a can of chicken noodle soup, a can of SpaghettiOs.

The next morning, after the children went to school, Marilyn pulled a scrap of paper from her dresser drawer. Tom Lawson's phone number still stood out, sharp black against the pale blue college rule.

"Tom?" she said when he answered. "Dr. Lawson. It's Marilyn Lee." When he didn't reply, she added, "James Lee's wife. We met at the Christmas party. We talked about me maybe working in your lab."

A pause. Then, to Marilyn's surprise: laughter. "I hired an undergrad months ago," Tom Lawson said. "I had no idea you were actually serious about that. With your children and your husband and all."

Marilyn hung up without bothering to reply. For a long time, she stood in the

125

kitchen by the phone, staring through the window. Outside, it no longer felt like spring. The wind had turned biting and dry; the daffodils, tricked by the warm weather, bent their faces to the ground. All across the garden, they lay prostrate, stems broken, yellow trumpets withered. Marilyn wiped the table and pulled the crossword puzzle toward her, trying to forget the amusement in Tom Lawson's voice. The newsprint clung to the damp wood, and as she wrote in her first answer, the pen tore through the paper, leaving a blue "A" on the tabletop.

She took her car keys down from their hook and lifted her handbag from the entry table. At first she told herself she was just going out to clear her head. Despite the chill, she rolled the window down, and as she circled the lake once, twice, the breeze snaked its way beneath her hair to the nape of her neck. *With your children and husband and all.* She drove without thinking, all the way through Middlewood, past the campus and the grocery store and the roller rink, and only when she found herself turning into the hospital parking lot did she realize this was where she'd intended to come all along.

Inside, Marilyn settled in the corner of the waiting room. Someone had painted the room — walls, ceiling, doors — a pale, calming blue. White-hatted, white-skirted nurses glided in and out like clouds, bearing syringes of insulin, bottles of pills, rolls of gauze. Candy stripers buzzed by with carts of lunch trays. And the doctors: they strode unhurried through the bustle like jets cutting their steady way through the sky. Whenever they appeared, heads turned toward them; anxious husbands and hysterical mothers and tentative daughters stood up at their approach. They were all men, Marilyn noticed: Dr. Kenger, Dr. Gordon, Dr. McLenahan, Dr. Stone. What had made her think she could be one of them? It seemed as impossible as turning into a tiger.

Then, through the double doors from the emergency room: a slender dark-haired figure, hair pulled back in a neat bun. For a moment, Marilyn could not place her. "Dr. Wolff," one of the nurses called, lifting a clipboard from the counter, and Dr. Wolff crossed the room to take it, her heels clack-clacking on the linoleum. Marilyn had seen Janet Wolff only once or twice since she'd moved in a month before, but she would not have recognized her anyway. She had heard that Janet Wolff worked at the hospital — Vivian Allen, leaning over the garden fence, had whispered about late shifts, the

Wolff boy left to run wild — but she had pictured a secretary, a nurse. Not this graceful woman, no older than she, tall in black slacks, a white doctor's coat loose around her slim frame. This *Dr. Wolff,* a stethoscope looped around her neck like a shining silver necklace, who with expert hands touched and turned the bruised wrist of a workman, who called clear and confident across the room, "Dr. Gordon, may I have a word with you about your patient, please?" And Dr. Gordon put down his clipboard, and came.

It was not her imagination. Everyone repeated it, like a mantra. Dr. Wolff. Dr. Wolff. Dr. Wolff. The nurses, bottles of penicillin in hand: "Dr. Wolff, a quick question." The candy stripers, as they passed by: "Good morning, Dr. Wolff." Most miraculous of all, the other doctors: "Dr. Wolff, could I ask your opinion, please?" "Dr. Wolff, you're needed in patient room two." Only then did Marilyn finally believe.

How was it possible? How had she managed it? She thought of her mother's cookbook: *Make somebody happy today — bake a cake! Bake a cake — have a party. Bake a cake to take to a party. Bake a cake just because you feel good today.* She pictured her mother creaming shortening and sugar, sifting flour, greasing a pan. *Is there anything*

that gives you a deeper sense of satisfaction?
There was Janet Wolff striding across the
hospital waiting room, her coat so white it
glowed.

Of course it was possible for her: she had
no husband. She let her son run wild.
Without a husband, without children, perhaps it would have been possible. *I could
have done that,* Marilyn thought, and the
words clicked into place like puzzle pieces,
shocking her with their rightness. The
hypothetical past perfect, the tense of
missed chances. Tears dripped down her
chin. No, she thought suddenly. *I could do
that.*

And then, to her embarrassment and horror, there was Janet Wolff before her, bending solicitously in front of her chair.

"Marilyn?" she said. "It's Marilyn, right?
Mrs. Lee?"

To which Marilyn replied the only words
in her mind: "Dr. Wolff."

"What's wrong?" Dr. Wolff asked. "Are
you ill?" Up close, her face was surprisingly
young. Beneath her powder, a faint constellation of freckles still dotted her nose. Her
hand, gentle on Marilyn's shoulder, was
steady and assured, and so was her smile.
Everything will be fine, it seemed to say.

Marilyn shook her head. "No, no. Everything's fine." She looked up at Janet Wolff. "Thank you." And she meant it.

The next evening, after a dinner of canned ravioli and canned vegetable soup, she planned it out in her mind. She had all of her mother's savings, enough for a few months; when her mother's house was sold, she would have more, enough for a few years, at least. In a year, she could finish her degree. It would prove that she still could. That it was not too late. After that, at last, she would apply to medical school. Only eight years later than planned.

While the children were at school, she drove an hour to the community college outside Toledo and enrolled in organic chemistry, advanced statistics, anatomy: everything she'd planned for her last semesters. The next day, she made the drive again and found a furnished efficiency near the campus, signing a lease for the first of May. Two weeks away. Every night, when she was alone, she read the cookbook again, steeling herself with her mother's small and lonely life. *You don't want this,* she reminded herself. *There will be more to your life than this.* Lydia and Nath would be fine, she told herself again and again. She would not let herself think otherwise. James would be there. Look how they had managed while

130

she was in Virginia. It was still possible.

In the quiet dark, she packed her old college textbooks into cartons and tucked them in the attic, ready to go. As May approached, she cooked lavish meal after lavish meal: Swedish meatballs, beef Stroganoff, chicken à la king — everything James and the children liked best, everything from scratch, just as her mother had taught her. She baked a pink birthday cake for Lydia and let her eat as much as she wanted. On the first of May, after Sunday dinner, she sealed leftovers in Tupperware and put them in the freezer; she baked batch after batch of cookies. "It's like you're preparing for a famine," James said, laughing, and Marilyn smiled back, a fake smile, the same one she had given to her mother all those years. You lifted the corners of your mouth toward your ears. You kept your lips closed. It was amazing how no one could tell.

That night, in bed, she wrapped her arms around James, kissed the side of his neck, undressed him slowly, as she had when they were younger. She tried to memorize the curve of his back and the hollow at the base of his spine, as if he were a landscape she would never see again, beginning to cry — silently at first and then, as their bodies collided again and again, more fiercely.

"What is it?" James whispered, stroking her cheek. "What's wrong?" Marilyn shook her head, and he pulled her close, their bodies sticky and damp. "It's okay," he said, kissing her forehead. "Everything will be better tomorrow."

In the morning, Marilyn burrowed beneath the covers, listening to James dress. The zip as he fastened his trousers. The clink as he buckled his belt. Even with her eyes closed, she could see him straightening his collar, smoothing the cowlick in his hair, which still, after all these years, made him look a bit like a schoolboy. She kept them closed when he came to kiss her good-bye, because if she saw him, she knew the tears would come again.

At the bus stop, later that morning, she knelt on the sidewalk and kissed Nath and Lydia each on the cheek, not daring to look into their eyes. "Be good," she told them. "Behave. I love you."

After the bus had disappeared around the curve of the lake, she visited her daughter's room, then her son's. From Lydia's dresser she took a single barrette, cherry-colored Bakelite with a white flower, one of a pair she seldom wore. From the cigar box beneath Nath's bed she took a marble, not his favorite — the cobalt with white specks like stars — but one of the little dark ones, the ones he called oilies. From the inside of James's overcoat, the old one he'd worn in her college days, she snipped the spare button from the underside of the lapel. A tiny token from each, tucked into the pocket of her dress — a gesture that would resurface in her youngest child years later, though Marilyn would never mention this small theft to Hannah, or to anyone. Not something treasured and loved; something they might miss but would not grieve. No need to tear another hole, even a pinprick, in their lives. Then Marilyn took her boxes from their hiding place in the attic and sat down to write James a note. But how did you write something like this? It seemed wrong to write to him on her stationery, as if he were a stranger; more wrong still to write it on the scratch pad in the kitchen, as if it were no more important than a grocery list. At last she pulled a blank sheet from the typewriter and sat down at her vanity with a pen.

I realize that I am not happy with the life I lead. I always had one kind of life in mind and things have turned out very differently. Marilyn took a deep, ragged breath. *I have kept all these feelings inside me for a long time, but now, after being in my mother's house again, I think of her and realize I cannot put them aside any longer. I know you'll be fine without me.* She paused, trying to convince herself this was true.

I hope you can understand why I have to leave. I hope you can forgive me.

For a long time Marilyn sat, ballpoint in hand, unsure how to finish. In the end she tore up the note and tossed the shreds into the wastepaper basket. Better, she decided, just to go. To disappear from their lives as if she had never been there.

To Nath and Lydia, who that afternoon found themselves unmet at the bus stop, who let themselves into an unlocked and empty house, that was exactly how it seemed. Their father, when he came home two hours later to find his children huddled on the front steps, as if they were afraid to be in the house alone, kept asking questions. "What do you mean, *gone*?" he asked Nath, who could only repeat: *gone,* the only word he could find.

Lydia, meanwhile, said nothing at all during the confused rest of the evening, in which their father called the police and then all the neighbors but forgot about dinner, and bedtime, as the policemen took note after note until she and Nath fell asleep on the living room floor. She awoke in the middle of the night in her own bed — where her father had deposited her, shoes still on — and felt for the diary her mother had given her at Christmas. At last something important had occurred, something that she ought to write down. But she did not know how to explain what had happened, how everything had changed in just one day, how someone she loved so dearly could be there one minute, and the next minute: *gone*.

FIVE

Hannah knows nothing about that summer, of her mother's long-ago disappearance. For as long as she's been alive, the family has never spoken of it, and even if they had, it would have changed nothing. She is furious with her sister for vanishing, bewildered that Lydia would leave them all behind; knowing would only have made her more furious, more bewildered. *How could you,* she would have thought, *when you knew what it was like?* As it is, imagining her sister sinking into the lake, all she can think now is: *How?* And: *What was it like?*

Tonight she will find out. Again it is two A.M. by her glow-in-the-dark clock; all night she has lain patiently, watching the numbers tick by. Today, June 1, should have been her last day of school; tomorrow Nath was supposed to walk across the stage in his blue robe and mortarboard and collect his diploma. But they're not going to Nath's commencement; neither of them has gone back to school since — Her mind silences the thought.

She takes the squeaky sixth stair on her toes; she skips the middle rosette in the front-hall carpet and the creaky floorboard beneath, landing cat-soft just at the door. Although upstairs Marilyn and James and Nath all lie awake, searching for sleep, no one hears: Hannah's body knows all the secrets of silence. In the dark, her fingers slide back the bolt, then grasp the safety chain and unfasten it without rattling. This last is a new trick. Before the funeral, there was no chain.

She's been practicing this for three weeks now, toying with the lock whenever her mother wasn't looking. Now Hannah oozes her body around the door and steps barefoot onto the lawn, where Lydia must have been on her last night alive. Overhead, the moon hovers behind tree branches, and the yard and the walkway and the other houses slowly appear out of the grainy dark. This is what her sister would have seen that night: glints of moonlight reflected in Mrs. Allen's windowpanes, the mailboxes all leaning slightly away. The faint glimmer of the streetlamp on the corner, where the main road loops around the lake.

At the edge of the lawn Hannah stops, toes on the sidewalk, heels still on the grass, and pictures that thin figure marching into the shadows. She had not looked afraid. So Hannah heads straight down the middle of the road too, where the yellow line would be if their street were busy enough to need one. Through the darkened windows, the pale linings of curtains glow. There are no lights anywhere on their street, except for Mrs. Allen's front-door light, which she leaves on all the time, even during the day. When Hannah was younger, she had thought adults stayed up late every night, until two or three perhaps. She adds this to the list of things she's learned are untrue.

At the corner she stops, but sees only darkness both ways, no cars. Her eyes are used to the dark now, and she darts across the main road and onto the grassy bank of the lake, but she still can't see it. Only the slope of the ground tells her that she's getting close. She passes a clump of birches, all holding their stiff arms above their heads as if in surrender. Then, suddenly, her toes find the water. Below the low thrum of a high-up airplane she hears it: a faint lapping against her ankles, soft as the sound of her own tongue in her mouth. If she looks very hard, she can see a faint shimmer, like silver tulle.

Except for that, she would not have known that this was water.

"A beautiful location," the realtor had told James and Marilyn when they had first moved to Middlewood. Hannah has heard this story many times. "Five minutes to the grocery store and the bank. And think of it, the lake practically at your doorstep." He had glanced at Marilyn's rounded belly. "You and the kiddos can swim all summer. Like having your own private beach." James, charmed, had agreed. All her life, Hannah has loved this lake. Now it is a new place.

The dock, smoothed by years of use, is the same silvery-gray by moonlight that it is in the day. At the end one small lamp, set on a post, stretches its light over a thin circle of the water. She will set out in the boat, as Lydia must have. She will row to the middle of the lake, where her sister somehow ended up, and peer down into the water. Maybe then she'll understand.

But the boat is gone. The city, belatedly cautious, has taken it away.

Hannah sinks back onto her heels and imagines her sister kneeling to unknot the rope, then pushing the boat away from the shore, so far out you couldn't tell the water from the darkness around it. At last she lies down on the dock, rocking herself gently, looking up into the night sky. It is as close to her sister's last night as she can get.

If this were another summer, the lake would still be a lovely place. Nath and Lydia would don swimsuits and spread towels across the grass. Lydia, gleaming with baby oil, would stretch out in the sun. If Hannah were very lucky, she would be allowed to rub a squirt of oil on her own arms, to retie the strings of Lydia's bikini after she had tanned her back. Nath would cannonball off the dock, spraying a fine mist that would bead up on their skin like pearls. On the very best days — though those were very, very rare — their parents would come, too. Their father would practice his breaststroke and his Australian crawl, and if he was in a good mood, he'd take Hannah out over her head, steadying her as she kicked. Their mother, shaded by a huge sun hat, would look up from her *New Yorker* when Hannah returned to the towel and let her curl quietly against her shoulder to peep at the cartoons. These things happened only at the lake.

They won't go to the lake this summer at all; they will never go again. She knows without having to ask. Her father has spent the past three weeks in his office, although the university had offered to have someone else finish out the term. Her mother has spent hours and hours in Lydia's room, looking and looking at everything but touching nothing. Nath roams the house like a caged beast, opening cupboards and shutting them, picking up one book after another, then tossing them down again. Hannah doesn't say a word. These are the new rules, which no one has outlined but which she already knows: Don't talk about Lydia. Don't talk about the lake. Don't ask questions.

She lies still for a long time, picturing her sister on the lake bed. Her face would point straight up, like this, studying the underside of the water. Her arms would stretch out, like this, as if she were embracing the whole world. She would listen and listen, waiting for them to come and find her. *We didn't know,* Hannah thinks. *We would have come.*

It doesn't help. She still doesn't understand.

Back home, Hannah tiptoes into Lydia's room and shuts the door. Then she lifts the dust ruffle and pulls out the slim velvet box hidden beneath the bed. Under the tent of Lydia's blanket, she opens the box and pulls out a silver locket. Their father had given it to Lydia for her birthday, but she had tucked it under her bed, letting the velvet grow shaggy with dust.

The necklace is broken now but, anyway, Hannah has promised Lydia that she will never put it on, and she does not break promises to people she loves. Even if they aren't alive anymore. Instead she rubs the fine chain between her fingers like a rosary. The bed smells like her sister sleeping: a warm and musky and sharp smell — like a wild animal — that emerged only when she was deep in slumber. She can almost feel the imprint of her sister's body in the mattress, wrapping her like a hug. In the morning, when the sunlight comes through the window, she remakes the bed and replaces the locket and returns to her room. Without thinking, she knows she will do this again the next night, and the next, and the next, smoothing the blanket when she wakes, stepping carefully over the scattered shoes and clothes as she makes her way to the door.

At breakfast time, Nath comes downstairs to find his parents arguing, and he stops in the hallway just outside the kitchen. "Unlocked all night," his mother is saying, "and you don't even care."

"It wasn't unlocked. The bolt was on." By the sharp little edges in his father's voice, he can tell this conversation has been going on for some time.

"Someone could have gotten in. I put that chain on for a reason." Nath tiptoes into the doorway, but his parents — Marilyn bent over the sink, James hunched in his chair — don't look up. On the far side of the table, Hannah squirms over her toast and milk. *I'm sorry,* she thinks, as hard as she can. *I forgot the chain. I'm sorry I'm sorry.* Her parents don't notice. In fact, they act as if she isn't even there.

Silence for a long moment. Then James says, "You really think a chain on the door would have changed anything?"

Marilyn clunks her teacup hard against the counter. "She would never have gone out on her own. I know she wouldn't. Sneaking out in the middle of the night? My Lydia? Never." She wrings the china with both hands. "Someone took her out there. Some nutcase."

James sighs, a deep trembling sigh, as if he's struggling to lift a very heavy weight. For the past three weeks Marilyn has been saying things like this. The morning after the funeral he woke up just after sunrise and everything came rushing back to him — the glossy casket, Louisa's skin slick against his, the soft little moan she had made as he climbed atop her — and he suddenly felt grimy, as if he were caked with mud. He turned the shower on hot, so hot he couldn't stand still beneath it and had to keep turning, like something on a spit, offering the steaming spray a new patch of flesh again and again. It hadn't helped. And when he came out of the bathroom, a faint scratching noise led him to the bottom of the stairs, where Marilyn was installing the chain on the front door.

He had wanted to say what had been growing in his mind for days: what had happened to Lydia was nothing they could lock out or scare away. Then the look on Marilyn's face stopped him: sad, and frightened, but angry too, as if he were to blame for something. For a moment she seemed like a different woman, a stranger. He had swallowed hard and touched his collar, buttoning it over his throat. "Well," he said, "I'm going in to school. My summer class." When he leaned in to kiss her, she flinched away as if his touch burned. On the front porch, the paperboy had deposited a newspaper. *Local Family Lays Daughter to Rest.*

He still has it locked in the bottom drawer of his desk. *As one of only two Orientals at Middlewood High — the other being her brother, Nathan — Lee stood out in the halls. However, few seemed to have known her well.*

Every day since then, there have been more articles: any death is a sensation in a small town, but the death of a young girl is a journalistic gold mine. *Police Still Searching for Clues in Girl's Death. Suicide Likely Possibility, Investigators Say.* Each time he sees one, he folds the newsprint over itself, as if wrapping up something rotten, before Marilyn or the children spot it. Only in the safety of his office does he unroll the paper to read it carefully. Then he adds it to the growing stack in the locked drawer.

Now he bows his head. "I don't think that's what happened."

Marilyn bristles. "What are you suggesting?"

Before James can answer, the doorbell rings. It is the police, and as the two officers step into the kitchen, Nath and Hannah simultaneously let out their breaths. At last their parents will stop arguing.

"We just wanted to give you folks an update," says the older one — Officer Fiske, Nath remembers. He pulls a notebook from his pocket and nudges his glasses up with a stubby finger. "Everyone at the station is truly sorry for your loss. We just want to find out what happened."

"Of course, officer," James murmurs.

"We've spoken to the people you listed."

Officer Fiske consults his notebook. "Karen Adler, Pam Saunders, Shelley Brierley — they all said they barely knew her."

Hannah watches redness spread across her father's face, like a rash.

"We've talked to a number of Lydia's classmates and teachers as well. From what we can tell, she didn't have many friends." Officer Fiske looks up. "Would you say Lydia was a lonely girl?"

"Lonely?" James glances at his wife, then — for the first time that morning — at his son. *As one of only two Orientals at Middlewood High — the other being her brother, Nathan — Lee stood out in the halls.* He knows that feeling: all those faces, fish-pale and silent and staring. He had tried to tell himself that Lydia was different, that all those friends made her just one of the crowd. "Lonely," he says again, slowly. "She did spend a lot of time alone."

"She was so busy," Marilyn interrupts. "She worked very hard in her classes. A lot of homework to do. A lot of studying." She looks earnestly from one policeman to the other, as if afraid they won't believe her. "She was very smart."

"Did she seem sad at all, these past few weeks?" the younger officer asks. "Did she ever give any sign she might want to hurt

146

herself? Or —"

Marilyn doesn't even wait for him to finish. "Lydia was very happy. She loved school. She could have done anything. She'd never go out in that boat by herself." Her hands start to shake, and she clutches the teacup again, trying to keep them steady — so tightly Hannah thinks she might squeeze it to pieces. "Why aren't you looking for whoever took her out there?"

"There's no evidence of anyone else in the boat with her," says Officer Fiske. "Or on the dock."

"How can you tell?" Marilyn insists. "My Lydia would never have gone out in a boat alone." Tea sloshes onto the counter. "You just never know, these days, who's waiting around the corner for you."

"Marilyn," James says.

"Read the paper. There are psychos everywhere these days, kidnapping people, shooting them. Raping them. What does it take for the police to start tracking *them* down?"

"Marilyn," James says again, louder this time.

"We're looking into all possibilities," Officer Fiske says gently.

"We know you are," says James. "You're doing all you can. Thank you." He glances at Marilyn. "We can't ask for more than

147

that." Marilyn opens her mouth again, then closes it without a word.

The policemen glance at each other. Then the younger one says, "We'd like to ask Nathan a few more questions, if that's okay. Alone."

Five faces swivel toward Nath, and his cheeks go hot. "Me?"

"Just a couple of follow-ups," says Officer Fiske. He puts his hand on Nath's shoulder. "Maybe we can just step out onto the front porch."

When Officer Fiske has shut the front door behind them, Nath props himself against the railing. Under his palms, a few shreds of paint work loose and flutter to the porch floor. He has been wrestling with the idea of calling the police himself, of telling them about Jack and how he must be responsible. In another town, or another time, they might have shared Nath's suspicions already. Or if Lydia herself had been different: a Shelley Brierley, a Pam Saunders, a Karen Adler, a normal teenage girl, a girl they understood. The police might have looked at Jack more closely, pieced together a history of small complaints: teachers protesting graffitied desks and insolent remarks, other brothers taking umbrage at his liberties with their sisters. They might have listened to Nath's complaints — *after school all spring every day* — and come to similar conclusions. A girl and a boy, so much time together, alone — it would not be so hard to understand, after all, why Nath eyed Jack so closely and bitterly. They, like Nath, might have found suspicious signs in everything Jack has ever said or done.

But they won't. It complicates the story, and the story — as it emerges from the teachers and the kids at school — is so obvious. Lydia's quietness, her lack of friends. Her recent sinking grades. And, in truth, the *strangeness* of her family. A family with no friends, a family of misfits. All this shines so brightly that, in the eyes of the police, Jack falls into shadow. A girl like that and a boy like him, who can have — does have — any girl he wants? It is impossible for them to imagine what Nath knows to be true, let alone what he himself imagines. To his men, Officer Fiske often says, "When you hear hoofbeats, think horses, not zebras." Nath, they would have said, is only hysterical. Hearing zebras everywhere. Now, face-to-face with the police, Nath can see that there is no point in mentioning Jack at all: they have already decided who is to blame.

Officer Fiske settles himself against the railing too. "We just wanted to chat a little,

Nathan, in private. Maybe you'll think of something you forgot. Sometimes brothers and sisters know things about each other their parents don't, you know?"

Nath tries to agree, but nothing comes out. He nods. Today, he suddenly remembers, should have been his graduation.

"Was Lydia in the habit of sneaking out alone?" Officer Fiske asks. "There's no need to worry. You're not in trouble. Just tell us what you know." He keeps saying *just,* as if it's a tiny favor he wants, a little offhand thing. Talk to us. Tell us her secrets. Tell us everything. Nath starts to tremble. He's positive the policemen can see him shaking.

"Had she ever snuck out by herself before, at night?" the younger policeman asks. Nath swallows, tries to hold himself still.

"No," he croaks. "No, never."

The policemen glance at each other. Then the younger one perches on the railing beside Nath, like a kid leaning against a locker before school, as if they're friends. This is his role, Nath realizes. To act like the buddy, to coax him to talk. His shoes are polished so bright they reflect the sun, a blurry smudge of light at each big toe.

"Did Lydia usually get along with your parents?" The policeman shifts his weight, and the railing creaks.

150

Maybe you should join some clubs, too, honey, meet some new people. Would you like to take a summer class? That could be fun.

"Our parents?" Nath says. He hardly recognizes the voice that comes out as his. "Sure she did."

"Did you ever see either of them hit her?"

"Hit her?" Lydia, so fussed over, so carefully tended, like a prize flower. The one perpetually on their mother's mind, even when she was reading, dog-earing pages of articles Lydia might like. The one their father kissed first, every night, when he came home. "My parents would never hit Lydia. They *loved* her."

"Did she ever talk about hurting herself?"

The porch railing starts to blur. All he can do is shake his head, hard. No. No. No.

"Did she seem upset the night before she disappeared?"

Nath tries to think. He had wanted to tell her about college, the lush green leaves against the deep red brick, how much fun it was going to be. How for the first time in his life he'd stood up straight, how from that new angle the world had looked bigger, wider, brighter. Except she had been silent all dinner, and afterward she'd gone right up to her room. He had thought she was

151

tired. He had thought: *I'll tell her tomorrow.*

And suddenly, to his horror, he begins to cry: wet, messy tears that dribble down his nose and into the collar of his shirt.

Both policemen turn away then, and Officer Fiske closes his notebook and fishes in his pocket for a handkerchief. "Keep it," he says, holding it out to Nath, and he squeezes him on the shoulder once, hard, and then they're gone.

Inside, Marilyn says to James, "So I have to ask your permission now, to speak in company?"

"That's not what I meant." James props his elbows on the table and rests his forehead on his hands. "You just can't go making wild accusations. You can't go berating the police."

"Who's berating? I'm just asking questions." Marilyn drops her teacup into the sink and turns on the water. An angry soap froth rises in the drain. "Looking into all possibilities? He didn't even listen when I said it could be a stranger."

"Because you're acting hysterical. You hear one news report and you get all these ideas in your head. Let it go." James still hasn't lifted his head from his hands. "Marilyn, just let it *go.*"

In the brief silence that follows, Hannah slips under the table and huddles there, hugging her knees to her chest. The table-cloth casts a half-moon shadow on the linoleum. As long as she stays inside it, she thinks, curling her toes in closer, her parents will forget she's there. She has never heard her parents fight before. Sometimes they bicker over who forgot to screw the cap back onto the toothpaste, or who left the kitchen light on all night, but afterward her mother squeezes her father's hand, or her father kisses her mother's cheek, and all is well again. This time, everything is different.

"So I'm just a hysterical housewife?" Marilyn's voice is cool and sharp now, like the edge of a steel blade, and under the table Hannah holds her breath. "Well, someone is responsible. If I have to find out what happened to her myself, I will." She scrubs at the counter with the dish towel and tosses it down. "I would think you'd want to know, too. But listen to you. *Of course, officer. Thank you, officer. We can't ask for more, officer.*" The foam chokes its way down the drain. "I know how to think for myself, you know. Unlike some people, I don't just kowtow to the police."

In the blur of her fury, Marilyn doesn't

think twice about what she's said. To James, though, the word rifles from his wife's mouth and lodges deep in his chest. From those two syllables — *kowtow* — explode bent-backed coolies in cone hats, pigtailed Chinamen with sandwiched palms. Squinty and servile. Bowing and belittled. He has long suspected that everyone sees him this way — Stanley Hewitt, the policemen, the checkout girl at the grocery store. But he had not thought that *everyone* included Marilyn.

He drops his crumpled napkin at his empty place and pushes his chair from the table with a screech. "I have class at ten," he says. Below the hem of the tablecloth, Hannah watches her father's stocking feet — a tiny hole just forming at one heel — retreat toward the garage stairs. There's a pause as he slips on his shoes, and a moment later, the garage door rumbles open. Then, as the car starts, Marilyn snatches the teacup from the sink and hurls it to the floor. Shards of china skitter across the linoleum. Hannah stays absolutely still as her mother runs upstairs and slams her bedroom door, as her father's car backs out of the driveway with a mechanical little whine and growls away. Only when everything is completely quiet does she dare to crawl out from under the tablecloth, to pick the fragments of porcelain from the puddle of soapy water.

The front door creaks open, and Nath reappears in the kitchen, his eyes and nose red. From this she knows he has been crying, but she pretends not to notice, keeping her head bent, stacking the pieces one by one in her cupped palm.

"What happened?"

"Mom and Dad had a fight." She tips the broken cup into the garbage can and wipes her damp hands on the thighs of her bellbottoms. The water, she decides, will dry on its own.

"A fight? About what?"

Hannah lowers her voice to a whisper. "I don't know." Although there is no sound from their parents' bedroom overhead, she is antsy. "Let's go outside."

Outside, without discussing it, she and Nath both head for the same place: the lake. All the way down the block, she scans the street carefully, as if their father might still be around the corner, no longer angry, ready to come home. She sees nothing but a few parked cars.

Hannah's instincts, however, are good. Pulling out of the driveway, James too had been drawn to the lake. He had made a loop around it, once, twice, Marilyn's words echoing in his mind. *Kowtowing to the police.* Over and over he hears it, the palpable disgust in her voice, how little she thought of him. And he cannot blame her. How could Lydia have been happy? *Lee stood out in the halls. Few seemed to have known her well. Suicide Likely Possibility.* He passes the dock where Lydia would have climbed into the boat. Then their little dead-end street. Then the dock again. Somewhere in the center of this circle his daughter, friendless and alone, must have dived into the water in despair. *Lydia was very happy,* Marilyn had said. *Someone is responsible.* Someone, James thinks, and a deep spike carves its way down his throat. He cannot bear to see the lake again. And then he knows where he wants to be.

He has rehearsed in his mind what to say to Louisa so often that this morning, he awoke with it on his lips. *This was a mistake. I love my wife. This must never happen again.* Now, when she opens the door, what comes out of his mouth is: "Please." And Louisa gently, generously, miraculously opens her arms.

In Louisa's bed, he can stop thinking — about Lydia, about the headlines, about the lake. About what Marilyn must be doing at home. About who is *responsible.* He focuses on the curve of Louisa's back and the pale silk of her thighs and the dark sweep of her hair, which brushes his face again and again and again. Afterward, Louisa wraps her arms around him from behind, as if he is a child, and says, "Stay." And he does.

What Marilyn has been doing is pacing Lydia's room, tingling with fury. It's obvious what the police think, with all their hinting: *No evidence of anyone in the boat with her. Would you say Lydia was a lonely girl?* It's obvious, too, that James agrees. But her daughter could not have been so unhappy. Her Lydia, always smiling, always so eager to please? *Sure, Mom. I'd love to, Mom.* To say she could have done such a thing to herself — no, she had loved them too much for that. Every single night, before she went up to bed, she found Marilyn wherever she was — in the kitchen, in the study, in the laundry room — and looked her full in the face: *I love you, Mom. See you tomorrow.* Even that last night she had said it — *tomorrow* — and Marilyn had given her a quick squeeze and a little smack on the shoulder and said, "Hurry up now, it's late." At this thought, Marilyn sinks to the carpet. If she had known, she'd have held Lydia a little longer. She would have kissed her. She would have put her arms around her daughter and never let go.

Lydia's bookbag lies slouched against her desk, where the police had left it after they'd searched it, and Marilyn pulls it into her lap. It smells of rubber erasers, of pencil shavings, of spearmint gum — precious, schoolgirl smells. In her embrace, books and binders shift under the canvas like bones under skin. She cradles the bag, sliding the straps over her shoulders, letting its weight hug her tight.

Then, in the half-unzipped front pocket, she spots something: a flash of red and white. Hidden beneath Lydia's pencil case and a bundle of index cards, a slit gapes in the lining of the bag. A small tear, small enough to slip by the busy policemen, intended to escape an even sharper eye: a mother's. Marilyn works her hand inside and pulls out an open package of Marlboros. And, beneath that, she finds something else: an open box of condoms.

She drops both, as if she has found a snake, and pushes the bookbag out of her lap with a thud. They must belong to someone else, she thinks; they could not be Lydia's. Her Lydia did not smoke. As for the condoms —

Inside, Marilyn cannot quite convince herself. That first afternoon, the police had asked, "Does Lydia have a boyfriend?" and she had answered, without hesitation, "She's barely sixteen." Now she looks down at the two tiny boxes, caught in the hammock of her skirt, and the outlines of Lydia's life — so sharp and clear before — begin to waver. Dizzy, she rests her head against the side of Lydia's desk. She will find out everything she doesn't know. She will keep searching until she understands how this could have happened, until she understands her daughter completely.

At the lake, Nath and Hannah settle on the grass and stare out over the water in silence, hoping for the same enlightenment. On a normal summer day, at least half a dozen kids would be splashing in the water or jumping off the pier, but today, the lake is deserted. Maybe the kids are afraid to swim now, Nath thinks. What happened to bodies in the water? Did they dissolve, like tablets? He doesn't know, and as he contemplates the possibilities, he is glad that his father allowed no one to see Lydia's body but himself.

He stares out over the water, letting time tick away. Only when Hannah sits up and

159

waves to someone does he emerge from his daze, his attention slowly centering on the street: Jack, in a faded blue T-shirt and jeans, walking home from graduation with a robe slung over his arm — as if it were just an ordinary day. Nath hasn't seen him since the funeral, though he's been peeking out at Jack's house two or three times a day. As Jack spots Nath, his face changes. He looks away, quickly, as if pretending he hasn't seen either of them, and walks faster. Nath pushes himself to his feet.

"Where are you going?"

"To talk to Jack." In truth he's not sure what he's going to do. He's never been in a fight before — he's skinnier and shorter than most of the boys in his class — but he has vague visions of grabbing Jack by the front of his T-shirt and pinning him to a wall, of Jack suddenly admitting his culpability. *It was my fault: I lured her, I persuaded her, I tempted her, I disappointed her.* Hannah lunges forward and grabs his wrist.

"Don't."

"It's because of him," Nath says. "She never went wandering out in the middle of the night before *he* came along."

Hannah yanks his arm, dragging him back to his knees, and Jack, almost jogging now, blue commencement robe fluttering behind him, reaches their street. He glances back at them over his shoulder and there's no mistaking it: fear in the hunch of his shoulders, fear in the way his gaze flicks to Nath, then quickly away. Then he turns the corner and disappears. In a few seconds, Nath knows, Jack will climb the stairs of his porch and open the door and be out of reach. He tries to wrench himself free, but Hannah's nails sink into his skin. He had not known a child could be so strong.

"Get off me —"

Both of them tumble back into the grass, and at last Hannah lets go. Nath sits up slowly, breathless. By now, he thinks, Jack is safe inside his house. Even if he rang the doorbell and banged on the door, Jack would never come out.

"What the hell did you do that for?"

With one hand, Hannah combs a dead leaf from her hair. "Don't fight with him. Please."

"You're crazy." Nath rubs his wrist, where her fingers have scratched five red welts. One of them has begun to bleed. "Jesus Christ. All I wanted was to talk to him."

"Why are you so mad at him?"

Nath sighs. "You saw how weird he was at the funeral. And just now. Like there's something he's afraid I'll find out." His voice drops. "I know he had something to do with this. I can feel it." He kneads his chest with his fist, just below his throat, and thoughts he has never voiced fight their way to the surface. "You know, Lydia fell in the lake once, when we were little," he says, and his fingertips begin to quiver, as if he has said something taboo.

"I don't remember that," Hannah says.

"You weren't born yet. I was only seven."

Hannah, to his surprise, slides over to sit beside him. Gently, she puts her hand on his arm, where she's scratched it, and leans her head against him. She has never dared sit so close to Nath before; he and Lydia and their mother and father are too quick to shrug her off or shoo her away. *Hannah, I'm busy. I'm in the middle of something. Leave me alone.* This time — she holds her breath — Nath lets her stay. Though he says nothing more, her silence tells him she is listening.

Six

The summer Lydia fell in the lake, the summer Marilyn went missing: all of them had tried to forget it. They did not talk about it; they never mentioned it. But it lingered, like a bad smell. It had suffused them so deeply it could never wash out.

Every morning, James called the police. Did they need more photographs of Marilyn? Was there any more information he could give? Were there any more people he could call? By mid-May, when Marilyn had been gone for two weeks, the officer in charge of the case told him, gently, "Mr. Lee, we appreciate all the help you've provided. And we're keeping an eye out for the car. I can't promise we'll find anything, though. Your wife took clothes with her. She packed suitcases. She took her keys." Officer Fiske, even then, hated to give out false hopes. "This kind of thing happens sometimes. Sometimes people are just too different." He did not say *mixed,* or *interracial,* or *mismatched,* but he didn't have to. James heard it anyway, and he would remember Officer Fiske very clearly, even a decade later.

To the children, he said, "The police are looking. They'll find her. She'll come home soon."

Lydia and Nath remembered it this way: weeks passed and their mother was still *gone.* At recess the other children whispered and teachers gave them pitying looks and it was a relief when school finally ended. After that their father stayed in his study and let them watch television all day, from *Mighty Mouse* and *Underdog* in the morning to *I've Got a Secret* late at night. When Lydia asked, once, what he did in the study, he sighed and said, "Oh, I just putter around." She thought of her father wearing soft rubber shoes and taking small steps on the smooth floor: putter putter putter. "It means reading books and things, stupid," Nath said, and the soft rubber shoes turned into her father's plain brown ones with the fraying laces.

What James actually did, each morning, was take a small envelope from his breast pocket. After the police had gone that first night with a snapshot of Marilyn and assurances they'd do all they could, after he had scooped the children up and tucked them in bed with their clothes still on, he had noticed the shredded scraps of paper in the bedroom wastebasket. One by one he plucked them from the cotton balls, the old newspapers, the tissues smudged with his wife's lipsticked kiss. He had pieced them together on the kitchen table, matching torn edge to torn edge. *I always had one kind of life in mind and things have turned out very differently.* The bottom half of the sheet was blank, but he hadn't stopped until every fragment was placed. She had not even signed it.

He read the note over and over, staring at the tiny cracks of wood grain snaking between the patches of white, until the sky outside shifted from navy to gray. Then he slipped the scraps of paper into an envelope. Every day — though he promised himself *this* time would be the last time — he settled Nath and Lydia in front of the television, locked the door to his study, and pulled out the shreds of note again. He read it while the children moved from cartoons to soap operas to game shows, while they sprawled, unsmiling, in front of *Bewitched* and *Let's Make a Deal* and *To Tell the Truth*, while — despite Johnny Carson's best zingers — they sank into sleep.

When they had married, he and Marilyn had agreed to forget about the past. They would start a new life together, the two of them, with no looking back. With Marilyn gone, James broke that pact again and again. Each time he read the note, he thought of her mother, who had never referred to him by name, only indirectly — to Marilyn — as *your fiancé.* Whose voice he had heard on their wedding day, echoing out into the marble lobby of the courthouse like an announcement on the P.A. system, so loud heads had turned: *It's not right, Marilyn. You know it's not right.* Who had wanted Marilyn to marry someone *more like her.* Who had never called them again after their wedding. All this must have come back to Marilyn as she ate at her mother's table and slept in her mother's bed: what a mistake she'd made, marrying him. How her mother had been right all along. *I have kept all these feelings inside me for a long time, but now, after being in my mother's house again, I think of her and realize I cannot put them aside any longer.* In kindergarten, he had learned how to make a bruise stop hurting: you pressed it over and over with your thumb. The first time it hurt so much your eyes watered. The second time it hurt a little less. The tenth time, it was barely an ache. So he read the note again and again. He remembered everything he could: Marilyn kneeling to lace Nath's sneaker; Marilyn lifting his collar to slide in the stays. Marilyn as she was that first day in his office: slender and serious and so focused that he didn't dare look at those eyes directly.

It didn't stop hurting. His eyes didn't stop watering.

When he heard the station's late-night sign-off and the national anthem begin to play, he would slip the scraps of Marilyn's note into the envelope and tuck it back into his shirt pocket. Then he tiptoed into the living room, where the children lay curled up together on the floor by the sofa, illuminated by the test pattern on the television. The Indian at the top of the screen glared as James carried first Lydia, then Nath, to bed. Then — because, without Marilyn, the bed felt too empty, like a barren plateau — he returned to the living room, swaddling himself in an old crocheted afghan on the sofa and studying the circles on the screen until the signal cut off. In the morning, it all began again.

Each morning Lydia and Nath, finding themselves back in their beds, wondered for just a moment if the universe had righted itself: perhaps they might enter the kitchen and find their mother at the stove, waiting for them with love and kisses and hard-boiled eggs. Neither ever mentioned this most tender hope, but each morning, when they met in the kitchen and found no one there but their father, in rumpled pajamas, setting out two empty bowls, they looked at each other and knew. Still *gone.*

They tried to keep busy, trading the marshmallows from their cereal to make breakfast last as long as they could: a pink for an orange, two yellows for a green. At lunchtime, their father made sandwiches, but he never got it right — not enough peanut butter, or not enough jelly, or cut crosswise instead of in triangles like their mother would have. Lydia and Nath, suddenly tactful, said nothing, even at dinner, when there would be peanut butter and jelly again.

The only time they left the house was for the grocery store. "Please," Nath begged one day on the way home, as the lake glided past the car windows. "Please can we swim. Just an hour. Just five minutes. Just ten seconds." James, his eyes on the rearview mirror, did not slow the car. "You know Lydia doesn't know how," he said. "I'm not ready to play lifeguard today." He turned onto their street, and Nath slid across the backseat and pinched Lydia's arm.

"Baby," he hissed. "We can't swim because of *you.*"

Across the street, Mrs. Allen was weeding her garden, and when the car doors opened, she waved them over. "James," she said. "James, I haven't seen you in a while." She held a sharp little rake and wore pink and purple gloves, but when she leaned on the inside of the garden gate and peeled them off, Lydia spotted half-moons of dirt under her fingernails.

"How is Marilyn?" Mrs. Allen asked. "She's been away quite a while, hasn't she? I do hope everything is all right." Her eyes were excited and bright, as if — Nath thought — she might get a present.

"We're holding down the fort," James said.

"How long will she be away?"

James glanced down at the children and hesitated. "Indefinitely," he said. Beside him, Nath kicked Mrs. Allen's gate with the toe of his sneaker. "Don't do that, Nath. You're leaving a scuff."

Mrs. Allen peered down at them, but the children, in unison, looked away. Her lips were too thin, her teeth too white. Under the heel of Lydia's shoe, a wad of bubble gum stuck her to the concrete like glue.

Even if she were allowed, she thought, she could not run away.

"You two be good now, and your mother will be home soon, isn't that right?" Mrs. Allen said. She shifted her thin-lipped smile to James, who didn't meet her eye. "Our groceries must be melting," James said, though he and Lydia and Nath knew there was nothing in the bag but a quart of milk, two jars of Jif, and a loaf of bread. "It's nice seeing you, Vivian." He tucked the paper sack under his arm and took each of the children by a hand and turned away, and the gum under Lydia's shoe stretched and snapped, leaving a long, dried-out worm on the sidewalk.

At dinner, Nath asked, "What does *indefinitely* mean?"

Their father looked suddenly at the ceiling, as if Nath had pointed out a bug and he wanted to find it before it ran away. Lydia's eyes went hot, as if she were staring into the oven. Nath, remorseful, prodded his sandwich with his knuckle, squeezing peanut butter onto the tablecloth, but their father didn't notice.

"I want you to forget everything Mrs. Allen said," James said finally. "She's a silly woman and she doesn't know your mother at all. I want you to pretend we never even

170

talked to her." He patted their hands and tried to smile. "This isn't anyone's fault. Especially not yours."

Lydia and Nath both knew he was lying, and they understood that this was how things would be for a long time.

The weather grew warm and sticky. Every morning Nath counted up the number of days his mother had been gone: Twenty-seven. Twenty-eight. Twenty-nine. He was tired of staying inside in the stale air, tired of the television, tired of his sister, who more and more stared glassy-eyed at the screen in silence. What was there to say? Their mother's absence gnawed at them quietly, a dull and spreading hurt. One morning in early June, when Lydia nodded off during a commercial break, he tiptoed toward the front door. Their father had told them not to leave the house, but the porch steps, he decided, were still the house.

At the far end of the street, Jack perched on his own porch railing, chin propped on bent-up knees. Ever since that day at the pool, Nath had not spoken to Jack, not even hi. When they got off the school bus together, Nath tugged at the straps of his bookbag, walking home as fast as he could. At recess, if he saw Jack coming toward him, he ran to the other side of the playground.

It was starting to be a habit, disliking Jack. Now, though, as Jack turned his head and spotted him and bounded down the street, Nath stayed put. Talking to anyone — even Jack — was better than more silence.

"Want one?" Jack asked when he reached the steps. Nestled in his outstretched palm: a half-dozen red candies, fish-shaped, the size of his thumb. Head to tail, tail to head, they glistened like jewels. Jack grinned, and even the tips of his ears perked up. "Got them at the five-and-dime. Ten cents a scoop."

Instantly Nath was flooded with intense longing: for the shelves of scissors and paste and crayons, the bins of bouncy balls and wax lips and rubber rats, the foil-wrapped chocolate bars lined up at the front counter, and, by the register, the big glass jar of ruby-colored candy, the cherry scent wafting out the moment you lifted the lid.

Jack bit the head off one of the fish and held out his hand again. "They're good." Close up, Jack's eyelashes were the same sandy color as his hair, the tips golden where they caught the sunlight. Nath slipped one of the candies into his mouth and let the sweetness seep into him and counted the freckles on Jack's cheek: nine.

"You'll be okay," Jack said suddenly. He

leaned closer to Nath, as if he were telling a secret. "My mom says kids only *need* one parent. She says if my dad doesn't care enough to see me, it's his loss, not mine."

Nath's tongue went stiff and thick, like a piece of meat. Suddenly he could not swallow. A trickle of syrupy spit nearly choked him, and he spat the half-chewed candy into the grass.

"Shut up," he hissed. "You — you shut up." He spat again, for good measure, trying to expel the taste of cherry. Then he stumbled to his feet and back inside, slamming the door so hard that the screen shook. Behind him, Jack lingered at the bottom of the steps, looking down at the fish trapped inside his fist. Later on, Nath would forget exactly what Jack had said to make him so angry. He would remember only the anger itself, which smoldered as if it had always been there.

Then, a few days later, the most wonderful distraction arrived — for Nath, at least. One morning Nath turned on the television, but there were no cartoons. There was Walter Cronkite, serene at his desk just as if he were doing the evening news — but it was barely eight A.M., and his desk stood outside, the Cape Kennedy wind ruffling his papers and his hair. A rocket stood poised on the launchpad behind him; at the bottom of the screen, a countdown clock ticked. It was the launch of *Gemini 9*. Had Nath known the word, he would have thought: *surreal*. When the rocket shot upward in a billow of sulfur-colored smoke, he crept so close to the television that his nose smudged the glass. The counters on the bottom of the screen showed impossible numbers: seven thousand miles an hour, nine thousand, ten. He had not known anything could fly so high.

All morning Nath absorbed the news reports, savoring each new term like a fancy bonbon: *Rendezvous. Orbital map.* Lydia curled up on the sofa and went to sleep while, all afternoon, Nath repeated *Gemini. Gemini. GEM-in-i.* Like a magic spell. Long after the rocket faded into blue, the camera stayed trained on the sky, on the fading plume of white it left behind. For the first time in a month, he forgot, for a moment, about his mother. Up there — eighty-five miles high, ninety, ninety-five, the counter said — everything on earth would be invisible. Mothers who disappeared, fathers who didn't love you, kids who mocked you — everything would shrink to pinpoints and vanish. Up there: nothing but stars.

For the next day and a half, despite

Lydia's complaints, Nath refused to switch to *I Love Lucy* reruns or *Father Knows Best.* He began to refer to the astronauts — Tom Stafford and Gene Cernan — by first name, as if they were friends. As the first transmission from the astronauts was patched through, Lydia heard only garbled, scratchy gibberish, as if the voices had been pressed through a grinder. Nath, however, had no trouble making out the words: Gene, breathless, whispering, "Boy, it sure is beautiful out here." NASA had no television feed of the men in orbit, so the station aired a simulation: an actor on wires, a prop set on a soundstage in Missouri. But when the space-suited figure lumbered out of the capsule and floated gracefully, effortlessly upward — feet to the sky, tethered by *nothing* — Nath forgot it wasn't real. He forgot everything. He forgot to breathe.

At lunch, while they ate their peanut butter sandwiches, Nath said, "The astronauts eat *shrimp cocktail* and *beef stew* and *pineapple cake.*" At dinner, he said, "Gene is the youngest man ever to go into space, and they're going to do the longest spacewalk ever." In the morning, as his father poured cereal that Nath was too excited to eat, he said, "The astronauts wear *iron pants* to protect their legs from the boosters."

James, who should have loved astronauts — what were they but modern cowboys, after all, venturing into the newest frontier? — did not know any of these things. Tangled in his thoughts, Marilyn's torn-up note pressed to his heart, he saw his son's new obsession through the other end of the telescope. The astronauts, far off in the sky, were mere specks. Two little men in a sardine can, tinkering with nuts and bolts, while here on earth people were disappearing, even dying, and others were struggling just to stay alive one more day. So frivolous, so ridiculous: actors playing dress-up, strung on wires, pretending to be brave. Dancing with their feet above their heads. Nath, mesmerized, stared at the screen all day with a serene smile, and James felt a hot resentful flare in his gullet.

On Sunday evening, Nath said, "Daddy, can you believe people can go practically to the moon and *still come back*?" and James slapped him, so hard Nath's teeth rattled. "Shut up about that nonsense," he said. "How can you think about things like that when —"

He had never hit Nath before, and he never would again. But something between them had already broken. Nath, clutching his cheek, darted out of the room, as did

Lydia, and James, left alone in the living room with the image of his son's shocked, reddening eyes, kicked the television to the floor in a burst of glass and sparks. And although he took the children on a special trip to Decker's Department Store on Monday to buy another, he would never again think of astronauts, of space, without recoiling, as if shielding his eyes from shards of glass.

Nath, on the other hand, took down the *Encyclopaedia Britannica* and began to read: *Gravity. Rocket. Propulsion.* He began to scan the newspapers for articles about the astronauts, about their next mission. Surreptitiously he clipped them and saved them in a folder, poring over them when he woke up in the night dreaming of his mother. Tented by his blanket, he pulled a flashlight from under his pillow and reread the articles in order, memorizing every detail. He learned the name of each launch: *Freedom. Aurora. Sigma.* He recited the names of the astronauts: Carpenter. Cooper. Grissom. Glenn. By the time he reached the end of the list, he was able to sleep again.

Lydia had nothing to keep her mind off the mother-shaped hole in her world, and with Nath distracted by *docking adaptors* and *splashdowns* and *apogees,* she noticed something: the house smelled different without her mother in it. Once she noticed this, she could not stop noticing. At night she dreamed terrible things: she was crawling with spiders, she was tied up with snakes, she was drowning in a teacup. Sometimes, when she woke in the dark, she could hear the creak of the sofa springs downstairs as their father turned over, then turned again. Those nights, she never fell back asleep again, and the days grew sticky and thick, like syrup.

Only one thing in the house still reminded Lydia of her mother: the big red cookbook. While her father locked himself in his office and Nath bent his head over the encyclopedia, she would go into the kitchen and take it down from the counter. At five, she could already read some — though not nearly as well as Nath — and she sounded out the recipes: Chocolate Joy Cake. Olive Loaf. Onion Slim-Dip. Each time she opened the cookbook, the woman on the front looked a little more like her mother — the smile, the folded-back collar, the way she looked not right at you but over your shoulder, just past you. After her mother had come back from Virginia, she had read this book every day: in the afternoon, when Lydia came home from school; in the evening, before Lydia went to bed. In the mornings, sometimes, it was still on the table, as if her mother had been reading it all night. This cookbook, Lydia knew, was her mother's favorite book, and she leafed through it with the adoration of a devotee touching a Bible.

The third day of July, when her mother had been gone for two months, she curled up in her favorite spot under the dining table with the cookbook once again. That morning, when she and Nath had asked their father about hot dogs and sparklers and s'mores, he had said only, "We'll see," and they all knew this meant no. Without their mother, there would be no barbeques, no lemonade, no walking down to the lake to watch the fireworks. There would be nothing but peanut butter and jelly and the house with the curtains pulled shut. She flipped the pages, looking at the photos of cream pies and cookie houses and standing rib roasts. And, there, on one page: a line drawn down the side. She sounded out the words.

What mother doesn't love to cook with her little girl?

Beneath that:

And what little girl doesn't love learning with Mom?

Little bumps pocked the page all over, as

if it had been out in the rain, and Lydia stroked them like Braille with her fingertip. She did not understand what they were until a tear splashed against the page. When she wiped it away, a tiny goose bump remained.

Another formed, then another. Her mother must have cried over this page, too.

It's not your fault, her father had said, but Lydia knew it was. They'd done something wrong, she and Nath; they'd made her angry somehow. They hadn't been what she wanted.

If her mother ever came home and told her to finish her milk, she thought, the page wavering to a blur, she would finish her milk. She would brush her teeth without being asked and stop crying when the doctor gave her shots. She would go to sleep the second her mother turned out the light. She would never get sick again. She would do everything her mother told her. Everything her mother wanted.

Far off in Toledo, Marilyn did not hear the silent promise her young daughter was making. On the third of July, while Lydia huddled beneath the dining table, Marilyn bent over a new book: *Advanced Organic Chemistry*. Her midterm was in two days, and she had been studying all morning. With her notebook in hand, Marilyn felt like an undergraduate again; even her signature had gone soft and round, like it had been before she married, before her handwriting stiffened and tightened. All the other students in her course were college kids, some diligently trying to get ahead, some reluctantly trying to catch up from failed classes and bad semesters. To her surprise, they treated her no differently than they treated each other: quiet, polite, focused. In the cool lecture hall, they all sketched molecules, labeling them *ethyl, methyl, propyl, butyl;* at the end of the class, they compared notes and hers were exactly the same: beautiful little hieroglyphs of hexagons and lines. Proof, she told herself, that I'm just as smart as the others. That I belong.

Yet often, when she opened her books, Marilyn's mind whirled. Equations jumbled and rejumbled, hidden messages jumping out at her. NaOH became *Nath,* his small face wide-eyed and reproachful. One morning, consulting the periodic table, instead of *helium* she thought *He* and James's face floated up in her mind. Other days, the messages were more subtle: a typo in the textbook — "the common acids, *egg.* nitric,

181

acetic . . ." — left her in tears, thinking of hard-boiled, sunny-side up, scrambled. At these times she slipped her fingertips into her pocket for the barrette, the marble, the button. She turned them over and over until again her mind was smooth.

Some days, though, even these talismans lost their power. Two weeks after she left home, she woke in her rented twin bed, her body one sharp ache. Suddenly she felt drowned in the incredible wrongness of the moment, that she should be here, so far away from them. At last, caped in a blanket, she tiptoed to the telephone in the kitchen. It was six forty-one in the morning, but it took only two rings. "Hello?" James had said. A long pause. "Hello?" She said nothing, not daring to speak, just letting that voice soak into her heart. He had sounded hoarse — just static, she told herself, though she did not truly believe this. At last, she pressed the hook down with one finger and held it there, a long time, before replacing the receiver again. All day she listened to that voice in her head, like a familiar and loved lullaby.

From then on, she called every few days, when the yearning for home became too much. No matter what time it was, James picked up the phone, and she worried, imagining him sleeping at the kitchen table, or in his study beside the extension. Yet the one time she received no answer — James and the children, out of food, had been forced to the grocery store at last — she had panicked, imagining house fires or earthquakes or meteor strikes, and called again and again, every five minutes, then every two, until James's voice had come across the line at last. Another time, when she called in the middle of the morning, James, exhausted, had fallen asleep at his desk, and Nath had picked up instead. "Lee residence," he had answered dutifully, just as she'd trained him, and Marilyn wanted to say, *Are you all right? Are you being good?* but found her throat swollen shut with longing. Nath, to her surprise, didn't hang up at the silence. He had knelt on the kitchen chair, which he'd climbed to reach the phone, listening. After a moment, Lydia had tiptoed in from the doorway and crouched beside him, the handset sandwiched between their ears, for two minutes, three minutes, four, as if they could hear everything their mother was feeling and wishing in the gentle hiss on the line. They had been the ones to hang up first, and after the click, Marilyn had cradled the phone for a long time, hands trembling.

Nath and Lydia never mentioned this to their father, and James never reported the calls to the police. He had already begun to suspect that they were not much interested in helping him, and deep inside, where his old fears lay coiled, he thought he understood their reasoning: it had only been a matter of time before a wife like Marilyn left a husband like him. Officer Fiske continued to be very kind, but James resented this even more; the politeness made it even harder to bear. For her part, Marilyn told herself each time she put down the receiver that it was the last time, that she would not call again, that this was proof her family was fine, that she had begun a new life. She told herself this so firmly that she believed it completely, until the next time she found herself dialing their number.

She told herself that everything was possible now, in this new life. She subsisted on cereal and sandwiches and spaghetti from the pizza joint down the street; she had not known it was possible to live without owning a single pot. Eight more credits, she calculated, and she would finish her degree. She tried to forget everything else. She rolled Nath's marble between her fingers as she wrote away for medical school brochures. She snapped the clip of Lydia's barrette — one-two, one-two — as she penned tiny notes in the margins of her textbook. She concentrated so hard that her head ached.

That third day of July, Marilyn flipped a page in her textbook and black cotton clouded her view. Her head went heavy as a melon, pulling her off balance, buckling her knees, dragging her toward the floor. In a moment, her vision cleared, then her mind. She discovered a spilled glass of water trickling off the tabletop, her notes scattered across the tiles, her blouse clammy and damp. Only when her own handwriting came back into focus did she stand again.

She had never fainted before, never even come close, even during the hottest days of summer. Now she was tired, almost too tired to stand up. Easing herself onto the sofa cushions, Marilyn thought, *Maybe I'm sick, maybe I caught a bug from someone.* Then another thought arrived and her whole body went cold. It was the third; she was sure of this; she had been counting down the days to this exam. That meant she was nearly — she counted on her fingers, alert now, as if she'd been doused with icy water — three weeks late. No. She thought back. Since before she left home almost nine weeks ago. She hadn't realized it had been so long.

She wiped her hands on her jeans and tried to stay calm. After all, she *had* been late before. When she'd been stressed, or sick, as if her body hadn't enough attention to keep everything running, as if something had to be put on hold. Working as hard as she was, perhaps her body could not keep up. *You're just hungry,* Marilyn told herself. She hadn't eaten all day and it was nearly two o'clock. There was nothing in the cupboard, but she would go to the store. She would get food and eat it and then she would feel much better. Then she would get back to studying.

In the end, Marilyn would never take that exam. At the store, she put cheese and bologna and mustard and soda into her cart. She lifted a loaf of bread from the shelf. *It's nothing,* she told herself again. *You're fine.* With the grocery sack under her arm and the six-pack of bottles in her hand, she headed to her car, and without warning the parking lot spiraled around her. Knees, then elbows, slammed into asphalt. The paper sack tumbled to the ground. Soda bottles shattered on the pavement, exploding in a spray of fizz and glass.

Marilyn sat up slowly. Her groceries lay scattered around her, the loaf of bread in a puddle, the jar of mustard slowly rolling away toward a green VW van. Cola dripped down her shins. She had cut herself on the glass: a deep gash right across the center of her palm, straight as a ruler's edge. It did not hurt at all. She turned her hand from side to side, letting the light play on the layers of skin like sandstone strata: clearish pink, like watermelon, with flecks of snowy white. At the bottom, a river of rich red welled up.

She dug in her purse for a handkerchief and touched its corner to her palm and suddenly the cut was drained dry, the handkerchief blotched scarlet. The beauty of her hand amazed her: the pureness of the colors, the clarity of the white flecks and the thin lines on the muscle. She wanted to touch it, to lick it. To taste herself. Then the cut began to sting, and blood began to pool in her cupped palm, and she realized she would have to go to the hospital.

The emergency room was almost empty. The next day it would be full of Fourth of July accidents: food poisoning from bad egg salad, burned hands from grill fires, singed eyebrows from rogue fireworks. That afternoon, though, Marilyn walked up to the front desk and held out her hand, and in a few minutes she found herself on a cot, a petite young blonde in white taking her pulse and examining her palm. And when the young blonde said, "Let's get you stitched up," and took a bottle of anesthetic from a cupboard, Marilyn blurted out, "Shouldn't the doctor do that?"

The blond woman laughed. "I'm Dr. Greene," she said. Then, as Marilyn stared, she added, "Would you like to see my hospital badge?"

As the young woman closed the gash with neat black stitches, Marilyn's hands began to ache. She clenched her teeth, but the ache spread into her wrists, up to her shoulders, down her spine. It wasn't the surgery. It was disappointment: that like everyone else, she heard *doctor* and still thought — would forever think — *man.* The rims of her eyes started to burn, and when Dr. Greene tied off the last stitch and smiled and said, "How are you feeling?" Marilyn blurted out, "I think I'm pregnant," and burst into tears.

After that everything happened very fast. There were tests to be run, vials of blood to be drawn. Marilyn didn't remember exactly how it worked but knew it involved rabbits. "Oh, we don't use rabbits anymore," the pretty young doctor laughed, slipping the needle into the soft crook of Marilyn's arm.

"We use frogs now. Much faster and easier. Isn't modern science wonderful?" Someone got Marilyn a cushioned chair and a blanket to drape over her shoulders; someone asked for her husband's phone number, which Marilyn, in a daze, recited. Someone brought her a glass of water. The cut on her hand was closed and mute now, black sutures binding the raw flesh shut. Hours passed, but it seemed only a few minutes before James was there, radiant with amazement, holding her good hand while the young doctor said, "We'll call you with the results on Tuesday, Mr. and Mrs. Lee, but it looks like you'll be due in January." Then, before Marilyn could speak, she stepped into the long white hallway and disappeared.

"Marilyn," James whispered when the doctor had gone. His tone made her name a question that she could not yet bring herself to answer. "We've missed you so much."

Marilyn touched her unwounded hand to her belly for a long time. She could not take classes pregnant. She could not start medical school. All she could do was go home. And once she was home, she would see her children's faces, and there would be a new baby, and — she admitted it to herself slowly, with an ache more painful than her hand — she would never have the strength to leave them again. There was James, kneeling on the floor beside her chair as if in prayer. There was her old life, soft and warm and smothering, pulling her into its lap. Nine weeks. Her grand plan had lasted nine weeks. Everything she had dreamed for herself faded away, like fine mist on a breeze. She could not remember now why she thought it had all been possible.

This is it, Marilyn told herself. *Let it go. This is what you have. Accept it.*

"I was so foolish," she said. "I made such a terrible mistake." She leaned into James, breathing in the heavy sweet smell of his neck. It smelled like home. "Forgive me," she whispered.

James guided Marilyn to the car — his car — with his arm around her waist and helped her into the front seat as if she were a child. The next day, he would take a taxi from Middlewood back to Toledo and make the hour-long drive again in Marilyn's car, warm and aglow at knowing his wife would be there when he got home. For now, though, he drove carefully, scrupulously obeying the speed limit, reaching over every few miles to pat Marilyn's knee, as if reassuring himself that she was still there. "Are you too cold? Are you too warm? Are you thirsty?" he asked again and again. *I'm not an invalid,* Marilyn wanted to say, but her mind and tongue seemed to move in slow motion: they were already home, he had already gone to get her a cold drink and a pillow for the small of her back. He was so happy, she thought; look at that little bounce at the end of each step, look at how he tucked the blanket so carefully around her feet. When he came back, she said only, "Where are the children?" and James said he had left them across the street with Vivian Allen, not to worry, he would take care of everything.

Marilyn leaned back against the couch cushions and woke to the sound of the doorbell. It was almost dinnertime; James had retrieved the children from Mrs. Allen's and a pizza deliveryman stood at the door with a stack of boxes. By the time Marilyn wiped the sleep from her eyes, James had already counted out the tip and taken the boxes and shut the door. She followed him, dozily, into the kitchen, where he put the pizza down right in the center of the table, between Lydia and Nath.

"Your mother's home," he said, as if they couldn't see her standing there in the doorway behind him. Marilyn touched a hand to her hair and felt frizz. Her braid had come undone; her feet were bare; the kitchen was overly warm, overly bright. She felt like a child who'd overslept, wandering downstairs, late to everything. Lydia and Nath stared at her warily across the table, as if she might suddenly do something unexpected, like scream, or explode. Nath's mouth puckered, as if he were sucking something sour, and Marilyn wanted to stroke his hair and tell him that she hadn't planned any of this, hadn't meant for this to happen. She could see the question in their eyes.

"I'm home," she repeated, nodding, and they ran to hug her then, warm and solid, slamming into her legs, burying their faces in her skirt. One tear trickled down Nath's cheek, one ran along Lydia's nose, catching in her lips. Marilyn's hand burned and throbbed, as if she were holding a hot little heart in her palm.

"Were you good while I was away?" she asked, crouching on the linoleum beside them. "Did you behave?"

To Lydia, her mother's return was nothing short of a miracle. She had made a promise and her mother had heard it and come home. She would keep her word. That afternoon, when her father had hung up the phone and said those astonishing words —

192

Your mother is coming home — she had made a decision: her mother would never have to see that sad cookbook again. At Mrs. Allen's, she had made a plan, and after her father had picked them up — *Shh, not a peep, your mother is sleeping* — she had taken it away. "Mama," she said into her mother's hip now. "While you were gone. Your cookbook." She swallowed. "I — lost it."

"You did?" To her astonishment, Marilyn felt no anger. No: she felt pride. She pictured her daughter tossing the cookbook onto the grass and stomping it into the mud with her shiny Mary Janes and walking away. Tossing it into the lake. Setting it ablaze. To her own surprise, she smiled. "Did you do that," she said, curling her arm around her small daughter, and Lydia hesitated, then nodded.

It was a sign, Marilyn decided. For her it was too late. But it wasn't too late for Lydia. Marilyn would not be like her own mother, shunting her daughter toward husband and house, a life spent safely behind a deadbolt. She would help Lydia do everything she was capable of. She would spend the rest of her years guiding Lydia, sheltering her, the way you tended a prize rose: helping it grow, propping it with stakes, arching each stem

193

toward perfection. In Marilyn's belly, Hannah began to fidget and kick, but her mother could not yet feel it. She buried her nose in Lydia's hair and made silent promises. Never to tell her to sit up straight, to find a husband, to keep a house. Never to suggest that there were jobs or lives or worlds not meant for her; never to let her hear *doctor* and think only *man.* To encourage her, for the rest of her life, to do more than her mother had.

"All right," she said, releasing her daughter at last. "Who's hungry?"

James was already taking plates from the cupboard, distributing napkins, lifting the lid of the top box in a whiff of meat-scented steam. Marilyn put a slice of pepperoni pizza on each of their plates, and Nath, with a deep, contented sigh, began to eat. His mother was home, and tomorrow there would be hard-boiled eggs for breakfast, hamburgers and hot dogs for supper, strawberry shortcake for dessert. Across the table, Lydia stared down at her portion in silence, at the red circles dotting the surface, at the long thin threads of cheese tying it back to the box.

Nath was only half-right: the next day there were hot dogs and hamburgers, but no eggs, no shortcake. James grilled the meat himself, charring it slightly, but the family, determined to celebrate, ate it anyway. In fact, Marilyn would refuse to cook at all after her return, each morning popping frozen waffles into the toaster, each evening heating a frozen potpie or opening a can of SpaghettiOs. She had other things on her mind. Math, she thought that Fourth of July; she will need math, this daughter of mine. "How many buns inside the bag?" she asked, and Lydia tapped each with her finger, counting up. "How many hot dogs are on the grill? How many won't have buns?" At each right answer, her mother smoothed her hair and cuddled her against her thigh.

All day Lydia added up. If everybody ate one hot dog, how many would be left over for tomorrow? If she and Nath got five sparklers each, how many would they have all together? By the time dark fell and fireworks blossomed in the sky, she counted ten kisses from her mother, five caresses, three times her mother called her *my smart girl.* Every time she answered a question, a dimple appeared in her mother's cheek like a little fingerprint. "Another," she begged, every time her mother stopped. "Mama, ask me another." "If that's really what you want," her mother said, and Lydia nodded.

"Tomorrow," Marilyn said, "I'll buy you a book and we'll read it together."

Instead of just one book, Marilyn bought a stack: *The Science of Air. Why There Is Weather. Fun with Chemistry.* At night, after she tucked Nath in, she perched on the edge of Lydia's bed and lifted one from the top. Lydia huddled against her, listening to the deep, underground drum of her mother's heartbeat. When her mother breathed in, she breathed in. When her mother breathed out, she breathed out. Her mother's voice seemed to come from within her own head. "Air is everywhere," her mother read. "Air hovers all around you. Though you can't see it, it is still there. Everywhere you go, air is there." Lydia snuggled deeper into her mother's arms, and by the time they reached the last page, she was almost asleep. "Read me another," she murmured, and when Marilyn, thrilled, whispered, "Tomorrow, all right?" Lydia nodded so hard her ears rang.

That most important word: *tomorrow.* Every day Lydia cherished it. Tomorrow I'll take you to the museum to look at the dinosaur bones. Tomorrow we'll learn about trees. Tomorrow we'll study the moon. Every night a small promise extracted from her mother: that she would be there in the morning.

And in return, Lydia kept her own promise: she did everything her mother asked. She learned to write the plus sign, like a little stunted *t*. She counted on her fingers every morning, adding up over the cereal bowl. Four plus two. Three plus three. Seven plus ten. Whenever her mother stopped, she asked for more, which made her mother glow, as if Lydia had flicked on a light. She stood on the step stool over the sink, aproned from neck to ankle, and pinched baking soda into a jar of vinegar. "That's a chemical reaction," her mother said, and Lydia nodded as the foam gurgled down the drain. She played store with her mother, making change with pennies and nickels: two cents for a hug, four cents for a kiss. When Nath plunked down a quarter and said, "Bet you can't do that one," their mother shooed him away.

Inside Lydia could feel it: everything that was to come. One day the books would have no pictures. The problems would grow longer and harder. There would be fractions, decimals, exponents. The games would get trickier. Over meat loaf her mother would say, "Lydia, I'm thinking of a number. If you multiply by two and add one, you get seven." She would count her way back until she got the right answer, and her mother would smile and bring in the dessert. One day her mother would give her a real stethoscope. She would undo the top two buttons of her blouse and press the chestpiece to her skin and Lydia would hear her mother's heart directly. "Doctors use these," her mother would say. It was far away then, tiny in the distance, but Lydia already knew it would happen. The knowledge hovered all around her, clinging to her, every day getting thicker. Everywhere she went, it was there. But every time her mother asked, she said *yes, yes, yes.*

Two weeks later, Marilyn and James drove to Toledo to retrieve her clothes and books. "I can go alone," Marilyn insisted. By then the marble and the barrette and the button nestled quietly, forgotten, in the pocket of her dress in the closet. Already the dress was growing tight and soon Marilyn would give it away to Goodwill, with her tiny, forgotten talismans still tucked inside. Still, her eyes stung at the thought of emptying that apartment, sealing her books back into cartons, tossing her half-filled notebooks into the rubbish. She wanted privacy for this little funeral. "Really," she said. "You don't have to come." James, however, insisted. "I don't want you lifting anything heavy in your condition," he said. "I'll ask Vivian Allen to stop by and watch the kids for the afternoon."

As soon as James and Marilyn had gone, Mrs. Allen turned the TV to a soap opera and sat down on the couch. Lydia hugged her knees under the dining table, cookbook-less; Nath picked lint from the carpet and glowered. His mother woke him up and tucked him in, but Lydia filled up all the spaces in between. He knew the answer to every question their mother asked, but whenever he tried to jump in, she shushed him while Lydia counted on her fingers. At the museum, he wanted to watch the star show in the planetarium, but they spent the whole day looking at the skeletons, the model of the digestive system, whatever Lydia wanted. That very morning, he had come down to the kitchen early, clutching his folder of news clippings, and his mother, still in her bathrobe, gave him a sleepy smile over the rim of her teacup. It was the first time she had really *looked* at him since she came home, and something fluttered in his throat like a little bird. "Can I have a hard-boiled egg?" he asked, and, like a miracle, she said, "All right." For a moment he forgave her everything. He decided he would show her the pictures of the astronauts he'd been collecting, his lists of launches, everything. She would understand them. She would be impressed.

Then, before he could say a word, Lydia padded down the steps, and his mother's attention flitted away and alighted on Lydia's shoulders. Nath pouted in the corner, flicking the edges of his folder, but no one paid any attention to him until his father came into the kitchen. "Still mooning over those astronauts?" he said, plucking an apple from the fruit bowl on the counter. He laughed at his own joke and bit into the apple, and even across the kitchen Nath had heard the hard crunch of teeth piercing skin. His mother, listening to Lydia recount last night's dream, had not. She had forgotten all about his egg. The little bird in his throat had died and swelled so that he could hardly breathe.

On the couch, Mrs. Allen let out a little stuttering snore. A thread of spit oozed down her chin. Nath headed outside, leaving the front door half-open, and jumped down off the porch. The ground slammed into his heels like a jolt of electricity. Above him the sky stretched out pale steel gray.

"Where are you going?" Lydia peeked around the door.

"None of your business." He wondered if Mrs. Allen would hear, if she would wake and come out and call them back, but nothing happened. Without looking, he knew Lydia was watching, and he strode right down the middle of the street, daring her to follow. And in a moment, she did.

She followed him all the way to the lake and to the end of the little pier. The houses on the other side of the water looked like dollhouses, tiny and scaled-down and perfect. Inside, mothers were boiling eggs or baking cakes or making pot roasts, or maybe fathers were poking the coals in the barbecue, turning the hot dogs with a fork so that the grill made perfect black lines all over. Those mothers had never gone far away and left their children behind. Those fathers had never slapped their children or kicked over the television or laughed at them.

"Are you going swimming?" Lydia peeled off her socks and tucked one in each shoe, then perched at the end of the dock beside him, dangling her feet over the edge. Someone had left a Barbie doll in the sand, naked and muddy, one of its arms gone. Nath pried off the other and threw it into the water. Then the leg, which was harder. Lydia began to fidget.

"We better go home."

"In a minute." In his hands, the head of the Barbie had turned around to face her back.

"We'll get in trouble." Lydia reached for a sock.

The other leg wouldn't come off, and Nath turned on his sister. He felt himself unsteady, struggling for balance, as if the world had tipped to one side. He did not know exactly how it had happened but everything had gone askew, like a teeter-totter unevenly weighted. Everything in their life — their mother, their father, even he himself — slid, now, toward Lydia. Like gravity, there was no resisting it. Everything orbited her.

Later on, Nath would never be able to disentangle what he said and what he thought and what he only felt. He would never be sure whether he said anything at all. All Nath would know, for sure, was this: he pushed Lydia into the water.

Whenever he remembered this moment, it lasted forever: a flash of complete separateness as Lydia disappeared beneath the surface. Crouched on the dock, he had a glimpse of the future: without her, he would be completely alone. In the instant after, he knew it would change nothing. He could feel the ground still tipping beneath him.

Even without Lydia, the world would not level. He and his parents and their lives would spin into the space where she had been. They would be pulled into the vacuum she left behind.

More than this: the second he touched her, he knew that he had misunderstood everything. When his palms hit her shoulders, when the water closed over her head, Lydia had felt relief so great she had sighed in a deep choking lungful. She had staggered so readily, fell so eagerly, that she and Nath both knew: that she felt it, too, this pull she now exerted, and didn't want it. That the weight of everything tilting toward her was too much.

In reality, it was only a few seconds before Nath jumped into the water. He ducked under, grabbed Lydia's arm, pulled her to the surface, pedaling furiously.

Kick, he gasped. Kick. *Kick.*

They floundered their way to the edge of the lake, moving slowly toward the shallows until their feet hit the sandy bottom and they lurched aground. Nath wiped mud from his eyes. Lydia vomited a mouthful of lake water into the grass. For a minute, two, three, they lay facedown, catching their breath. Then Nath pushed himself to his feet, and to his surprise, Lydia reached up to clutch his hand. *Don't let go,* she meant, and, dizzy with gratitude, Nath gave it.

They trudged home in silence, making damp slodges on the sidewalk. Except for Mrs. Allen's snores, there was no noise but the sound of water dripping from their clothes to the linoleum. They had been gone only twenty minutes, but it felt as though eons had passed. Quietly they tiptoed upstairs and hid their wet clothes in the hamper and put on dry, and when their parents returned with suitcases and boxes of books, they said nothing. When their mother complained about the water spots on the floor, Nath said he had spilled a drink. At bedtime, Nath and Lydia brushed their teeth sociably at the sink, taking turns to spit, saying goodnight as if it were any other night. It was too big to talk about, what had happened. It was like a landscape they could not see all at once; it was like the sky at night, which turned and turned so they couldn't find its edges. It would always feel too big. He pushed her in. And then he pulled her out. All her life, Lydia would remember one thing. All his life, Nath would remember another.

Middlewood Elementary held its annual welcome-back picnic on the last weekend in

August. Their mother pressed one hand to her belly, where Hannah grew heavier every day; their father carried Lydia on his shoulders as they walked across the parking lot. After lunch, there were contests: who could hit a Wiffle ball the farthest, who could toss the most beanbags into a coffee can, who could guess the number of jelly beans in the one-gallon Mason jar. Nath and James entered the father-son egg race, each balancing a raw egg in a teaspoon like an offering. They made it almost all the way to the finish line before Nath tripped and dropped his. Miles Fuller and his father crossed the line first and Mrs. Hugard, the principal, gave them the blue ribbon.

"It's okay," James said, and for a moment Nath felt better. Then his father added, "Now, if they had a contest for reading all day —" All month he had been saying things like this: things that sounded like jokes but weren't. Every time, as he heard his own voice, James bit the tip of his tongue, too late. He did not understand why he said these things to Nath, for that would have meant understanding something far more painful: that Nath reminded him more and more of himself, of everything he wanted to forget from his own boyhood. He knew only that it was becoming a reflex, one that left him smarting and ashamed, and he glanced away. Nath looked down at his broken egg, yolk trickling between blades of grass, whites seeping into the soil. Lydia gave him a small smile, and he ground the shell into the dirt with his sneaker. When his father turned his back, Nath spat into the lawn at his feet.

And then came the three-legged race. A teacher looped a handkerchief around Lydia's and Nath's ankles and they hobbled to the starting line, where other children were tethered to their parents, or to siblings, or to each other. They had hardly begun to run when Lydia caught the edge of Nath's shoe under her own and stumbled. Nath threw an arm wide for balance and wobbled. He tried to match Lydia's stride, but when Lydia swung her leg forward, Nath pulled back. The handkerchief around their ankles was tied so tight their feet throbbed. It didn't loosen, yoking them together like mismatched cattle, and it didn't come undone, even when they jerked in opposite directions and tumbled face-forward onto the soft, damp grass.

SEVEN

Ten years later it had still not come undone.
Years passed. Boys went to war; men went
to the moon; presidents arrived and resigned
and departed. All over the country, in
Detroit and Washington and New York,
crowds roiled in the streets, angry about
everything. All over the world, nations
splintered and cracked: North Vietnam, East
Berlin, Bangladesh. Everywhere things came
undone. But for the Lees, that knot per-
sisted and tightened, as if Lydia bound them
all together.

Every day, James drove home from the
college — where he taught his cowboy class
term after term after term, until he could
recite the lectures word for word — mulling
over the slights of the day: how two little
girls, hopscotching on the corner, had seen
him brake at the stop sign and thrown
pebbles at his car; how Stan Hewitt had
asked him the difference between a spring

207

roll and an egg roll; how Mrs. Allen had smirked when he drove past. Only when he reached home and saw Lydia did the bitter smog dissipate. For her, he thought, everything would be different. She would have friends to say, *Don't be an idiot, Stan, how the hell would she know?* She would be poised and confident; she would say, *Afternoon, Vivian,* and look right at her neighbors with those wide blue eyes. Every day, the thought grew more precious.

Every day, as Marilyn unboxed a frozen pie or defrosted a Salisbury steak — for she still refused to cook, and the family quietly accepted this as the price of her presence — she made plans: Books she would buy Lydia. Science fair projects. Summer classes. "Only if you're interested," she told Lydia, every time. "Only if you want to." She meant it, every time, but she did not realize she was holding her breath. Lydia did. *Yes,* she said, every time. *Yes. Yes.* And her mother would breathe again. In the newspaper — which, between loads of washing, Marilyn read front to back, metering out the day, section by section — she saw glimmers of hope. Yale admitted women, then Harvard. The nation learned new words: *affirmative action; Equal Rights Amendment; Ms.* In her mind, Marilyn spun out Lydia's future in one long golden thread, the future she was positive her daughter wanted, too: Lydia in high heels and a white coat, a stethoscope round her neck; Lydia bent over an operating table, a ring of men awed at her deft handiwork. Every day, it seemed more possible.

Every day, at the dinner table, Nath sat quietly while his father quizzed Lydia about her friends, while his mother nudged Lydia about her classes. When they turned, dutifully, to him, he was tongue-tied, because his father — still seared by the memory of a smashed television and his son's slapped face, did not ever want to hear about space. And that was all Nath read or thought about. In his spare moments, he worked his way through every book in the school card catalog. *Spaceflight. Astrodynamics. See also: combustion; propulsion; satellites.* After a few stuttering replies, the spotlight would swivel back to Lydia, and Nath would retreat to his room and his aeronautics magazines, which he stashed under his bed like pornography. He did not mind this permanent state of eclipse: every evening, Lydia rapped at his door, silent and miserable. He understood everything she did not say, which at its core was: *Don't let go.* When Lydia left — to struggle over her homework or a science fair project — he turned his telescope outward, looking for faraway stars, far-off places where he might one day venture alone.

And Lydia herself — the reluctant center of their universe — every day, she held the world together. She absorbed her parents' dreams, quieting the reluctance that bubbled up within. Years passed. Johnson and Nixon and Ford came and went. She grew willowy; Nath grew tall. Creases formed around their mother's eyes; their father's hair silvered at the temples. Lydia knew what they wanted so desperately, even when they didn't ask. Every time, it seemed such a small thing to trade for their happiness. So she studied algebra in the summertime. She put on a dress and went to the freshman dance. She enrolled in biology at the college, Monday, Wednesday, Friday, all summer long. *Yes. Yes. Yes.*

(What about Hannah? They set up her nursery in the bedroom in the attic, where things that were not wanted were kept, and even when she got older, now and then each of them would forget, fleetingly, that she existed — as when Marilyn, laying four plates for dinner one night, did not realize her omission until Hannah reached the table. Hannah, as if she understood her

210

place in the cosmos, grew from quiet infant to watchful child: a child fond of nooks and corners, who curled up in closets, behind sofas, under dangling tablecloths, staying out of sight as well as out of mind, to ensure the terrain of the family did not change.)

A decade after that terrible year, everything had turned upside down. For the rest of the world, 1976 was a topsy-turvy time, too, culminating in an unusually cold winter and strange headlines: *Snow Falls on Miami.* Lydia was fifteen and a half, and winter break had just begun. In five months she would be dead. That December, alone in her room, she opened her bookbag and pulled out a physics test with a red fifty-five at the top.

The biology course had been hard enough, but by memorizing *kingdom, phylum,* and *class* she'd passed the first few tests. Then, as the course got tougher, she had gotten lucky: the boy who sat to her right studied hard, wrote large, and never covered up his answers. "My daughter," Marilyn had said that fall to Mrs. Wolff — *Doctor* Wolff — "is a genius. An A in a *college* class, and the only girl, too." So Lydia had never told her mother that she didn't understand the Krebs cycle, that she couldn't explain mitosis. When her mother framed the grade report from the college, she hung it on her wall and pretended to smile.

After biology, Marilyn had other suggestions. "We'll skip you ahead in science this fall," she'd said. "After college biology, I'm sure high school physics will be a snap." Lydia, knowing this was her mother's pet subject, had agreed. "You'll meet some of the older students," her father had told her, "and make some new friends." He'd winked, remembering how at Lloyd, older had meant *better.* But the juniors all talked to each other, comparing French translations due next period or memorizing Shakespeare for the quiz that afternoon; to Lydia they were merely polite, with the distant graciousness of natives in a place where she was a foreigner. And the problems about car crashes, shooting cannons, skidding trucks on frictionless ice — she couldn't make the answers turn out. Race cars on banked tracks, roller coasters with loops, pendulums and weights: around and around, back and forth she went. The more she thought about it, the less sense it made. Why *didn't* the race cars tip over? Why *didn't* the roller coaster fall from its track? When she tried to figure out why, gravity reached up and pulled down the cars like a trailing ribbon. Each night when she sat down with her book, the equations — studded with *k* and *M* and theta — seemed pointed and dense as brambles. Above her desk, on the postcard her mother had given her, Einstein stuck out his tongue.

Each test score had been lower than the last, reading like a strange weather forecast: ninety in September, mid-eighties in October, low seventies in November, sixties before Christmas. The exam before this one, she'd managed a sixty-two — technically passing, but hardly passable. After class, she'd shredded it into penny-sized scraps and fed it down the third-floor toilet before coming home. Now there was the fifty-five, which, like a bright light, made her squint, even though Mr. Kelly hadn't written the *F* at the top of the page. She'd stashed it in her locker for two weeks under a stack of textbooks, as if the combined weight of algebra and history and geography might snuff it out. Mr. Kelly had been asking her about it, hinting that he could call her parents himself, if necessary, and finally Lydia promised to bring it back after Christmas break with her mother's signature.

All her life she had heard her mother's heart drumming one beat: *doctor, doctor, doctor.* She wanted this so much, Lydia knew, that she no longer needed to say it. It was always there. Lydia could not imagine another future, another life. It was like trying to imagine a world where the sun went around the moon, or where there was no such thing as air. For a moment she considered forging her mother's signature, but her handwriting was too round, too perfectly bulbous, like a little girl's script. It would fool no one.

And last week, something even more terrifying had happened. Now, from under her mattress, Lydia extracted a small white envelope. Part of her hoped that, somehow, it would have changed; that over the past eight days the words would have eroded so she could blow them away like soot, leaving nothing but a harmless blank page. But when she blew, just one quick puff, the paper quivered. The letters clung. *Dear Mr. Lee: We thank you for your participation in our new early admission process and are very pleased to welcome you to the Harvard Class of 1981.*

For the past few weeks, Nath had checked the mail every afternoon, even before he said hello to their mother, sometimes before he took off his shoes. Lydia could feel him aching to escape so badly that everything else was falling away. Last week, at breakfast, Marilyn had leaned Lydia's marked-up math homework against the box of Wheaties. "I checked it last night after you went to bed," she said. "There's a mistake in number twenty-three, sweetheart." Five years, a year, even six months earlier, Lydia would have found sympathy in her brother's eyes. *I know. I know.* Confirmation and consolation in a single blink. This time Nath, immersed in a library book, did not notice Lydia's clenched fingers, the sudden red that rimmed her eyes. Dreaming of his future, he no longer heard all the things she did not say.

He had been the only one listening for so long. Since their mother's disappearance and return, Lydia had been friendless. Every recess that first fall, she had stood to the side, staring at the First Federal clock in the distance. Each time a minute ticked by, she squeezed her eyes shut and pictured what her mother might be doing — scrubbing the counter, filling the kettle, peeling an orange — as if the weight of all those details could keep her mother there. Later she would wonder if this had made her miss her chance, or if she had ever had a chance at all. One day she had opened her eyes and found Stacey Sherwin standing before her: Stacey Sherwin of the waist-long golden hair, surrounded by a gaggle of girls. In

215

Middlewood's kindergarten class, Stacey Sherwin was the kingmaker, already adept at wielding her power. A few days earlier, she had announced, "Jeannine Collins stinks like garbage water," and Jeannine Collins had peeled away from the group, ripping her glasses from her tear-smudged face, while the other girls in Stacey's coterie tittered. Lydia, from a safe distance, had watched this unfold with awe. Only once, on the first day of kindergarten, had Stacey spoken to her directly: "Do Chinese people celebrate Thanksgiving?" And: "Do Chinese people have belly buttons?"

"We're all going over to my house after school," Stacey said now. Her eyes flicked briefly to Lydia's, then slid away. "You could come, too."

Suspicion flared in Lydia. Could she really have been chosen by Stacey Sherwin? Stacey kept looking at the ground and wound a ribbon of hair round her finger and Lydia stared, as if she might be able to see right into Stacey's mind. Shy or sly? She couldn't tell. And she thought, then, of her mother, her face peering through the kitchen window, waiting for her to arrive.

"I can't," she said at last. "My mom said I have to come straight home."

Stacey shrugged and walked away, the

other girls trailing behind her. In their wake came a swell of sudden laughter, and Lydia could not tell if she had been left out of the joke or if she had been the joke herself.

Would they have been kind to her or mocked her? She would never know. She would say no to birthday parties, to roller-skating, to swimming at the rec center, to everything. Each afternoon she rushed home, desperate to see her mother's face, to make her mother smile. By the second grade, the other girls stopped asking. She told herself she didn't care: her mother was still there. That was all that mattered. In the years to come, Lydia would watch Stacey Sherwin — her golden hair braided, then ironed flat, then feathered — waving to her friends, pulling them toward her, the way a rhinestone caught and held the light. She would see Jenn Pittman slip a note to Pam Saunders and see Pam Saunders unfold it beneath her desk and snicker; she would watch Shelley Brierley share out a pack of Doublemint and breathe in the sugar-spearmint scent as the foil-wrapped sticks passed her by.

Only Nath had made it bearable all that time. Every day, since kindergarten, he saved her a seat — in the cafeteria, a chair across the table from him; on the bus, his books placed beside him on the green vinyl seat. If she arrived first, she saved a seat for him. Because of Nath, she never had to ride home alone while everyone else chatted sociably in pairs; she never needed to gulp out, "Can I sit here?" and risk being turned away. They never discussed it, but both came to understand it as a promise: he would always make sure there was a place for her. She would always be able to say, *Someone is coming. I am not alone.*

Now Nath was leaving. More letters were on their way. *In a few days we will send a packet of information and forms should you choose to accept your place.* Still, for a moment, Lydia allowed herself to fantasize: slipping the next letter out of the mail pile, and the next, and the next, tucking them between mattress and box spring where Nath couldn't find them, so that he would have no choice but to stay.

Downstairs, Nath riffled through the pile of mail: a grocery circular, an electric bill. No letter. That fall, when the guidance counselor had asked Nath about his career plans, he had whispered, as if telling her a dirty secret. "Space," he'd said. "Outer space." Mrs. Hendrich had clicked her pen twice, in-out, and he thought she was going to laugh. It had been nearly five years since the last trip to the moon, and the nation, having bested the Soviets, had turned its attention elsewhere. Instead Mrs. Hendrich told him there were two routes: become a pilot or become a scientist. She flipped a folder open to his printed-out transcript. B-minus in phys ed; A-plus in trigonometry, calculus, biology, physics. Though Nath dreamed of MIT, or Carnegie Mellon, or Caltech — he'd even written for pamphlets — he knew there was only one place his father would approve: Harvard. To James, anything else was a failing. Once he got to college, Nath told himself, he would take advanced physics, material science, aerodynamics. College would be a jumping-off point for a million places he had never been, a stop-off at the moon before shooting into space. He would leave everything and everyone behind — and though he wouldn't admit it to himself, *everyone* meant Lydia, too.

Lydia was fifteen now, taller, and at school, when she tied her hair up and put on lipstick, she looked grown up. At home, she looked like the same startled five-year-old who had clung to his hand as they crawled back ashore. When she stood near, the little-girl scent of her perfume — even its name childish, Baby Soft — wafted from her skin. Ever since that summer, he had felt something still binding their ankles and tugging him off balance, fettering her weight to his. For ten years, that something had not loosened, and now it had begun to chafe. All those years, as the only other person who understood their parents, he had absorbed her miseries, offering silent sympathy or a squeeze on the shoulder or a wry smile. He would say, *Mom's always bragging about you to Dr. Wolff. When I got that A-plus in chem, she didn't even notice.* Or, *Remember when I didn't go to the ninth grade formal? Dad said, "Well, I guess if you can't get a date . . ."* He had buoyed her up with how too much love was better than too little. All that time, Nath let himself think only: *When I get to college* — He never completed the sentence, but in his imagined future, he floated away, untethered.

It was almost Christmas now, and still no letter from Harvard. Nath went into the living room without turning on the lamp, letting the colored lights on the tree guide his way. Each blackened windowpane reflected back a tiny Christmas tree. He would have to type new essays and wait for a second or third or fourth choice, or maybe he'd have to stay home forever. His father's voice carried from the kitchen: "I think she'll really like it. As soon as I saw it, I thought of her." No need for an antecedent — in their family, *she* was always Lydia. As the Christmas lights blinked on and off, the living room appeared, dimly, then disappeared again. Nath closed his eyes when the lights came on, opened them as they went off, so that he saw only uninterrupted darkness. Then the doorbell rang.

It was Jack — not yet suspicious in Nath's eyes, only long distrusted and disliked. Though it was below freezing, he wore just a hooded sweatshirt, half-zipped over a T-shirt Nath couldn't quite read. The hems of his jeans were frayed and damp from the snow. He pulled his hand from his sweatshirt pocket and held it out. For a moment, Nath wondered if he was expected to shake it. Then he saw the envelope pinched between Jack's fingers.

"This came to our house," Jack said. "Just got home and saw it." He jabbed his thumb at the red crest in the corner. "I guess you'll be going to Harvard, then."

The envelope was thick and heavy, as if puffed with good news. "We'll see," Nath said. "It might be a rejection, right?"

Jack didn't smile. "Sure," he said with a shrug. "Whatever." Without saying good-bye, he turned home, crushing a trail of footprints across the Lees' snowy yard.

Nath shut the door and flipped on the living room light, weighing the envelope in both hands. All of a sudden the room felt unbearably hot. The flap came up in a ragged tear and he yanked out the letter, crumpling its edge. *Dear Mr. Lee: Let us once again congratulate you on your early admission to the Class of 1981.* His joints went loose with relief.

"Who was it?" Hannah, who had been listening from the hallway, peeked around the doorframe.

"A letter" — Nath swallowed — "from Harvard." Even the name tingled on his tongue. He tried to read the rest, but the text wouldn't focus. *Congratulate. Once again.* The mailman must have lost the first one, he thought, but it didn't matter. *Your admission.* He gave up and grinned at Hannah, who tiptoed in and leaned against the couch. "I got in."

"To Harvard?" James said, coming in from the kitchen.

Nath nodded.

"The letter got delivered to the Wolffs," he said, holding it out. But James barely glanced at it. He was looking at Nath, and for once he was not frowning, and Nath realized he had grown as tall as his father, that they could look at each other eye to eye.

"Not bad," James said. He smiled, as if half-embarrassed, and put his hand on Nath's shoulder, and Nath felt it — heavy and warm — through his shirt. "Marilyn. Guess what?"

His mother's heels clattered in from the kitchen. "Nath," she said, kissing him hard, on the cheek. "Nath, really?" She plucked the letter from his grip. "My god, Class of 1981," she said, "doesn't that make you feel old, James?" Nath wasn't listening. He thought: *It's happening. I did it, I made it, I'm going.*

At the top of the stairs, Lydia watched her father's hand tighten on Nath's shoulder. She could not remember the last time he had smiled at Nath like that. Her mother held the letter to the light, as if it were a precious document. Hannah, elbows hooked over the arm of the sofa, swung her feet in glee. Her brother himself stood silent, awed and grateful, 1981 glistening in his eyes like a beautiful far-off star, and something wobbled inside Lydia and tumbled into her chest with a clang. As if they heard it, everyone looked up toward her, and just as Nath opened his mouth to shout out the good news, Lydia called, "Mom, I'm failing physics. I'm supposed to let you know."

That night, while Nath brushed his teeth, the bathroom door creaked open and Lydia appeared, leaning against the doorjamb. Her face was pale, almost gray, and for a moment he felt sorry for her. Over dinner, their mother had moved from frantic questions — how could she let this happen, didn't she realize — to blunt statements: "Imagine yourself older and unable to find a job. Just imagine it." Lydia hadn't argued, and faced with her daughter's silence, Marilyn had found herself repeating that dire warning again and again. "Do you think you'll just find a man and get married? Is that all you plan for your life?" It had been all she could do to keep from crying right there at the table. After half an hour, James said, "Marilyn —" but she had glared so fiercely that he subsided, prodding shreds of pot roast in the separating onion-soup gravy. Everyone had forgotten about Harvard, about Nath's letter, about Nath himself.

After dinner, Lydia had found Nath in the living room. The letter from Harvard lay on the coffee table, and she touched the seal where it said *VERITAS*.

"Congratulations," she said softly. "I knew you'd get in." Nath had been too angry to speak to her and fixed his eyes on the television screen, where Donny and Marie were singing in perfect harmony, and before the song was over Lydia had run upstairs to her room and slammed the door. Now there she stood in the doorway, ashen and barefoot on the bathroom tiles.

He knew what Lydia wanted now: for him to offer reassurance, a humiliation, a moment he'd rather forget. Something to make her feel better. *Mom will get over it. It will be okay. Remember when . . . ?* But he didn't want to remember all the times his father had doted on Lydia but stared at him with disappointment flaring in his eyes, all the times their mother had praised Lydia but looked over and past and through him, as if he were made of air. He wanted to savor the long-awaited letter, the promise of getting away at last, a new world waiting as white and clean as chalk.

He spat fiercely into the sink without looking at her, swishing the last bit of froth down the drain with his fingers.

"Nath," Lydia whispered as he turned to go, and he knew by the tremble in her voice that she'd been crying, that she was about to begin again.

"Goodnight," he said, and closed the door behind him.

The next morning, Marilyn thumbtacked the failed test to the kitchen wall across from Lydia's seat. For the next three days, from breakfast until dinner, she plopped the physics book in front of her daughter and sat down beside her. All Lydia needed, she thought, was a little encouragement. Momentum and inertia, kinetic and potential — these things still lingered in the corners of her own mind. She read aloud over Lydia's shoulder: *For every action, there is an equal and opposite reaction.* She worked through the failed test with Lydia again and again until Lydia could solve every problem correctly.

What Lydia did not tell her mother was that, by the third time through, she had simply memorized the right answers. All day, while she huddled over her physics book at the table, she waited for her father to intercede: *That's enough, Marilyn. It's Christmas break, for God's sake.* But he said nothing. Lydia had refused to speak to Nath since *that night* — as she thought of it — and she suspected, correctly, that he was angry at her as well; he avoided the kitchen entirely, except for meals. Even Hannah would have been some comfort — a small and silent buffer — but as usual, she was nowhere to be seen. In actuality, Hannah had planted herself under the end table in the foyer, just out of sight of the kitchen, listening to the scratch of Lydia's pencil. She hugged her knees and sent soft and patient thoughts, but her sister did not hear them. By Christmas morning, Lydia was furious at them all, and even the discovery that Marilyn had at last unpinned the test from the wall failed to cheer her up.

Sitting down around the Christmas tree felt sullied now, too. James lifted one ribboned package after another from the pile, handing each around, but Lydia dreaded the gift from her mother. Usually her mother gave her books — books that, although neither of them fully realized it, her mother secretly wanted herself, and which, after Christmas, Marilyn would sometimes borrow from Lydia's shelf. To Lydia, they were always too hard no matter what age she was, less presents than unsubtle hints. Last year, it was *The Color Atlas of Human Anatomy,* so large it wouldn't fit on the shelf upright; the year before, she had received a thick volume called *Famous Women of Science.* The famous women had bored her. Their stories were all the same:

told they couldn't; decided to anyway. Because they really wanted to, she wondered, or because they were told not to? And the anatomy had made her queasy — men and women with their skin peeled off, then their muscles stripped away, until they were nothing but skeletons laid bare. She'd flipped through some of the color plates and slammed the book and squirmed in her seat, as if she could shake off the feeling like a dog shook rain off its fur.

Nath, watching his sister's eyes blink and redden, felt a twinge of pity cut through his anger. He had read the letter from Harvard eleven times now and had finally convinced himself it was real: they had actually accepted him. In nine months, he would be gone, and that knowledge took the sting out of all that had happened. So what if his parents cared more about Lydia's failure than his success? He was leaving. And when he got to college — Lydia would have to stay behind. The thought, finally put into words, was bittersweet. As his father passed him a present wrapped in red foil, Nath flashed Lydia a tentative smile, which she pretended not to see. After three comfortless days, she was not ready to forgive him yet, but the gesture warmed her, like a gulp of tea on a cold winter day.

If she had not looked up at the ceiling just then, Lydia might have forgiven her brother after all. But something caught her eye — a Rorschach of white above their heads — and a tiny memory ballooned in her mind. They had been quite small. Her mother had taken Hannah to a doctor's appointment and she and Nath, home alone, had spotted a huge spider crawling just above the window frame. Nath had climbed the sofa and crushed it with their father's shoe, leaving a black smudge and half a footprint on the ceiling. "Say you did it," he'd begged, but Lydia had a better idea. She fetched the bottle of Liquid Paper from beside their father's typewriter and painted over each spot, one by one. Their parents never noticed the dots of white against the cream of the ceiling, and for months afterward, she and Nath would glance up and share a smile.

Now, looking carefully, Lydia could still see the faint tread of their father's shoe, the bigger splotch where the spider had been. They had been a team. They had stuck together, even in this small, silly thing. She had never expected a time when that would not be true. Morning light splashed across the wall, making shadows and spots of glare. She squinted, trying to distinguish white from off-white.

"Lydia?" Everyone else had been busy, unwrapping gifts: across the room, Nath fed a roll of film into a new camera; a ruby pendant on a gold chain gleamed against her mother's robe. In front of her, her father held out a package, small and compact and sharp-edged, like a jewel box. "From me. I picked it out myself." He beamed. Usually James left the Christmas shopping to Marilyn, allowing her to sign each tag *Love, Mom and Dad.* But he had picked this gift out himself, and he could not wait to bestow it.

A present he picked out himself, Lydia thought, must be something special. At once she forgave her father for not interceding. Beneath this wrapping was something delicate and precious. She imagined a gold necklace like some girls at school wore and never took off, little gold crosses they'd received at their confirmations, or tiny charms that nestled between their collarbones. A necklace from her father would be like that. It would make up for the books from her mother, for all of the past three days. It would be a little reminder that said *I love you. You're perfect just as you are.*

She slid her finger under the wrapping paper, and a squat gold and black book fell into her lap. *How to Win Friends and Influ-*

ence People. A bright band of yellow slashed the cover in two. *Fundamental Techniques in Handling People. Six Ways of Making People Like You.* At the top, in deep red letters: *The More You Get Out of This Book, the More You'll Get Out of Life!* James beamed.

"I thought you could use this," he said. "It's supposed to — well, help you win friends. Be popular." His fingers grazed the title on the cover.

Lydia felt her heart in her chest like a pellet of ice, sliding down out of reach. "I have friends, Daddy," she said, though she knew this was a lie.

Her father's smile flickered. "Of course you do. I just thought — you know, you're getting older, and in high school now — people skills are so important. It'll teach you how to get along with everyone." His eyes darted from her face to the book. "It's been around since the thirties. Supposed to be the best on the subject."

Lydia swallowed, hard.

"It's great," she said. "Thanks, Daddy."

There was no hope for the other presents in her lap, but Lydia opened them anyway. A fluffy Orlon scarf from Nath. A Simon and Garfunkel album from Hannah. Books from her mother, as usual: *Women Pioneers in Science. Basic Physiology.* "Some things I thought you might be interested in," Marilyn said, "since you did so well in biology." She sipped her tea with a slurp that grated all the way down Lydia's spine. When nothing was left beneath the tree but balled-up wrapping paper and shreds of ribbon, Lydia stacked her gifts carefully, the book from her father on top. A shadow fell over it: her father, standing behind her.

"Don't you like the book?"

"Sure I like it."

"I just thought it would be helpful," he said. "Though you probably know everything about that already." He pinched her cheek. "How to win friends. I wish —" He stopped, swallowing the words back down: *I wish I'd had it when I was your age.* Perhaps, he thought, everything would have been different; if he'd known how to *handle people,* how to make them like him, perhaps he'd have fit in at Lloyd, he'd have charmed Marilyn's mother, they'd have hired him at Harvard. He'd have *gotten more out of life.* "I thought you'd like it," he finished lamely.

Though her father had never mentioned his schooldays, though she had never heard the story of her parents' marriage or their move to Middlewood, Lydia felt the ache of it all, deep and piercing as a foghorn. More than anything, her father fretted over her being well liked. Over her fitting in. She opened the book in her lap to the first section. *Principle 1. Don't criticize, condemn, or complain.*

"I love it," she said. "Thanks, Daddy."

James could not miss the edge in her voice, but he brushed it aside. Of course she's annoyed, he thought, at a present she doesn't need. Lydia already had plenty of friends; almost every evening she was on the phone with someone, after she'd finished all of her homework. How foolish of him to have bought this book at all. He made a mental note to come up with something better for her next gift.

The truth was this: at thirteen, at her father's urging, Lydia had called up Pam Saunders. She hadn't even known Pam's number and had had to look it up in the book, which lolled on her lap as she ticked the dial around. Aside from the phone in the kitchen, and the one in her father's study, the only other phone in the house was on the landing, a little window seat halfway up the stairs where her mother kept a few throw pillows and a wilting African violet. Anyone passing by downstairs could overhear. Lydia waited for her father to head into the living room before she dialed the last digit.

233

"Pam?" she said. "It's Lydia."

A pause. She could almost hear Pam's brow crinkling. "Lydia?"

"Lydia Lee. From school."

"Oh." Another pause. "Hi."

Lydia wormed her finger into the phone cord and tried to think of something to say. "So — what did you think of the geography quiz today?"

"It was okay, I guess." Pam snapped her gum, a tiny *tsk* of a sound. "I hate school."

"Me too," Lydia said. For the first time, she realized this was true, and saying it emboldened her. "Hey, do you want to go roller-skating on Saturday? I bet my dad would drive us." A sudden vision of her and Pam, whizzing around the roller rink, giddy and giggling, flashed through her mind. Behind them, in the stands, how delighted her father would be.

"Saturday?" Sharp, startled silence. "Oh, sorry, I can't. Maybe some other time?" A murmur in the background. "Hey, I gotta go. My sister needs the phone. Bye, Lydia." And the clunk of the receiver being set back on the hook.

Stunned by how suddenly Pam had hung up, Lydia was still clutching the handset to her ear when her father appeared at the foot of the stairs. At the sight of her on the phone, a lightness crossed his face, like clouds shifting after strong wind. She saw him as he must have looked when he was young, long before she had been born: boyishly hopeful, possibilities turning his eyes into stars. He grinned at her and, on exaggerated tiptoe, headed into the living room.

Lydia, phone still pressed to her cheek, could hardly believe how easy it had been to bring that bright flush of joy to her father. It seemed, at the time, like such a small thing. She remembered this the next time she lifted the receiver and held it to her ear, murmuring, "mm-hmm, mm-hm — she *did*?" until her father passed through the front hallway, paused below, smiled, and moved on. As time went by, she would picture the girls she watched from afar and imagine what she'd say if they were truly friends. "Shelley, did you watch *Starsky and Hutch* last night? Oh my *god,* Pam, can you believe that English essay — ten pages? Does Mrs. Gregson think we have nothing better to do? Stacey, your new hairdo makes you look *exactly* like Farrah Fawcett. I wish my hair would do that." For a while, it remained a small thing, the dial tone humming in her ear like a friend. Now, with the book in her hand, it no longer seemed so small.

After breakfast, Lydia settled cross-legged in the corner by the tree and opened the book again. *Be a good listener. Encourage others to talk about themselves.* She turned a few pages. *Remember that the people you are talking to are a hundred times more interested in themselves and their wants and problems than they are in you and your problems.*

Across the living room, Nath put his eye to the viewfinder of his new camera, zooming in on Lydia, pushing her in and out of focus. He was apologizing for giving her the silent treatment, for shutting the door in her face when all she'd wanted was not to be alone. Lydia knew this, but she was not in the mood to make up. In a few months he would be gone, and she would be left alone to win friends and influence people and pioneer in science. Before Nath could snap the photo, she dropped her gaze back to the book, hair curtaining her face. *A smile says, "I like you. You make me happy. I am glad to see you." That is why dogs make such a hit. They are so glad to see us that they almost jump out of their skins.* Dogs, Lydia thought. She tried to picture herself as a dog, something docile and friendly, a golden retriever with a black smile and a fringy tail, but she did not feel friendly and purebred and blond. She felt unsociable and suspicious, like the Wolffs' dog down the street, a mutt, braced for hostility.

"Lyds," Nath called. He would not give up. "Lydia. Lyd-i-a." Through the screen of her hair, Lydia saw the zoom lens of the camera like a giant microscope trained on her. "Smile."

You don't feel like smiling? Then what? Force yourself to smile. Act as if you were already happy, and that will tend to make you happy.

Lydia pulled her hair back over her shoulder in a slowly untwisting rope. Then she stared straight into the black eye of the camera, refusing to smile, even the slightest bend in her lips, even after she heard the shutter click.

By the time school started again, Lydia was relieved to escape the house, even if physics class was the first thing she had to face. She set the failed test — signed now by her mother — facedown on Mr. Kelly's desk. Mr. Kelly himself was already at the chalkboard, drawing a diagram. *Unit II: Electricity and Magnetism,* he wrote at the top. Lydia slid into her seat and rested her cheek on the desktop. Someone had etched a dime-sized *FUCK YOU* into the surface with a pushpin. She pressed her thumb against it, and when she lifted her hand a backward *FUCK* rose on her fingertip like a welt.

"Good vacation?" It was Jack. He slouched into the next seat, one arm slung over the back, as if it were a girl's shoulder. At this point she hardly knew Jack at all, though he lived just on the corner, and hadn't talked to him in years. His hair had darkened to the color of beach sand; the freckles she remembered from their childhood had faded but not disappeared. But she knew that Nath didn't like him at all, never had, and for this reason alone she was pleased to see him.

"What are you doing here?"

Jack glanced at the board. "Electricity and Magnetism."

Lydia blushed. "I mean," she said, "this is a junior class."

Jack pulled a capless ballpoint from his knapsack and rested his foot on his knee. "Did you know, Miss Lee, that physics is required to graduate? Since I failed the second unit of physics last year, here I am again. My last chance." He began to trace the tread of his tennis-shoe sole in blue ink. Lydia sat up.

"You *failed*?"

"I *failed*," he said. "Fifty-two percent.

Below below-average. I know that's a hard concept to grasp, Miss Lee. Since you've never failed anything."

Lydia stiffened. "As a matter of fact," she said, "I'm failing physics myself."

Jack didn't turn his head, but she saw one eyebrow rise. Then, to her surprise, he leaned across the aisle and doodled a tiny zero on the knee of her jeans.

"Our secret membership sign," he said as the bell rang. His eyes, a deep blue-gray, met hers. "Welcome to the club, Miss Lee."

All through class that morning, Lydia traced that tiny zero with her fingertip, watching Jack out of the corner of her eye. He was focused on something she couldn't see, ignoring Mr. Kelly's drone, the pencils scratching around him, the fluorescent light buzzing overhead. One thumb drummed a pitter-pat on the desktop. *Does Jack Wolff want to be friends?* she wondered. *Nath would kill him. Or me.* But after that first day, Jack didn't say another word to her. Some days he came late, then put his head down on his desk for the entire period; some days he did not come at all. The zero washed out in the laundry. Lydia kept her head bent over her notes. She copied down everything Mr. Kelly wrote on the board, turning the pages of her textbook back and forth so

239

often that the corners softened and frayed.

Then, at the end of January, at dinner, her mother passed the salad and the dish of Hamburger Helper and looked at Lydia expectantly, tilting her head this way and that, like a pair of rabbit ears trying to catch the signal. Finally, she said, "Lydia, how is physics class?"

"It's fine." Lydia speared a carrot coin on her fork. "Better. It's getting better."

"How much better?" her mother said, a touch of sharpness in her voice.

Lydia chewed the carrot to a pulp. "We haven't had a test yet. But I'm doing okay on the homework." This was only half a lie. The first test of the term was the next week. In the meantime she stumbled through the assignments, copying the odd-numbered problems from the answers at the back of the book and fudging the even ones as best she could.

Her mother frowned, but she scooped up a piece of macaroni. "Ask your teacher if you can do some extra credit," she said. "You don't want this grade to sink you. With all your potential —"

Lydia jabbed her fork into a wedge of tomato. Only the wistfulness in her mother's voice stopped her from screaming. "I know, Mom," she said. She glanced across the table at Nath, hoping he'd change the subject, but Nath, who had other things on his mind, didn't notice.

"Lydia, how's Shelley doing?" James asked. Lydia paused. Last summer, at her father's urging, she'd invited Shelley over once, to hang out. Shelley, though, had seemed more interested in flirting with Nath, trying to get him to play catch in the yard, asking him whether he thought Lynda Carter or Lindsay Wagner was hotter. They hadn't spoken since.

"Shelley's good," she said. "Busy. She's secretary of the student council."

"Maybe you can get involved, too," James said. He wagged his fork at her, with the air of a wise man delivering an aphorism. "I'm sure they'd love your help. And how about Pam and Karen?"

Lydia looked down at her plate, at the picked-over salad and the sad clump of beef and cheese beside it. The last time she'd talked to Karen was over a year ago, when her father had chauffeured them home from a matinee of *One Flew Over the Cuckoo's Nest*. At first she'd been proud that, for once, her plans had not been a lie. Karen had just moved to town and Lydia, emboldened by her newness, had suggested a movie and Karen had said, "Okay, sure, why not."

Then, for the whole ride, her father had tried to show off how *cool* he was: "Five brothers and sisters, Karen? Just like the Brady Bunch! You watch that show?" "Dad," Lydia had said. *"Dad."* But he'd kept going, asking Karen what the hot new records were these days, singing a line or two from "Waterloo," which was already two years old. Karen had said, "Yeah," and "No," and "I don't know" and fiddled with the bottom bead of her earring. Lydia had wanted to melt and seep into the seat cushions, deep down where the foam would block every bit of sound. She thought of saying something about the movie, but couldn't think of anything. All she could think of was Jack Nicholson's vacant eyes as the pillow came down to smother him. The silence swelled to fill the car until they pulled up in front of Karen's house.

The next Monday, at lunch, she had paused beside Karen's table and tried to smile. "Sorry about my dad," she said. "God, he's so embarrassing."

Karen had peeled the lid from her yogurt and licked the foil clean and shrugged. "It's okay," she said. "Actually, it was sort of cute. I mean, he's obviously just trying to help you fit in."

Now Lydia glared at her father, who

grinned brightly at her, as if proud to know so much about her *friends,* to remember their names. A dog, she thought, waiting for a treat.

"They're great," she said. "They're both great." At the other end of the table, Marilyn said quietly, "Stop badgering her, James. Let her eat her dinner," and James said, a little less quietly, "I'm not the one nagging about her homework." Hannah prodded a pebble of hamburger on her plate. Lydia caught Nath's eye. *Please,* she thought. *Say something.*

Nath took a deep breath. He had been waiting to bring something up all evening. "Dad? I need you to sign some forms."

"Forms?" James said. "What for?"

"For Harvard." Nath set down his fork. "My housing application, and one for a campus visit. I could go in April, over a weekend. They have a student who'll host me." Now that he had started, the words tumbled out in a breathless blur. "I have enough saved for a bus ticket and I'll only miss a few days of school. I just need your permission."

Miss a few days of school, Lydia thought. Their parents would never allow it.

To her surprise, they nodded.

"That's smart," Marilyn said. "You'll get

a taste of campus life, for next year, when you're there for real." James said, "That's an awfully long bus ride. I think we can afford a plane ticket for such a special occasion." Nath grinned at his sister in double triumph: *They're off your back. And they said yes.* Lydia, making trails in the cheese sauce with the tip of her knife, could think only one thing: *He can't wait to leave.*

"You know who's in my physics class now?" she said suddenly. "Jack Wolff, from down the street." She nibbled a shred of iceberg and measured her family's reaction. To her parents, the name slid past as if she hadn't spoken. Her mother said, "Lyddie, that reminds me, I could help you go over your notes on Saturday, if you want." Her father said, "I haven't seen Karen in a while. Why don't you two go to a movie sometime? I'll drive you." But Nath's head, across the table, jerked up as if a rifle had gone off. Lydia smiled back down at her plate. And right then she decided that she and Jack were going to be friends.

At the beginning, it seemed impossible. Jack hadn't come to class in nearly a week, and she hovered near his car after school for days before she caught him alone. The first day, he came out of the building with a blond junior she didn't know, and she ducked behind a bush and watched through the branches. Jack slid his hands into the girl's pocket, then inside her coat, and when she pretended to be offended and pushed him away, he tossed her over his shoulder, threatening to throw her into the snowbank, while she squealed and giggled and hammered his back with her fists. Then Jack set her down and opened the door of the Beetle, and the blond girl climbed in, and they drove off, steam billowing from the tailpipe, and Lydia knew they wouldn't be back. The second day, Jack didn't show up at all, and Lydia eventually trudged home. The snow was calf-deep; there had been record low temperatures all winter. A hundred miles north, Lake Erie had frozen; in Buffalo, snow drowned the roofs of houses, swallowing power lines. At home, Nath, who had sat alone on the bus for the first time he could remember, demanded, "What happened to you?" and Lydia stomped upstairs without replying.

On the third day, Jack came out of the building alone, and Lydia took a deep breath and ran down to the curb. As usual, Jack wore no coat, no gloves. Two bare, red fingertips pinched a cigarette.

"Mind giving me a ride home?" she said.

"Miss Lee." Jack kicked a clump of snow off the front tire. "Aren't you supposed to be on your school bus?"

She shrugged, tugging her scarf back up to her neck. "Missed it."

"I'm not going straight home."

"I don't mind. It's too cold to walk."

Jack fumbled in his hip pocket for his keys. "Are you sure your brother wants you hanging out with a guy like me?" he said, one eyebrow raised.

"He's not my keeper." It came out louder than she meant, and Jack laughed out a puff of smoke and climbed into the driver's seat. Lydia, cheeks scarlet, had nearly turned away when he leaned over and popped up the knob on the passenger side.

Now that she was in the car, she didn't know what to say. Jack started the engine and eased the car into gear, and the big speedometer and gas gauge on the dashboard flicked to life. There were no other dials. Lydia thought of her parents' cars: all the indicators and warning lights to tell you if the oil was too low, if the engine was too hot, if you were driving with the parking brake on or the door or the trunk or the hood open. They didn't trust you. They needed to check you constantly, to remind you what to do and what not to do. She had never been alone with a boy before — her mother had forbidden her to go out with boys, not that she had ever tried — and it occurred to her that she had never had an actual conversation with Jack before. She had only a vague idea about the things that happened in the backseat. Out of the corner of her eye, she studied Jack's profile, the faint stubble — darker than his sandy hair — that ran all the way up to his sideburns and all the way down to the soft part of his throat, like a smudge of charcoal waiting to be wiped away.

"So," she said. Her fingers twitched, and she tucked them into her coat pocket. "Can I bum a cigarette?"

Jack laughed. "You're so full of shit. You don't smoke." He offered the pack anyway, and Lydia plucked out a cigarette. She'd thought it would be solid and heavy, like a pencil, but it was light, like nothing at all. Without taking his eyes off the road, Jack tossed her his lighter.

"So you decided you didn't need your brother to chaperone you home today."

Lydia could not ignore the scorn in his voice, and she was unsure if he was laughing at her, or Nath, or both of them at once. "I'm not a child," she said, lighting the cigarette and putting it to her lips. The smoke burned in her lungs and made her head spin and suddenly she felt sharp and aware. Like cutting your finger, she thought: the pain, and the blood, reminded you that you were alive. She breathed out, a tiny cyclone funneling between her teeth, and held out the lighter. Jack waved a hand.

"Stick it in the glove compartment."

Lydia snapped open the catch and a small blue box fell out and landed at her feet. She froze, and Jack laughed.

"What's the matter? Never seen Trojans before, Miss Lee?"

Lydia, her face burning, scooped up the condoms and tucked them back into the open box. "Sure I have." She slid them back into the glove compartment, along with the lighter, and tried to change the subject. "So what did you think of the physics test today?"

Jack snorted. "I didn't think you cared about physics."

"Are you still failing?"

"Are you?"

Lydia hesitated. She took a long drag, imitating Jack, and tipped her head back as she exhaled. "I don't care about physics. I could give a rat's ass."

"Bullshit," Jack said. "Then how come whenever Mr. Kelly hands back an assignment, you look like you're going to cry?"

She hadn't realized it was so obvious, and a hot flush flared in her cheeks and trickled down her neck. Beneath her, the seat creaked and a spring prodded her thigh, like a knuckle.

"Little Miss Lee, smoking," Jack said, clucking his tongue. "Won't your brother be upset when he finds out?"

"Not as upset as he'd be to find out I was in your car." Lydia grinned. Jack didn't seem to notice. He rolled down the window and a cold rush of air burst into the car as he flicked his cigarette butt into the street.

"Hates me that much, does he?"

"Come on," Lydia said. "Everybody knows what happens in this car."

Abruptly, Jack pulled to the side of the road. They had just reached the lake, and his eyes were cold and still, like the iced-over water behind him. "Maybe you'd better get out, then. You don't want someone like me corrupting you. Ruining your chances of getting into Harvard like your brother."

He must really hate Nath, Lydia thought. *As much as Nath hates him.* She imagined them in class together all these years: Nath sitting close to the front, notebook out, one hand rubbing the little furrow between his eyebrows, the way he did when he was thinking hard. Utterly focused, oblivious to everything else, the answer right there, sealed inside his mouth. And Jack? Jack would be sprawled in the back corner, shirt untucked, one leg stretched into the aisle. So comfortable. So certain of himself. Not worried about what anyone thought. No wonder they couldn't stand each other.

"I'm not like him, you know," she said.

Jack studied her for a long moment, as if trying to decide if this were true. Beneath the backseat, the engine idled with a growl. The ash at the end of her cigarette length-ened, like a gray worm, but she said noth-ing, just breathed a thin cloud of fog into the frozen air and forced herself to meet Jack's narrowing gaze.

"How did you get blue eyes?" he said at last. "When you're Chinese and all?"

Lydia blinked. "My mom's American."

"I thought brown eyes won out." Jack propped his hand against her headrest and leaned in to study her carefully, like a jeweler with a gemstone. Under this ap-praisal, the back of Lydia's neck tingled, and she turned away and ashed her cigarette into the tray.

"Not always, I guess."

"I've never seen a Chinese person with

blue eyes."

Up close, she could see a constellation of freckles on Jack's cheek, faded now, but still there. As her brother had long ago, Lydia counted them: nine.

"You know you're the only girl in this school who's not white?"

"Yeah? I didn't realize." This was a lie. Even with blue eyes, she could not pretend she blended in.

"You and Nath, you're practically the only Chinese people in the whole of Middlewood, I bet."

"Probably."

Jack settled back into his seat and rubbed at a small dent in the plastic of the steering wheel. Then, after a moment, he said, "What's that like?"

"What's it like?" Lydia hesitated. Sometimes you almost forgot: that you didn't look like everyone else. In homeroom or at the drugstore or at the supermarket, you listened to morning announcements or dropped off a roll of film or picked out a carton of eggs and felt like just another someone in the crowd. Sometimes you didn't think about it at all. And then sometimes you noticed the girl across the aisle watching, the pharmacist watching, the checkout boy watching, and you saw yourself reflected in their stares: incongruous. Catching the eye like a hook. Every time you saw yourself from the outside, the way other people saw you, you remembered all over again. You saw it in the sign at the Peking Express — a cartoon man with a coolie hat, slant eyes, buckteeth, and chopsticks. You saw it in the little boys on the playground, stretching their eyes to slits with their fingers — *Chinese — Japanese — look at these* — and in the older boys who muttered *ching chong ching chong ching* as they passed you on the street, just loud enough for you to hear. You saw it when waitresses and policemen and bus drivers spoke slowly to you, in simple words, as if you might not understand. You saw it in photos, yours the only black head of hair in the scene, as if you'd been cut out and pasted in. You thought: *Wait, what's she doing there?* And then you remembered that *she* was *you.* You kept your head down and thought about school, or space, or the future, and tried to forget about it. And you did, until it happened again.

"I dunno," she said. "People decide what you're like before they even get to know you." She eyed him, suddenly fierce. "Kind of like you did with me. They think they know all about you. Except you're never who they think you are."

Jack stayed silent for a long time, staring down at the castle in the center of the steering wheel. They would never be friends now. He hated Nath, and after what she'd just said, he would hate her, too. He would kick her out of the car and drive away. Then, to Lydia's surprise, Jack pulled the pack of cigarettes from his pocket and held it out. A peace offering.

Lydia did not wonder where they would go. She did not think, then, about what excuse she'd offer her mother, the excuse that — with an inspired smirk — would be her cover for all her afternoons with Jack: that she'd stayed after school to do physics extra credit. She did not even think about Nath's shocked and anxious face when he learned where she had been. Looking out over the lake, she could not know that in three months she would be at its bottom. At that moment she simply took the proffered cigarette and, as Jack flicked the lighter, touched its tip to the flame.

EIGHT

James is all too familiar with this kind of forgetting. From Lloyd Academy to Harvard to Middlewood, he has felt it every day — that short-lived lull, then the sharp nudge to the ribs that reminded you that you didn't belong. It seemed a false comfort to him, like a zoo animal crouched in its cage, ignoring the gawking eyes, pretending it is still running wild. Now, a month after Lydia's funeral, he treasures those moments of forgetting.

Others might have found refuge in a pint of whiskey, or a bottle of vodka, or a six-pack of beer. James, though, has never liked the taste of alcohol, and he finds it does not dull his mind; it only turns him a dark beet-red, as if he has endured some terrible battering, while his mind races all the faster. He takes long drives, crisscrossing Middlewood, following the highway almost to Cleveland before turning back. He takes sleeping pills from the drugstore, and even in his dreams, Lydia is dead. Again and again, he finds only one place where he can stop thinking: Louisa's bed.

He tells Marilyn that he's going in to class, or to meet with students; on weekends, he says he has papers to grade. These are lies. The dean had canceled his summer class the week after Lydia's death. "Take some time for yourself, James," he had said, touching James gently on the shoulder. He did this with everyone he needed to soothe: students enraged over low grades, faculty slighted by the grants they did not receive. His job was to make losses feel smaller. But the students never turned their C-minuses into Bs; new funding never materialized. You never got what you wanted; you just learned to get by without it. And the last thing James wants is time for himself — being at home is unbearable. At every moment, he expects Lydia to appear in the doorway, or to hear the squeak of her floorboards overhead. One morning, he heard footsteps in her room, and before he could stop himself, he ran upstairs, breathless, only to find Marilyn pacing before Lydia's desk, opening and closing her desk drawers. *Get out,* he wanted to shout, as if this were a sacred space. Now, every morning, he picks up his briefcase, as if he is going to teach, and drives in to the college. Even in his office, he finds himself mesmerized by the family photo on his desk, where Lydia — barely fifteen, then — peers out, ready to leap through the frame's glass and leave everyone behind. By afternoon, he finds himself at Louisa's apartment, plunging into her arms, then between her legs, where, blessedly, his mind shuts off.

But after leaving Louisa's, he remembers again, and he is always angrier than before. On the way back to his car one evening, he seizes a stray bottle from the street and hurls it into the side of Louisa's building. Other nights, he fights the temptation to steer into a tree. Nath and Hannah try to stay out of his way, and he and Marilyn have barely exchanged a word in weeks. As the Fourth of July approaches, James passes the lake and finds that someone has festooned the dock with bunting and red and white balloons. He swerves to the side of the road and rips it all down, bursting each balloon under his heel. When everything has sunk beneath the surface of the water, and the dock lies solemn and barren, he heads home, still shaking.

The sight of Nath rummaging in the refrigerator sets him ablaze again. "You're wasting power," James says. Nath shuts the door, and his quiet obedience only makes James angrier. "Do you always have to be in the way?"

"Sorry," Nath says. He cups a hard-boiled egg in one hand, a paper napkin in the other. "I didn't expect you." Out of the car, with its lingering air of exhaust and engine grease, James realizes he can smell Louisa's perfume on his skin, musky and spicy-sweet. He wonders if Nath can, too.

"What do you mean, you didn't expect me?" he says. "Don't I have a right to come into my own kitchen after a hard day of work?" He sets his bag down. "Where's your mother?"

"In Lydia's room." Nath pauses. "She's been in there all day."

Under his son's eye, James feels a sharp prickle between his shoulder blades, as if Nath is blaming him.

"For your information," he says, "my summer course comes with a great deal of responsibility. And I have conferences. Meetings." His face flushes at the memory of that afternoon — Louisa kneeling before his chair, then slowly unzipping his fly — and this makes him angry. Nath stares, lips slightly pursed, as if he wants to frame a question but can't get past the *W—*, and suddenly, James is furious. For as long as he has been a father, James has believed that Lydia looked like her mother — beautiful, blue-eyed, poised — and that Nath looked like him: dark, hesitating in midspeech, preparing to stumble over his own words. He forgets, most of the time, that Lydia and Nath resemble each other, too. Now, in Nath's face, James suddenly sees a flash of his daughter, wide-eyed and silent, and the pain of this makes him cruel. "You're just home all day. Do you have any friends at all?"

His father has said things like this for years, but at this moment Nath feels something snap, like an overstretched wire. "None. I'm not like you. No conferences. No — meetings." He wrinkles his nose. "You smell like perfume. From your meetings, I guess?"

James grabs him by the shoulder, so hard his knuckles crack. "Don't you talk to me that way," he says. "Don't you question me. You don't know anything about my life." Then, before he even realizes the words are forming, they shoot from his mouth like spit. "Just like you didn't know anything about your sister's."

Nath's expression doesn't change, but his whole face stiffens, like a mask. James wants to snatch the words back out of the air, like moths, but they've already crawled into his son's ears: he can see it in Nath's eyes, which have gone shiny and hard as glass. He wants to reach out and touch his son — his hand, his shoulder, anywhere — and tell him he didn't mean it. That none of this is his fault. Then Nath punches the countertop so hard it leaves a crack in the old, worn laminate. He runs out of the room, footsteps thundering up the stairs, and James lets his bag fall to the floor and slumps back against the counter. His hand touches something cold and wet: the crushed remains of the hard-boiled egg, shards of shell driven deep into the tender white.

All night he thinks about this, his son's frozen face, and the next morning he rises early. Retrieving the newspaper from the front porch, he sees the date black and stark in the corner: July 3. Two months to the day since Lydia disappeared. It doesn't seem possible that just two months ago he had sat in his office grading papers, that he had been embarrassed to pluck a ladybug from Louisa's hair. Until two months ago, July 3 had been a happy date, secretly treasured for ten years — the day of Marilyn's miraculous return. How everything has changed. In the kitchen, James slides the rubber band from the newspaper and unrolls it. There, below the fold, he sees a small headline: *Teachers and Classmates Remember Departed Girl.* The articles about Lydia have grown shorter and sparser. Soon they would stop entirely, and everyone would forget about her. James cups the paper toward him. The day is cloudy, but he leaves the light off, as if the dimness will soften what he's about to read. From Karen Adler: *She seemed lonely. She didn't really hang out with anyone.* From Pam Saunders: *She didn't have a lot of friends, or even a boyfriend. I don't think the boys even noticed her.* At the bottom: *Lee's physics teacher, Donald Kelly, remembered her as the lone sophomore in a class of juniors, noting, "She worked hard, but of course she stood out."* Beside the article, a sidebar: *Children of Mixed Backgrounds Often Struggle to Find Their Place.*

Then the telephone rings. Every time, his first thought is: *They've found her.* In that instant, a tiny part of him shouts that it's all a mix-up, a case of mistaken identity, a bad dream. Then the rest of him, which knows better, pulls him down with a sickening thud: *You saw her.* And he remembers again, with awful clarity, her swollen hands, her pale and waxen face.

It is because of this that his voice, when he answers the phone, always trembles.

"Mr. Lee?" It's Officer Fiske. "I hope it's not too early to call. How are you this morning?"

"Fine," James says. Everyone asks this, and by now it is an automatic lie.

"Well, Mr. Lee," Officer Fiske says, and James knows now it is bad news. No one called you by name so insistently unless they were trying to be kind. "I'm calling to let you know that we've decided to close our investigation. We are ruling this case a suicide."

James has to repeat these words to himself before he understands. "Suicide?"

Officer Fiske pauses. "Nothing in police work is ever *sure*, Mr. Lee. I wish it were. It's not like the movies — things are hardly ever clear-cut." He does not like breaking bad news, and he takes refuge in official language. "Circumstances suggest suicide is by far the most likely scenario. No evidence of foul play. A history of loneliness. Her grades were slipping. Going out on the lake when she knew she couldn't swim."

James bows his head, and Officer Fiske continues. His tone is gentler now, like a father consoling a young child. "We know

261

this isn't easy for you and your family, Mr. Lee. We hope this at least helps you move on."

"Thank you," James says. He sets the receiver back on its hook. Behind him, Marilyn hovers in the doorway, one hand on the jamb.

"Who was it?" she asks. By the way she clutches her robe, tight over her heart, James knows she's already heard everything. She flicks the light switch, and in the sudden brightness, he feels exposed and raw.

"They can't close the case," Marilyn says. "Whoever did this is still out there."

"Whoever did this? The police think —" James pauses. "They don't think there was anyone else involved."

"They don't know her. Someone must have taken her out there. Lured her." Marilyn hesitates, the cigarettes and condoms surfacing in her mind, but anger muscles them aside and turns her voice shrill. "She wouldn't have gone out there by herself. Do you think I don't know my own daughter?"

James does not reply. All he can think is: *If we'd never moved here. If she had never seen the lake.* The silence between them thickens, like ice, and Marilyn shivers.

"You believe them, don't you?" she says. "You think she did this thing." She cannot bring herself to use the word *suicide;* the mere thought of it sets her aboil again. Lydia would never do such a thing to her family. To her mother. How could James believe it? "They just want to close the case. Easier to stop looking than to do any real work." Marilyn's voice quivers, and she clenches her hands, as if stilling them will still the trembling inside her. "If she were a white girl, they'd keep looking."

A rock plummets into James's gut. In all their time together, white has been only the color of paper, of snow, of sugar. Chinese — if it is mentioned at all — is a kind of checkers, a kind of fire drill, a kind of takeout, one James doesn't care for. It did not bear discussion any more than that the sky was up, or that the earth circled the sun. He had naively thought that — unlike with Marilyn's mother, unlike with everyone else — this thing made no difference to them. Now, when Marilyn says this — *If she were a white girl* — it proves what James has feared all along. That inside, all along, she'd labeled everything. *White* and *not white.* That this thing makes all the difference in the world.

"If she were a white girl," he says, "none of this would ever have happened."

Marilyn, still fuming at the police, does

263

not understand, and her confusion makes her angrier. "What do you mean?" Under the kitchen light, her wrists are pale and thin, her lips set, her face cold. James remembers: long ago, when they were young and the worst thing they could imagine was not being together, he had once leaned in to touch her, and his fingertips had left a trail of goose bumps across her shoulder blade. Every tiny hair on his arm had stood up, electrified. That moment, that connection, seems far away and small now, like something that happened in another life.

"You know what I mean. If she'd been a white girl —" The words are ash-bitter on his tongue. *If she'd been a white girl. If I'd been a white man.* "She would have fit in."

For moving would never have been enough; he sees that now. It would have been the same anywhere. *Children of Mixed Backgrounds Often Struggle to Find Their Place.* The mistake was earlier, deeper, more fundamental: it had happened the morning they'd married, when the justice of the peace had looked at Marilyn and she had said yes. Or earlier, on that first afternoon they'd spent together, when he had stood beside the bed, naked and shy, and she had twined her legs around his waist and pulled him toward her. Earlier yet: on that first day, when she'd leaned across his desk and kissed him, knocking the breath out of him like a swift, sharp punch. A million little chances to change the future. They should never have married. He should never have touched her. She should have turned around, stepped out of his office into the hallway, walked away. He sees with utter clarity: none of this was supposed to happen. A mistake.

"Your mother was right, after all," he says. "You should have married someone more like you."

Before Marilyn can say anything — before she knows whether to be angry or sad or hurt, before she really understands what James has said — he is gone.

This time, he does not bother to stop at the college. He drives straight to Louisa's, speeding through every traffic light, arriving out of breath, as though he'd run there on foot. "Is everything all right?" she says when she opens the door, still smelling of the shower, dressed but wet-haired, hairbrush in hand. "I didn't expect you so early." It's only quarter to nine, and James hears the questions that ripple behind her surprise: Has he come to stay? What about his wife? He does not know the answers. Now that he has finally pushed those words out into the air, he feels strangely light. The room wobbles and spins, and he sinks down onto the sofa.

"You need to eat something," Louisa says. She steps into the kitchen and returns with a small Tupperware. "Here." Gently, she pries open the lid and nudges the box toward him. Inside lie three snow-colored buns, tops ruffled like peony heads ready to blossom, revealing a glint of deep tawny red within. The sweet scent of roast pork wafts up to his nose.

"I made them yesterday," Louisa says. She pauses. "You know what these are?"

His mother had made these, long ago, in their tiny cinder-colored apartment. She had roasted the pork and crimped the dough and arranged the buns in the bamboo steamer she'd brought all the way from China. His father's favorite. *Char siu bau.*

Louisa beams, and only then does James realize he has spoken aloud. He has not said a word in Chinese in forty years, but he is amazed at how his tongue still curls around their familiar shape. He has not had one of these buns since he was a child. His mother had packed them in his lunches until he told her to stop, he'd rather eat what the other kids were eating. "Go on," Louisa says now. "Taste."

Slowly he lifts a bun from the box. It is lighter than he remembers, cloudlike, yielding beneath his fingertips. He had forgotten that anything could be so tender. He breaks the bun open, revealing glossy bits of pork and glaze, a secret red heart. When he puts it to his mouth, it is like a kiss: sweet and salty and warm.

He does not wait for her to wrap her arms around him, as if he is a small and hesitant child, or for her to coax him into the bedroom. Instead he pushes her to the floor as he reaches for his fly, tugging her skirt up and pulling her onto him right there in the living room. Louisa moans, arching her back, and James fumbles with the buttons on her blouse, peeling it away and unsnapping her bra and catching her breasts, heavy and round, in his cupped hands. As she grinds herself against him, he focuses on her face, on the dark hair that tumbles down into his mouth, on the deep brown eyes that close as her breath grows faster, her thrusts more urgent. This is the sort of woman, he thinks, he should have fallen in love with. A woman who looked just like this. A woman just like him.

"You're the kind of girl I should have married," he whispers afterward. It is the kind of thing every man says to his lover, but to him it feels like a revelation. Louisa, half-asleep in the crook of his arm, does not hear him, but the words snake into her ear, giving her the tangled dreams of every other other woman. *He will leave her — he will marry me — I will make him happy — there will be no other woman.*

At home, when Nath and Hannah come downstairs, Marilyn sits motionless at the kitchen table. Though it is past ten o'clock, she is wearing her bathrobe still, hugged so tightly around her that they cannot see her neck, and they know there is bad news even before she chokes out the word *suicide.* "Was it?" Nath asks slowly, and, turning for the stairs without looking at either of them, Marilyn says only, "They say it was."

For half an hour, Nath pokes at the dregs of cereal in the bottom of his bowl while Hannah watches him nervously. He has been checking the Wolffs' house every day, looking for Jack, trying to catch him — though for what, he isn't quite sure. One time he even climbed the porch steps and peeked in the window, but no one is ever home. Jack's VW hasn't puttered down the street in days. At last, Nath pushes the bowl away and reaches for the telephone. "Get out," he says to Hannah. "I want to make a phone call." Halfway up the stairs, Hannah pauses, listening to the slow clicks as Nath dials. "Officer Fiske," he says after a moment, "this is Nathan Lee. I'm calling about my sister." His voice drops, and only bits and pieces come through: *Ought to reexamine. Tried to talk to him. Acting evasive.* Toward the end, only one word is audible. *Jack. Jack.* As if Nath cannot say the name without spitting.

After Nath puts the phone down, so hard the bells jangle, he shuts himself in his room. They think he's being hysterical, but he knows there's something there, that there's some connection to Jack, some missing piece of the puzzle. If the police don't believe him, his parents won't either. His father is hardly home these days anyway, and his mother has locked herself in Lydia's room again; through the wall he can hear her pacing, like a prowling cat. Hannah raps at his door, and he puts on a record, loud, until he can't hear the sound of her knuckles, or his mother's footsteps, anymore. Later, none of them will remember how the day passes, only a numbed blur, overshadowed by all that would happen the next day.

When evening falls, Hannah opens her door and peers through the crack. A razor of light slices under Nath's door, another under Lydia's. All afternoon Nath had played his record over and over, but he has finally let it wind to a stop, and now a thick silence, like fog, seeps out onto the landing. Tiptoeing downstairs, she finds the house dark, her father still gone. The kitchen faucet drips: *plink, plink, plink.* She knows she should turn it off, but then the house will be silent, and at the moment this is unbearable. Back in her room, she imagines the faucet dripping to itself in the kitchen. With every *plink,* another bead of water would form on the brushed steel of the sink.

She longs to climb into her sister's bed and sleep, but with her mother there, she cannot, and to console herself, Hannah circles the room, checking her treasures, pulling each from its hiding place and examining it. Tucked between mattress and box spring: the smallest spoon from her mother's tea set. Behind the books on the shelf: her father's old wallet, the leather worn thin as tissue. A pencil of Nath's, his toothmarks revealing wood grain beneath the yellow paint. These are her failures. The successes are all gone: the ring on which her father kept his office keys; her mother's best lipstick, *Rose Petal Frost;* the mood ring Lydia used to wear on her thumb. They were wanted and missed and hunted down in Hannah's hands. *These aren't a toy,* said her father. *You're too young for makeup,* said her mother. Lydia had been more blunt: *Stay out of my things.* Hannah had folded her hands behind her back, savoring the lecture, nodding solemnly as she memorized the shape of them standing there beside the bed. When they were gone, she repeated each sentence under her breath, redrawing them in the empty spot where they'd been.

All she has left are things unwanted, things unloved. But she doesn't put them back. To make up for them being unmissed, she counts them carefully, twice, rubs a spot of tarnish from the spoon, snaps and un-snaps the change pocket of the wallet. She's had some of them for years. No one has ever noticed they were gone. They slipped away silently, without even the *plink* of a drop of water.

She knows Nath is convinced, no matter what the police say, that Jack brought Lydia to the lake, that he had something to do with it, that it's his fault. In his mind, Jack dragged her into the boat, Jack pushed her underwater, Jack's fingerprints are pressed into her neck. But Nath is all wrong about Jack.

This is how she knows. Last summer, she and Nath and Lydia had been down at the lake. It was hot and Nath had gone in for a swim. Lydia sunbathed on a striped towel in her swimsuit on the grass, one hand over her eyes. Hannah had been listing Lydia's many nicknames in her mind. Lyd. Lyds. Lyddie. Honey. Sweetheart. Angel. No one ever called Hannah anything but Hannah. There were no clouds, and in the sun, the water had looked almost white, like a puddle of milk. Beside her, Lydia let out a little sigh and settled her shoulders deeper into the towel. She smelled like baby oil and her skin gleamed.

As Hannah squinted, looking for Nath, she thought of possibilities. "Hannah Banana" — they might call her that. Or something that had nothing to do with her name, something that sounded strange but that, from them, would be warm and personal. *Moose,* she thought. *Bean.* Then Jack had strolled by, with his sunglasses perched atop his head, even though it was blindingly bright.

"Better watch out," he said to Lydia. "You'll have a white patch on your face if you lie like that." She laughed and uncovered her eyes and sat up. "Nath not here?" Jack asked, settling down beside them, and Lydia waved out toward the water. Jack pulled his cigarettes from his pocket and lit one, and suddenly there was Nath, glowering down at them. Water speckled his bare chest and his hair dripped down onto his shoulders.

"What are you doing here?" he'd said to Jack, and Jack stubbed the cigarette out in the grass and put on his sunglasses before looking up.

"Just enjoying the sun," he said. "Thought I might go for a swim." His voice didn't sound nervous, but from where she was sitting, Hannah could see his eyes behind the tinted lenses, how they fluttered to Nath, then away. Without speaking, Nath plunked himself down right between Jack and Lydia, bunching his unused towel in his hand. Blades of grass stuck to his wet swimsuit and his calves, like thin streaks of green paint.

"You're going to burn," he said to Lydia. "Better put on your T-shirt."

"I'm fine." Lydia shielded her eyes with her hand again.

"You're already turning pink," Nath said. His back was to Jack, as if Jack weren't there at all. "Here. And here." He touched Lydia's shoulder, then her collarbone.

"I'm fine," Lydia said again, swatting him away with her free hand and lying back again. "You're worse than Mom. Stop fuss-

273

ing. Leave me alone." Something caught Hannah's eye then, and she didn't hear what Nath said in return. A drop of water trickled out of Nath's hair, like a shy little mouse, and ran down the nape of his neck. It made its slow way between his shoulder blades, and where his back curved, it dropped straight down, as if it had jumped off a cliff, and splashed onto the back of Jack's hand. Nath, facing away from Jack, didn't see it, and neither did Lydia, peeking up through the slits between her fingers. Only Hannah, arms curled around knees, a little way behind them, saw it fall. In her ears, it made a noise, like a cannon shot. And Jack himself jumped. He stared at the drop of water without moving, as if it were a rare insect that might fly away. Then, without looking at any of them, he raised his hand to his mouth and touched his tongue to it, as if it were honey.

It happened so quickly that if she were a different person, Hannah might have wondered if she'd imagined it. No one else saw. Nath was still turned away; Lydia had her eyes shut now against the sun. But the moment flashed lightning-bright to Hannah. Years of yearning had made her sensitive, the way a starving dog twitches its nostrils at the faintest scent of food. She could not mistake it. She recognized it at once: love, one-way deep adoration that bounced off and did not bounce back; careful, quiet love that didn't care and went on anyway. It was too familiar to be surprising. Something deep inside her stretched out and curled around Jack like a shawl, but he didn't notice. His gaze moved away to the far side of the lake, as if nothing had happened. She stretched her leg and touched her bare foot to Jack's, big toe to big toe, and only then did he look down at her.

"Hey, kiddo," he said, ruffling her hair with his hand. Her whole scalp had tingled and she thought her hair might stand up, like static electricity. At the sound of Jack's voice, Nath glanced over.

"Hannah," he said, and without knowing why, she stood up. Nath nudged Lydia with his foot. "Let's go." Lydia groaned but picked up her towel and the bottle of baby oil.

"Stay away from my sister," Nath said to Jack, very quietly, as they left. Lydia, already walking away, shaking grass off her towel, didn't hear, but Hannah had. It sounded like Nath had meant her — Hannah — but she knew he'd really meant Lydia. When they stopped at the corner to let a car pass, she peeked back over her shoulder, one quick glance too fast for Nath to notice. Jack was watching them go. Anyone would think he was looking at Lydia, with the towel slung around her hips now, like a sarong. Hannah shot him a little smile, but he didn't smile back, and she could not tell if he hadn't seen her, or if her one little smile hadn't been enough.

Now she thinks of Jack's face as he looked down at his hands, as if something important had happened to them. No. Nath is wrong. Those hands could never have hurt anyone. She is sure of it.

On Lydia's bed, Marilyn hugs her knees like a little girl, trying to leap the gaps between what James has said and what he thinks and what he meant. *Your mother was right all along. You should have married someone more like you.* With such bitterness in his voice that it choked her. These words sound familiar and she mouths them silently, trying to place them. Then she remembers. On their wedding day, in the courthouse: her mother had warned her about their children, how they wouldn't fit in anywhere. *You'll regret it,* she had said, as if they would be flippered and imbecile and doomed, and out in the lobby, James must have heard everything. Marilyn had said only, *My mother just thinks I should marry someone more like me,* then brushed it away, like dust onto the floor. But those words had haunted James. How they must have wound around his heart, binding tighter over the years, slicing into the flesh. He had hung his head like a murderer, as if his blood were poison, as if he regretted that their daughter had ever existed.

When James comes home, Marilyn thinks, speechless with aching, she will tell him: *I would marry you a hundred times if it gave us Lydia. A thousand times. You cannot blame yourself for this.*

Except James does not come home. Not at dinner; not at nightfall; not at one, when the bars in town close. All night Marilyn sits awake, pillows propped against the headboard, waiting for the sound of his car in the driveway, his footsteps on the stairs. At three, when he still hasn't come home, she decides she will go to his office. All the way to campus, she pictures him huddled in his wheeled armchair, crushed with sadness, soft cheek pressed to hard desk. When she finds him, she thinks, she will convince him this is not his fault. She will bring him home. But when she pulls into the lot, it is empty. She circles his building three times, checking all the spots where he usually parks, then all the faculty lots, then all the meters nearby. No sign of him anywhere.

In the morning, when the children come downstairs, Marilyn sits stiff-necked and bleary-eyed at the kitchen table. "Where's Daddy?" Hannah asks, and her silence is enough of an answer. It is the Fourth of July: everything is closed. James has no friends on the faculty; he is not close with their neighbors; he loathes the dean. Could he have been in an accident? Should she call the police? Nath rubs his bruised knuckle across the crack in the counter and remembers the perfume on his father's skin, his reddening cheeks, his sharp and sudden fury. *I don't owe him anything,* he thinks, but even so, he has the feeling of leaping off a high cliff when he swallows hard and says at last, "Mom? I think I know where he is."

At first Marilyn will not believe it. It is so unlike James. Besides, she thinks, he doesn't know anyone. He does not have any female friends. There are no women in the history department at Middlewood, only a few women professors at the college at all. When would James meet another woman? Then a terrible thought occurs to her.

She takes down the phone book and skims down the Cs until she finds it, the only Chen in Middlewood: *L Chen 105 4th St*

#3A. A telephone number. She nearly reaches for the receiver, but what would she say? *Hello, do you know where my husband is?* Without shutting the phone book, she grabs her keys from the counter. "Stay here," she says. "Both of you. I'll be back in half an hour."

Fourth Street is near the college, a student-heavy area of town, and even as she turns down it, squinting at building numbers, Marilyn has no plan. Maybe, she thinks, Nath is all wrong, maybe she is making a fool of herself. She feels like an overtuned violin, strung too tight, so that even the slightest vibration sets her humming. Then, in front of number 97, she sees James's car, parked beneath a scrubby maple. Four stray leaves dot its windshield.

Now she feels strangely calm. She parks the car, lets herself into 105, and climbs the steps to the third floor, where with one steady fist she raps at 3A. It is nearly eleven, and when the door opens, just wide enough to reveal Louisa still in a pale blue robe, Marilyn smiles.

"Hello," she says. "It's Louisa, isn't it? Louisa Chen? I'm Marilyn Lee." When Louisa does not respond, she adds, "James Lee's wife."

"Oh, yes," Louisa says. Her eyes flick away

279

from Marilyn's. "I'm sorry. I'm not dressed yet —"

"I can see that." Marilyn sets her hand on the door, holding it open with one palm. "I'll just take a moment of your time. You see, I'm looking for my husband. He didn't come home last night."

"Oh?" Louisa swallows hard, and Marilyn pretends not to notice. "How terrible. You must be very worried."

"I am. Very worried." She keeps her eyes trained on Louisa's face. They have met only twice before, in passing at the college Christmas party and then at the funeral, and Marilyn studies her carefully now. Long ink-colored hair, long lashes over down-turned eyes, small mouth, like a doll's. A shy little thing. *As far from me*, she thinks with a twinge, *as a girl could be.* "Do you have any idea where he might be?"

Louisa blushes bright pink, and Marilyn feels almost sorry for her, she is so transparent. "Why would I know?"

"You're his assistant, aren't you? You work together every day." She pauses. "He speaks of you so often at home."

"He does?" Confusion and pleasure and surprise mingle in Louisa's face, and Marilyn can see exactly what is running through her mind. *That Louisa — she's so smart. So talented. So beautiful.* She thinks, *Oh Louisa. How young you are.*

"Well," Louisa says at last. "Have you checked his office?"

"He wasn't there earlier," Marilyn says. "Perhaps he's there now." She sets her hand on the doorknob. "Could I use your telephone?"

Louisa's smile vanishes. "I'm sorry," she says. "My phone's actually not working right now." She looks desperately at Marilyn, as if wishing she would just give up and go away. Marilyn waits, letting Louisa fidget. Her hands have stopped shaking. Inside she feels a quiet smoldering rage.

"Thank you anyway," she says. "You've been very helpful." She lets her eyes drift past Louisa, to the tiny sliver of living room she can see through the doorway, and Louisa glances back over her shoulder nervously, as if James might have wandered out of the bedroom unawares. "If you see him," Marilyn adds, raising her voice, "tell my husband that I'll see him at home."

Louisa swallows again. "I will," she says, and at last Marilyn lets her shut the door.

NINE

A few months earlier, a different illicit romance had been brewing. To Nath's immense disapproval, all spring Lydia had spent her afternoons out with Jack in his car: driving round and round town, or parking the VW near the green quad of the college, or by the playground, or in a deserted parking lot.

Despite what Nath thought, to Lydia's smug satisfaction, despite the whispers, now and then, when someone glimpsed her climbing into Jack's car — *She's not, is she? No way. Her? Can't be* — despite Lydia's own expectations, the truth was much less scandalous. While the college students scurried to class, or kindergartners scaled the slide, or bowlers trudged into the alley for a quick after-work game, something happened that Lydia had never expected: she and Jack talked. As they sat smoking, feet propped on the dashboard, she told him stories about her parents: how in second grade, she'd traced the diagram of the heart from the encyclopedia, labeling each ventricle with magic marker, and her mother had pinned it up on her bedroom wall as if it were a masterpiece. How at ten, her mother had taught her to take a pulse; how at twelve her mother had persuaded her to skip Cat Malone's birthday party — the only one she'd ever been invited to — to finish her science fair project. How her father had insisted she go to the freshman dance and bought her a dress, and she had spent the night standing in the darkest corner of the gym, counting the minutes until she could go home: how late was late enough? Eight thirty? Nine? At first she tried not to mention Nath, remembering how Jack hated him. But she could not talk about herself without Nath and, to her surprise, Jack asked questions: Why did Nath want to be an astronaut? Was he quiet at home like he was at school? So she told him how, after the moon landing, he had bounded across the lawn, pretending to be Neil Armstrong, for days. How, in the sixth grade, he'd convinced the librarian to let him borrow from the adults' section and brought home textbooks on physics, flight mechanics, aerodynamics. How he'd asked for a telescope for his fourteenth birthday and received a clock radio instead; how he'd saved his allowance and bought himself one. How, sometimes, at dinner, Nath never said a word about his day, because their parents never asked. Jack absorbed everything, lighting her next cigarette as she flicked the old butt out the window, tossing her his pack when she ran out. Week after week, she tamped down a flare of guilt at making Nath seem even more pathetic — because talking about Nath kept her in Jack's car every afternoon, and every afternoon she spent in Jack's car bothered Nath more and more.

Now, in mid-April, Jack had started teaching Lydia to drive. At the end of the month, she would be sixteen.

"Think of the gas pedal and the clutch as partners," he said. "When one goes up, the other goes down." Under Jack's direction, Lydia let the clutch out slowly and tapped the gas with her toe, and the VW crept forward across the empty parking lot of the roller rink on Route 17. Then the engine stalled, slamming her shoulders into the seat back. Even after a week of practice, the violence of this moment still surprised her, how the whole car jolted and fell silent, as if it had had a heart attack.

"Try again," Jack said. He set his foot on

the dashboard and pushed in the cigarette lighter. "Nice and slow. Clutch in, gas out."

At the far end of the parking lot, a police car pulled in and executed a neat U-turn, pointing its nose toward the street. *They're not looking for us,* Lydia told herself. Route 17, out at the edge of town, was a notorious speed trap. Still, the black-and-white car kept catching her eye. She turned the key and restarted the car and stalled again, almost at once.

"Try again," Jack repeated, pulling a pack of Marlboros from his pocket. "You're in too much of a hurry."

She had not realized this, but it was true. Even the two weeks until her birthday, when she could get her learner's permit, seemed eternal. When she had her license, Lydia thought, she could go anywhere. She could drive across town, across Ohio, all the way to California, if she wanted to. Even with Nath gone — her mind shied from the thought — she would not be trapped alone with her parents; she could escape anytime she chose. Just thinking about it made her legs twitch, as if itching to run.

Slowly, she thought, taking a deep breath. Just like partners. One goes up, the other goes down. James had promised to teach her to drive their sedan as soon as she had her permit, but Lydia did not want to learn in their car. It was sedate and docile, like a middle-aged mare. It buzzed gently, like a watchful chaperone, if you didn't fasten your seat belt. "After you get your license," her father said, "we'll let you take the car out on Friday nights with your friends." "If you keep your grades up," her mother would add, if she was around.

Lydia sank the clutch to the floor and started the engine again and reached for the gearshift. It was almost five thirty, and her mother would expect her soon. When she tried to let out the clutch, her foot slipped off the pedal. The car bucked and died. The eyes of the policeman in the cruiser flicked toward them, then back toward the road.

Jack shook his head. "We can try again tomorrow." The coils of the lighter glowed as he pulled it from the socket and pressed a cigarette to its center, the end singeing black against the hot metal, then orange, as if the color had bled. He passed it to Lydia and, once they had switched seats, lit another for himself. "You almost had it," he said, wheeling the car toward the exit of the parking lot.

Lydia knew this was a lie, but she nodded. "Yeah," she said hoarsely. "Next time." As they turned onto Route 17, she blew a long column of smoke out toward the police car.

"So are you going to tell your brother we've been hanging out, and I'm not such a bad guy?" Jack asked when they were nearly home.

Lydia grinned. She suspected that Jack still took other girls out — some days, he and the VW were nowhere to be found — but with her, he was practically gentlemanly: he had never even held her hand. So what, if they were only friends? Most days she was the one climbing into his car, and she knew this had not escaped Nath's attention. At dinnertime, while she spun stories for her mother about her grades and her *extra credit project,* or for her father about Shelley's new perm or Pam's obsession with David Cassidy, Nath watched her — half-angry, half-afraid — as if he wanted to say something but didn't know how. She knew what he was thinking, and she let him. Some evenings, she came into Nath's room, plopped down on his windowsill, and lit a smoke, daring him to say something.

Now, Lydia said, "He would never believe me."

She hopped out a block early, and Jack turned the corner and pulled into his driveway while she trotted home, as if she'd walked the whole way herself. Tomorrow, she thought, she would pop the car into first and they would roll across the parking lot, white lines whipping beneath the wheels. On top of the pedals, her feet would feel comfortable, her insteps supple. Soon she would glide down the highway, shifting into third, then fourth, speeding off somewhere all on her own.

It didn't turn out that way. At home, in her room, Lydia flicked on the record player, where the album Hannah had given her for Christmas was already in place — to Lydia's surprise, she had been playing it over and over. She set the needle an inch and a half from the edge, aiming for the start of her favorite song, but overshot, and Paul Simon's voice suddenly soared into the room: *Hey, let your honesty shine, shine, shine* —

A faint knocking punched through the music, and Lydia twisted the volume knob as loud as it would go. In a moment, Marilyn, knuckles smarting, opened the door and leaned in.

"Lydia. *Lydia.*" When her daughter didn't turn around, Marilyn lifted the arm of the record player and the room went quiet, the record spinning helplessly beneath her hand. "That's better. How can you think with that on?"

"It doesn't bother me."

"Are you done with your homework already?" No answer. Marilyn pursed her lips. "You know, you shouldn't be listening to music if you haven't finished your schoolwork."

Lydia picked at a hangnail. "I'll do it after dinner."

"Better to get started now, don't you think? Make sure you have time to finish it all and do a careful job?" Marilyn's face softened. "Sweetheart, I know high school may not feel important. But it's the foundation of the rest of your life." She perched on the arm of Lydia's chair and stroked her daughter's hair. It was so crucial to make her understand, but she didn't know how. A quiver had crept into Marilyn's voice, but Lydia didn't notice. "Trust me. Please. Don't let your life slip away from you."

Oh god, Lydia thought, *not again.* She blinked fiercely and focused on the corner of her desk, where some article her mother had clipped months ago still sat, furred now with dust.

"Look at me." Marilyn cupped Lydia's chin in her hand and thought of all the things her own mother had never said to her, the things she had longed, her entire life, to hear. "You have your whole life in front of you. You can do anything you want." She paused, looking over Lydia's shoulder at the shelf crammed with books, the stethoscope atop the bookshelf, the neat mosaic of the periodic table. "When I'm dead, that's all I want you to remember."

She meant: *I love you. I love you.* But her words sucked the breath from Lydia's lungs: *When I'm dead.* All through that long-ago summer, she had thought her mother might really be dead, and those weeks and months had left a persistent, insistent ache in her chest, like a pulsing bruise. She had promised: anything her mother wanted. Anything at all. As long as her mother stayed.

"I know, Mom," she said. "I know." She tugged her notebook from her bookbag. "I'll get started."

"That's my girl." Marilyn kissed her on the head, right where her hair parted, and Lydia inhaled at last: shampoo, detergent, peppermint. A scent she had known all her life, a scent that, every time she smelled it, she realized she had missed. She curled her arms around Marilyn's waist, pulling her close, so close she could feel her mother's heartbeat against her cheek.

"Enough of that," Marilyn said at last, swatting Lydia playfully on the behind. "Get to work. Supper will be ready in half an hour."

All through dinner, the conversation with her mother writhed inside Lydia. She steeled herself with one thought: later, she would tell Nath all about it, and then she would feel better. She excused herself early, leaving half her plate untouched. "I've got to finish my physics," she said, knowing her mother wouldn't protest. Then, on her way upstairs, she passed the hall table, where her father had set the mail just before supper, and one envelope caught her eye: a Harvard seal in the corner, and beneath that, *Admissions Office.* She slit it open with her finger.

Dear Mr. Lee, she read. *We look forward to you joining us on campus April 29–May 2 and have matched you with a host student for your visit.* She knew it had been coming, but it had not seemed real until now. The day after her birthday. Without thinking, she ripped the letter and envelope in two. And at that moment, Nath came out of the kitchen.

"Thought I heard you out here," he said. "Can I borrow —" He spotted the red crest on the torn envelope, the letter in pieces in Lydia's hand, and froze.

Lydia flushed. "It's nothing important. I didn't —" But she had crossed a line, and both of them knew it.

"Gimme that." Nath snatched the letter. "This is mine. Jesus. What are you doing?"

"I just —" Lydia could not think of a way to finish.

Nath pieced the ragged edges together, as if he could make the letter whole again. "This is about my visit. What the hell were you thinking? That if I didn't get this, I couldn't go?" Put so starkly, it sounded foolish and pathetic, and tears began to form in the corners of Lydia's eyes, but Nath did not care. It was as if Lydia had been stealing from him. "Get it through your head: I'm going. I'm going that weekend. And I'm going in September." He bolted for the stairs. "Jesus Christ. I can't get out of this house fast enough." In a moment, his door slammed overhead, and although Lydia knew he wouldn't open it — nor did she know what she would say if he did — this did not stop her from knocking, again and again and again.

The next afternoon, in Jack's car, she stalled the engine over and over until Jack said they'd better call it a day.

"I know what to do," Lydia said. "I just can't do it." Her hand had cramped into a claw around the gearshift and she pried it away. *Partners,* she reminded herself. The gas and the clutch were partners. It struck her now: that wasn't true. If one went up, the other had to go down. That was how everything went. Her grade in physics had gone up to a C-minus but her grade in history had slipped to a D. Tomorrow her English essay was due — two thousand words on Faulkner — but she could not even find her book. Maybe there was no such thing as partners, she thought. From all her studying, this flashed through her mind: *For every action, there is an equal and opposite reaction.* One went up and the other went down. One gained, the other lost. One escaped, the other was trapped, forever.

The thought haunted her for days. Although Nath — cooled down now from the incident of the letter — was speaking to her again, she could not bear to mention it, even to apologize. Each night after dinner, despite her mother's most pointed nagging, she stayed in her room alone instead of tiptoeing down the hall in search of sympathy. The night before her birthday, James rapped at her door.

"You've seemed down the past couple of weeks," he said. He held out a little blue velvet box the size of a deck of cards. "I thought an early present might cheer you up." It had taken him some time, this gift, and he was proud of it. He had gone so far as to ask Louisa for advice on what a teenage girl might like, and this time, he was sure Lydia would love it.

Inside the box lay a silver heart on a chain. "It's beautiful," Lydia said, surprised. At last, a present that was a present — not a book, not a hint — something she wanted, not something they wanted for her. This was the necklace she had longed for at Christmas. The chain slid through her fingers like a stream of water, so lithe it felt almost alive.

James touched her dimple with a fingertip and twisted it, an old joke of his. "It opens."

Lydia flipped the locket open and froze. Inside were two pictures the size of her thumbnail: one of her father, one of her — dolled up for the ninth-grade dance the year before. All the way home, she had told him what a wonderful time she'd had. The photo of her father smiled broadly, fondly, expectantly. The photo of herself looked away, serious, resentful, sullen.

"I know this year has been tough, and your mother's been asking a lot of you," James said. "Just remember, school isn't everything. It's not as important as friendship, or love." Already he could see a faint line worrying a crease between Lydia's brows, dark circles blooming beneath her eyes from late-night studying. He wanted to smooth that wrinkle with his thumb, to wipe the shadows away like dust. "Every time you look at this, just remember what really matters. Every time you look at this, I want you to smile. Promise?"

He fiddled with the clasp of the necklace, struggling with the tiny spring loop. "I wanted gold, but a reliable source told me everyone was wearing silver this year," he said. Lydia ran a finger along the velvet lining of the box. Her father was so concerned with what *everyone* was doing: *I'm so glad you're going to the dance, honey — everyone goes to the dance. Your hair looks so pretty that way, Lyddie — everyone has long hair these days, right?* Anytime she smiled: *You should smile more — everyone likes a girl who smiles.* As if a dress and long hair and a smile could hide everything about her that was different. If her mother let her go out like the other girls, she thought, it might not matter what she looked like — Jackie Harper had one blue eye and one green, and she'd been voted Most Social last year. Or if she looked like everyone else, perhaps it would not matter that she had to study all the time, that she could not go out on the weekends until she'd done all her homework, that she could not go out with boys at all. One or the other might be overcome. To be pulled both ways — no dress, no book, no locket could help that.

"There we go," James said, the catch springing open at last. He refastened it at her nape, and the metal cut a line of cold, like a ring of ice, around her throat. "What do you think? Do you like it?" Lydia understood: this was meant to remind her of all he wanted for her. Like a string tied around her finger, only this lay around her neck.

"It's beautiful," she whispered, and James mistook her hoarseness for deep gratitude.

"Promise me," he said, "that you'll get along with everyone. You can never have too many friends." And Lydia closed her eyes and nodded.

The next day, in honor of her birthday, she wore the necklace, as her father suggested. "Right after school," James told her, "I'll take you over to get your permit and we'll have our first driving lesson before dinner." Her mother said, "And after dinner, we'll have cake. And I've got some special presents for the birthday girl." Which meant books, Lydia thought. That night Nath would pack his suitcase. All day she consoled herself: *In six hours, I will have my permit. In two weeks, I will be able to drive away.*

At three o'clock, her father pulled up in front of the school, but when Lydia picked up her bookbag and started for the sedan, she was surprised to see someone already in the passenger seat: a Chinese woman — a girl, really — with long black hair.

"So nice to finally meet you," the girl said as Lydia climbed into the backseat. "I'm Louisa, your dad's teaching assistant."

James paused the car to let a cluster of junior boys meander across the street. "Louisa has an appointment and since I was coming this way anyway, I offered her a ride."

"I shouldn't have said yes," Louisa said. "I should have just canceled it. I *hate* the dentist."

As he crossed in front of the car, one of the juniors grinned at them through the windshield and pulled his eyes into slits with his fingers. The others laughed, and Lydia scrunched down in her seat. It occurred to her: the boys probably thought Louisa was her mother. Squirming, she wondered if her father was embarrassed, too, but in the front seat, James and Louisa hadn't noticed a thing.

"Ten bucks says you don't even have one

cavity," James said.

"Five," Louisa said. "I'm just a poor grad student, not a rich professor." She patted his arm playfully, and the tenderness in her face shocked Lydia. Her mother looked at her father this way, late at night, when he was caught up in his reading and she leaned against his armchair affectionately, before nudging him to bed. Louisa's hand lingered on her father's arm and Lydia stared at them, her father and this girl, cozy in the front seat like a little married couple, a tableau framed by the bright screen of the windshield, and she thought suddenly: *This girl is sleeping with my father.*

It had never occurred to her before to think of her father as a man with desires. Like all teenagers, she preferred — despite her very existence — to imagine her parents as eternally chaste. But there was something in the way her father and Louisa touched, in their easy banter, that shocked her innocent sensibilities. To her, the faint crackle between them blazed so hotly that her cheeks flushed. They were lovers. She was sure of it. Louisa's hand was still on her father's arm and her father didn't move, as if the caress were nothing unusual. In fact, James did not even notice: Marilyn often rested her hand on him just this way, and the feeling was too familiar to stand out. For Lydia, however, the way her father kept looking straight ahead, eyes still scanning the road, was all the confirmation she needed.

"So I hear it's your birthday today," Louisa said, twisting toward the backseat again. "Sixteen. I'm sure this will be a very special year for you." Lydia didn't respond, and Louisa tried again. "Do you like your necklace? I helped pick it out. Your dad asked my advice on what you might like."

Lydia hooked two fingers beneath the chain, fighting the urge to yank it from her neck. "How would you know what I like? You don't even know me."

Louisa blinked. "I had some ideas. I mean, I've heard so much about you from your dad."

Lydia looked her directly in the eye. "Really," she said. "Daddy's never mentioned you."

"Come on, Lyddie," James said, "you've heard me talk about Louisa. How smart she is. How she never lets those undergrads get away with anything." He smiled at Louisa, and Lydia's vision blurred.

"Daddy, where did you drive after you got *your* license?" she asked suddenly.

In the rearview mirror, James's eyes flicked

open in surprise. "To school, to swim practices and meets," he said. "And on errands, sometimes."

"But not on dates."

"No," James said. His voice cracked briefly, like a teenage boy's. "No, not on dates."

Lydia felt small and sharp and mean, like a tack. "Because you didn't date. Right?" Silence. "Why not? Didn't anybody want to go out with you?"

This time James kept his eyes on the road before them, and his hands on the wheel stiffened, elbows locking.

"Oh, now," Louisa said. "I don't believe that for a minute." She put her arm on James's elbow again, and this time she kept it there until they reached the dentist's office, until James stopped the car and said, to Lydia's outrage, "See you tomorrow."

Despite his daughter glowering in the backseat, James did not realize anything was wrong. At the DMV, he kissed her on the cheek and took a chair. "You'll do fine," he said. "I'll be right here when you're done." Thinking about how excited Lydia would be, permit in hand, he had forgotten all about the moment in the car. Lydia herself, still roiling with the secret she was sure she had discovered, turned away without a word.

In the test room, a woman handed her an exam booklet and a pencil and told her to take any empty seat. Lydia made her way toward the back corner of the room, stepping over bookbags and purses and the legs of the boy in the next-to-last row. Everything her father had ever said to her bounced back in a new tone: *You can never have too many friends.* She thought of her mother, sitting at home, doing the laundry, filling in a crossword, while her father — She was furious with him, furious with her mother for letting this happen. Furious with everyone.

At that moment Lydia realized the room had gone silent. Everyone's head was bent over the test. She looked up at the clock, but it told her nothing: not when they started, not when the test ended, only the time, three forty-one. The second hand tick-tick-ticked around from eleven to twelve and the minute hand, like a long iron needle, jumped forward another notch. Three forty-two. She flipped her booklet open. *What color is a stop sign?* She filled in the circle for B: *Red. What must you do if you see or hear an emergency vehicle coming from any direction?* In her haste, the pencil slipped outside the bubble in a jagged

301

claw. A few rows up, a girl with pigtails rose, and the woman at the front gestured her into the next room. A moment later, the boy sitting next to her did the same. Lydia looked down at her booklet again. Twenty questions. Eighteen left to go.

If your car begins to skid, you should . . . All of the answers seemed plausible. She skipped ahead. *When are roads and highways most slippery? How much distance should you leave between yourself and the vehicle in front of you under good road conditions?* To her right, a man with a mustache closed his booklet and put down his pencil. C, Lydia guessed. A. D. On the next page, she found a list of sentences she could not complete. *When driving behind a large truck on the freeway, you should . . . To safely navigate a curve, you should . . . When backing up, you should . . .* She repeated each question to herself and got stuck on the last words, like a scratched record: *you should, you should, you should.* Then someone touched her shoulder, softly, and the woman from the front of the room said, "I'm sorry, dear, time's up."

Lydia kept her head bent over the desk, as if the words would not be true until she saw the woman's face. A dark spot formed in the middle of the paper, and it took her a moment to realize it was the mark of a tear, that it was hers. She wiped the paper clean with her hand, then wiped her cheek. Everyone else had gone.

"It's okay," the woman said. "You only need fourteen right." But Lydia knew she had filled in only five circles.

In the next room, where a man fed answer sheets into the scoring machine, she jabbed her finger with the tip of her pencil. "Eighteen right," the man said to the girl in front of her. "Take this to the counter and they'll take your picture and print your permit. Congratulations." The girl gave a happy little skip as she passed through the door and Lydia wanted to slap her. There was a brief moment of silence as the man looked at Lydia's form, and she focused on the splotch of mud on his boot.

"Well," he said. "Don't feel bad. Lots of people fail the first time." He turned the paper faceup and again she saw the five dark circles, like moles, the rest of the sheet blank and bare. Lydia did not wait for her score. As the machine sucked in the answer sheet, she walked straight past him, back into the waiting room.

There was a long line at the counter for photos now; the man with the mustache counted the bills in his wallet, the girl who had skipped picked at her nail polish. The pigtailed girl and the boy had already gone. On the bench, James sat waiting. "So," he said, looking down at her empty hands. "Where is it?"

"I failed," she said. The two women beside her father on the bench looked up at her, then quickly away. Her father blinked, once, twice, as if he hadn't heard her properly.

"It's okay, honey," he said. "You can try again this weekend." In the cloud of disappointment and humiliation, Lydia did not remember, or care, that she could take the test again. In the morning, Nath would leave for Boston. All she could think was: *I will be here forever. I will never be able to get away.*

James put his arm around his daughter, but it weighed on her shoulders like a lead blanket, and she shrugged it off.

"Can we go home now?" she said.

"As soon as Lydia comes in," Marilyn said, "we'll say surprise. And then we'll have dinner, and presents after." Nath was up in his room, packing for his trip, and alone with her youngest, she was planning aloud, half talking to herself. Hannah, delighted to have her mother's attention even by default, nodded sagely. Under her breath she practiced

— *Surprise! Surprise!* — and watched her mother pipe Lydia's name in blue onto the sheet cake. It was supposed to look like a driver's license, a white-frosted rectangle with a photo of Lydia in the corner where the real photograph would be. Inside, it was chocolate cake. Because this was an extra-special birthday, Marilyn had baked this cake herself — from a box, true, but she had mixed it, one hand moving the mixer through the cake batter, the other holding the battered aluminum bowl still against the whirling blades. She had let Hannah pick out the tub of frosting, and now she squeezed out the last of the tube of decorator's icing spelling L-Y-D and reached into the grocery bag for another.

Such a special cake, Hannah thought, would taste extra-special, too. Better than just plain vanilla or chocolate. The box had shown a smiling woman hovering over a slice of cake and the words *You mix in the love.* Love, Hannah decided, would be sweet, like her mother's perfume, and soft as marshmallows. Quietly she extended a finger, gouging a small dip in the perfectly smooth surface of the cake. "Hannah!" Marilyn snapped, and swatted her hand away.

While her mother smoothed the dent with

the spatula, Hannah touched the frosting on her finger to her tongue. It was so sweet her eyes watered, and when Marilyn wasn't looking, she wiped the rest of it onto the backside of the tablecloth. She could tell by the little line between her mother's eyebrows that she was still upset, and she wanted to lean her head against Marilyn's aproned thigh. Then her mother would understand that she hadn't meant to mess up the cake. But as she reached out, Marilyn set down the tube of icing mid-letter and lifted her head, listening. "That can't be them already."

Beneath her feet, Hannah felt the floor shiver as the garage door groaned open. "I'll get Nath."

By the time Hannah and Nath arrived downstairs, though, Lydia and their father had already come from the garage into the hallway, and the moment for *Surprise* had passed. Instead Marilyn took Lydia's face between her hands and kissed her on the cheek, hard, leaving a red smudge of lipstick, like a welt.

"You're home early," she said. "Happy birthday. And congratulations." She held out a palm. "So? Let's see it."

"I failed," Lydia said. She glared from Nath to their mother, as if daring them to be upset.

Marilyn stared. "What do you mean, you failed?" she said, honest surprise in her voice, as if she had never heard the word.

Lydia said it again, louder: "I *failed.*" It was almost, Hannah thought, as if she were mad at their mother, mad at all of them. It could not be just the test. Her face was stony and still, but Hannah saw the tiny trembles — in her hunched shoulders, in her jaw clenched tight. As if she might shiver to pieces. She wanted to wrap her arms tight around her sister's body, to hold her together, but she knew Lydia would only push her away. No one else noticed. Nath and Marilyn and James glanced at each other, unsure what to say.

"Well," Marilyn said at last. "You'll just study the traffic rules and try again when you're ready. It's not the end of the world." She tucked a stray lock of hair behind Lydia's ear. "It's okay. It's not like you failed a school subject, right?"

On any other day, this would have made Lydia boil over inside. Today — after the necklace, after the boys in front of the car, after the test, after Louisa — there was no room left in her for anger. Something within her tipped and cracked.

"Sure, Mom," she said. She looked up at

307

her mother, around at her whole family, and smiled, and Hannah nearly ducked behind Nath. The smile was too wide, too bright, cheery and white-toothed and fake. On her sister's face it was terrifying; it made Lydia look like a different person, a stranger. Again no one else noticed. Nath's shoulders unhunched; James let out his breath; Marilyn wiped her hands, which had grown damp, on her apron.

"Dinner's not quite ready yet," she said. "Why don't you go up and take a shower and relax? We'll eat early, as soon as it's done."

"Great," Lydia said, and this time Hannah actually did turn her face away until she heard her sister's footsteps on the stairs.

"What happened?" Marilyn murmured to James, who shook his head. Hannah knew. Lydia hadn't studied. Two weeks ago, before Lydia had come home after school, Hannah had explored her room, looking for treasures. She'd pocketed Lydia's book from the floor of the closet and, beneath it, had found the rules and regulations pamphlet. When Lydia started to study, Hannah had thought, she would notice her book was missing. She would come looking for it. Every few days, she had checked, but the pamphlet hadn't moved. Yesterday it had

been half-covered by a pair of beige plat-
forms and Lydia's best bell-bottoms. And
the book was still tucked upstairs under
Hannah's pillow.

Upstairs, in her room, Lydia yanked at
the necklace, which wouldn't break. She
unhooked it and slammed it inside its box,
as if it were a wild thing, and pushed it deep
beneath the bed. If her father asked where
it was, she would say she was saving it for
special occasions. She would say she didn't
want to lose it, don't worry, she'd wear it
next time, Daddy. In the mirror, a fine red
line ringed her neck.

By the time Lydia came down to dinner
an hour later, the mark had faded away,
though the feeling that accompanied it had
not. She had dressed up as if for a party,
her hair ironed dry and straight and glossy
on the big ironing board, her lips coated
with jam-colored gloss. James, looking at
her, had a sudden memory of Marilyn when
they'd first met. "Don't you look nice," he
said, and Lydia forced herself to smile. She
sat bolt upright with that same fake smile at
the dinner table, like a doll on display, but
only Hannah spotted its fakeness. Her back
ached, watching Lydia, every bit of her did,
and she slouched in her own chair until she
nearly slid off the seat. As soon as dinner

was over, Lydia patted her mouth with her napkin and stood up.

"Wait," Marilyn said. "There's cake." She went into the kitchen and in a moment emerged bearing the cake on a tray, candles aglow. The photo of Lydia was gone, the top of the cake refrosted to plain white, with just Lydia's name. Hiding under the smooth white, Hannah thought, was the pretend driver's license, the *Congratulations* and the blue L-Y-D. Though you couldn't see it, it was there just underneath, covered up but smudged and unreadable and horrible. And you'd be able to taste it, too. Their father snapped picture after picture, but Hannah didn't smile. Unlike Lydia, she had not yet learned to pretend. Instead she half shut her eyes, like she did during the scary parts of TV shows, so that she could only half see what came next.

Which was this: Lydia waited for them to finish singing. As they reached the last line of the song, James held up the camera and she bent over the cake, lips pursed as if to kiss. Her perfectly made-up face smiled around the table, sweeping each of them in turn. Their mother. Their father. Nath. Hannah did not know everything Lydia thought she understood — the necklace, Louisa, *all I want you to remember* — but she knew that something had shifted inside her sister, that she was balanced on a dangerous, high-up ledge. She sat very still, as if one wrong move might tip Lydia off the edge, and Lydia blew out the flames with one quick puff.

TEN

Lydia had been wrong about Louisa, of course. Back then, on his daughter's birthday, James would have laughed at the very idea; the thought of anyone other than Marilyn in his bed, in his life, was preposterous. But back then, the thought of life without Lydia had been preposterous, too. Now both of those preposterous things have come true.

When Louisa shuts the apartment door and returns to the bedroom, James is already buttoning his shirt. "You're going?" she says. Inside, she still clings to the possibility that Marilyn's visit was just a coincidence, but she is fooling herself, and she knows it.

James tucks in his shirt and fastens his belt. "I have to," he says, and they both know this is true, too. "It may as well be now." He's not sure what to expect when he reaches home. Sobbing? Rage? A frying pan to the head? He doesn't know yet, either, what he will say to Marilyn. "I'll see you later," he says to Louisa, who kisses his cheek, and this is the one thing he's sure of.

When he enters the house, just after noon, there is no sobbing, no rage — just silence. Nath and Hannah sit side by side on the living room couch, eyeing him warily as he passes through. It is as if they are watching a doomed man march to the gallows, and this is how James himself feels as he climbs the stairs to his daughter's room, where Marilyn sits at Lydia's desk, eerily calm. For a long while, she says nothing, and he wills himself still, keeps his hands steady, until she finally speaks.

"How long?"

Outside, Nath and Hannah crouch on the top step in wordless accord, holding their breath, listening to the voices that carry down the hall.

"Since — the funeral."

"The funeral." Marilyn, still studying the carpet, presses her lips into a thin line. "She's very young. How old is she? Twenty-two? Twenty-three?"

"Marilyn. Stop it."

Marilyn doesn't stop it. "She seems sweet. Quite docile — that's a nice change, I suppose. I don't know why I'm surprised. I guess you're long overdue for a trade-in.

She'd make a very nice little wife."

James, to his surprise, blushes. "No one's talking about —"

"Not yet. But I know what she wants. Marriage. Husband. I know her type." Marilyn pauses, remembering her younger self, her mother's proud whisper: *a lot of wonderful Harvard men.* "My mother spent her whole life trying to turn me into that type."

At the mention of Marilyn's mother, James stiffens, as if he has turned to ice. "Oh, yes. Your poor mother. And then you went and married me." He chokes out a laugh. "What a disappointment."

"I *am* disappointed." Marilyn's head snaps up. "I thought you were different." What she means is: *I thought you were better than other men. I thought you wanted better than that.* But James, still thinking of Marilyn's mother, hears something else.

"You got tired of different, didn't you?" he says. "I'm too different. Your mother knew it right away. You think it's such a good thing, standing out. But look at you. Just look at you." He takes in Marilyn's honey-colored hair; her skin, even paler than usual from a month spent indoors. Those sky-colored eyes he has adored for so long, first in his wife's face and then in his child's. Things he has never said, never even hinted to Marilyn before, pour from his mouth. "You've never been in a room where no one else looked like you. You've never had people mock you to your face. You've never been treated like a stranger." He feels as if he has vomited, violently, and he drags the back of his hand across his lips. "You have no idea what it's like, being different."

For a moment James looks young and lonely and vulnerable, like the shy boy she'd met so long ago, and half of Marilyn wants to gather him in her arms. The other half of her wants to batter him with her fists. She gnaws her lip, letting the two sides struggle. "Sophomore year, in the lab, the men used to sneak up behind me and try to lift up my skirt," she says at last. "One time they came in early and pissed in all of my beakers. When I complained, the professor put his arm around me and said —" The memory catches in her throat, like a burr. "*Don't worry about it, honey. Life's too short and you're too beautiful.* You know what? I didn't care. I knew what I wanted. I was going to be a doctor." She glares at James, as if he has contradicted her. "Then — fortunately — I came to my senses. I stopped trying to be different. I did just what all the other girls were doing. I got married. I gave all

315

that up." A thick bitterness coats her tongue. "Do what everyone else is doing. That's all you ever said to Lydia. Make friends. Fit in. But I didn't want her to be just like everyone else." The rims of her eyes ignite. "I wanted her to be exceptional."

On the stairs, Hannah holds her breath. She is afraid to move anything, even a fingertip. Maybe if she stays perfectly still, her parents will stop talking. She can hold the world motionless, and everything will be all right.

"Well, now you can marry this one," Marilyn says. "She seems like the serious type. You know what that means." She holds up her left hand, where the wedding ring glints dully. "A girl like that wants the whole package. Matchbox house, picket fence. Two-point-three kids." She lets out one hard, sharp, terrifying bark of a laugh, and out on the landing, Hannah hides her face against Nath's arm. "I suppose she'll be more than happy to trade student life for all that. I just hope she doesn't regret it."

At this word — *regret* — something in James flares. A hot biting smell, like over-heating wires, pricks his nostrils. "Like you do?"

A sudden and stunned silence. Though Hannah's face is still pressed into Nath's shoulder, she can picture her mother exactly: her face frozen, the rims of her eyes a deep red. If she cries, Hannah thinks, it won't be tears. It will be little drops of blood.

"Get out," Marilyn says at last. "Get out of this house."

James touches his pocket for his keys, then realizes they are still in his hand: he had not even put them down. As if he had known inside, all along, that he would not be staying.

"Let's pretend," he says, "that you never met me. That she was never born. That none of this ever happened." Then he is gone.

Out on the landing, there is no time to run: Hannah and Nath have not even stood up when their father emerges into the hallway. At the sight of his children, James stops short. It is clear they've heard everything. For the past two months, every time he sees one of them, he sees a fragment of their missing sister — in the tilt of Nath's head, in the long sweep of hair half screening Hannah's face — and he leaves the room abruptly, without truly understanding why. Now, with both of them watching, he edges past, not daring to meet their eyes. Hannah presses herself to the wall, letting their father pass, but Nath stares straight at him, silently, with a look James can't quite parse. The sound of his car as it whines out of the driveway, then speeds away, has the ring of finality; all of them hear it. Silence settles over the house like ash.

Then Nath leaps to his feet. *Stop,* Hannah wants to say, but she knows Nath won't. Nath pushes Hannah aside. His mother's keys dangle from their hook in the kitchen, and he takes them and heads for the garage.

"Wait," Hannah calls, out loud this time. She is not sure whether he is chasing their father or if he is running away as well, but she knows that what he has planned is dreadful. "Nath. Wait. Don't."

He doesn't wait. He backs out of the garage, nicking the lilac bush beside the door, and then he, too, is gone.

Upstairs, Marilyn hears none of this. She shuts the door of Lydia's room, and a thick, heavy quiet wraps itself around her like a smothering blanket. With one finger, she strokes Lydia's books, the neat binders in a row, each labeled in marker with the class and date. A coarse fur of dust now coats everything — the row of blank diaries, the old science fair ribbons, the pinned-up postcard of Einstein, the covers of each binder, the spines of each book. She imagines emptying Lydia's room piece by piece. The tiny holes and unfaded patches that will mar the wallpaper when the posters and pictures come down; the carpet, crushed beneath the furniture, that will never rise again. Like her own mother's house after everything had been cleared away.

She thinks of her mother coming home alone all those years to an empty house, the bedroom kept just as it was, with fresh bed-sheets, for the daughter who would never return, her husband long since gone, in some other woman's bed now. You loved so hard and hoped so much and then you ended up with nothing. Children who no longer needed you. A husband who no longer wanted you. Nothing left but you, alone, and empty space.

With one hand, she pulls Einstein from the wall and tears him in two. Then the periodic table, useless now. She yanks the earpieces from Lydia's stethoscope; she ravels the prize ribbons to satin shreds. One by one she topples the books from the shelf. *The Color Atlas of Human Anatomy. Women Pioneers of Science.* With each one, Marilyn's breath becomes more fierce. *How Your Body Works. Chemistry Experiments for Children. The Story of Medicine.* She remembers every single one. It is like rewinding time, working her way backward through Lydia's entire life. An avalanche piles up at her feet. Downstairs, huddled beneath the hall table, Hannah hears heavy thumps, like stone after stone thudding to the floor.

At last, perched in the far corner of the bookcase: the very first book Marilyn had ever bought for Lydia. Slender as a pamphlet, it teeters alone on the shelf, then tips. *Air hovers all around you,* the splayed pages read. *Though you can't see it, it is still there.* Marilyn wants to burn the books that litter the carpet, to peel the wallpaper from the walls. Everything that reminds her of Lydia and all she could have been. She wants to stomp the very bookshelf to splinters. Stripped bare, it lists unsteadily, as if it is tired, and with one push she knocks it to the floor.

And there, in the hollow below the bottom shelf: a book. Thick. Red. A Scotch-taped spine. Even before Marilyn sees the photo, she knows what it is. But she turns it over anyway, with suddenly unsteady hands, still astonished to find Betty Crocker's face implausibly, impossibly staring up at her.

Your cookbook, Lydia had said. *I lost it.* Marilyn had been thrilled, had considered it an omen: her daughter had read her mind. Her daughter would never be confined to a kitchen. Her daughter wanted more. It had been a lie. She flips the pages she has not seen in years, tracing her mother's pencil marks with her fingertip, smoothing the pockmarked pages where she had cried all those nights, in the kitchen, alone. Somehow Lydia had known: that this book had pulled on her mother like a heavy, heavy stone. She hadn't destroyed it. She had hidden it, all those years; she had piled book after book atop it, weighting it down, so her mother would never have to see it again.

Lydia, five years old, standing on tiptoe to watch vinegar and baking soda foam in the sink. Lydia tugging a heavy book from the shelf, saying, *Show me again, show me another.* Lydia, touching the stethoscope, ever so gently, to her mother's heart. Tears blur Marilyn's sight. It had not been science that Lydia had loved.

And then, as if the tears are telescopes, she begins to see more clearly: the shredded posters and pictures, the rubble of books, the shelf prostrate at her feet. Everything that she had wanted for Lydia, which Lydia had never wanted but had embraced anyway. A dull chill creeps over her. Perhaps — and this thought chokes her — that had dragged Lydia underwater at last.

The door creaks open, and Marilyn slowly

321

raises her head, as if Lydia might somehow, impossibly, appear. For a second the impossible happens: a small blurred ghost of little-girl Lydia, dark-haired, big-eyed. Hesitating in the doorway, clinging to the jamb. Please, Marilyn thinks. In this word is all she cannot phrase, even to herself. Please come back, please let me start over, please stay. Please.

Then she blinks, and the figure sharpens: Hannah, pale and trembling, her face glossy with tears.

"Mom," she whispers.

Without thinking, Marilyn opens her arms, and Hannah stumbles into them.

Across town, at the liquor store, Nath sets a fifth of whiskey on the counter. He has tasted alcohol exactly once in his life: at Harvard, his host student had offered him a beer. He'd gulped down four, more excited by the idea of it than the flavor — it had tasted, to him, like fizzy urine — and for the rest of the evening, the room had wobbled slightly on its axis. Now he wants the world to spin loose and careen away.

The man behind the counter studies Nath's face, then squints at the bottle of whiskey. Nath's fingers twitch. At eighteen, he is allowed to buy only three-two beer,

322

that watery stuff his classmates chugged at parties. But 3.2 percent isn't strong enough for what he needs now. The clerk eyes him again and Nath prepares himself: *Go home, sonny, you're too young for this stuff.*

Instead the clerk says, "Your sister that girl who died?"

Nath's throat goes raw, like a wound. He nods, focusing on the shelf behind the counter, where cigarettes rise in neat red-and-white stacks.

Then the clerk takes down a second bottle of whiskey and puts it in a bag with the first. He slides the bag toward Nath, along with the ten-dollar bill Nath has set on the counter.

"Good luck to you," he says, and turns away.

The quietest spot Nath knows is out on the edge of town, near the county line. He parks by the side of the road and pulls out one of the bottles. One gulp of whiskey, then another, burns its way down, and he pictures it torching away everything raw and red and painful inside him. It's almost one, and by the time the first bottle is gone, only one car has passed by, a dark-green Studebaker with an old lady at the wheel. The whiskey isn't working the way he'd hoped. He'd thought it would wipe his mind clean, like a sponge on a blackboard, but instead the world sharpens with each swallow, dizzying him with its details: the spatter of mud on the driver's side mirror; the last digit of the odometer, frozen between 5 and 6; the stitching in the car seat, just beginning to fray. A stray leaf, caught between windshield and wiper, rattles in the breeze. As he works through the second bottle, he thinks, suddenly, of his father's face as he'd walked out the door: the way he hadn't even glanced at them, as if he were focused on something far-off on the horizon or deep, deep in the past. Something neither he nor Hannah could see, something they couldn't touch even if they'd wanted to. The air inside the car grows thick, filling his lungs like cotton. Nath cranks the window down. Then — as the cool breeze rushes in — he pitches over the side and vomits both bottles of whiskey onto the curb.

In his own car, James too mulls over that moment on the stairs. After he'd pulled out of the driveway, he had driven without thinking, jamming his foot onto the gas pedal, heading wherever he can slam his foot to the floor. This is how he finds himself driving not back to Louisa's, but across town, right past campus, onto the highway, nudging the needle to sixty, sixty-five, seventy. Only when a sign — *Toledo 15 miles* — flashes wide and green overhead does he realize how far he's gone.

How appropriate, he thinks. Toledo. It strikes him that there is a beautiful symmetry to life. Ten years ago, Marilyn had fled here, leaving everything behind. Now it is his turn. He takes a deep breath and presses the pedal more firmly. He has said it at last, what he had been most afraid to say, what she had most longed to hear: *Pretend that you never met me. That none of this ever happened.* He has undone the great mistake of her life.

Except — and he can't deny this, no matter how he tries — Marilyn had not seemed grateful. She had flinched, as if he'd spat in her face. She had bitten her lips once, twice, as if swallowing a hard, painful seed. The car veers toward the shoulder, gravel shuddering under its wheels.

She left first, James reminds himself, nudging the car to the center of the road again. This is what she's wanted all along. Yet even as he thinks this, he knows it is untrue. The yellow line wavers and weaves. To James, years of unabashed stares prickling his spine, as if he were an animal in the zoo, years of mutters in the street — *chink, gook, go home* — stinging his ears, *different* has always been a brand on his forehead, blazoned there between the eyes. It has tinted his entire life, this word; it has left its smudgy fingerprints on everything. But *different* had been different for Marilyn.

Marilyn: young and unafraid in a classroom of men. Draining the urine from her flasks, plugging her ears by filling her head with dreams. A white blouse in a sea of navy-blue blazers. How she had longed for *different:* in her life, in herself. It is as if someone has lifted his world and turned it sideways and set it down again. Marilyn, packing those dreams away in lavender for their daughter, disappointment layered beneath her smile. Triply sequestered by house and dead-end street and tiny college town, her hands soft and uncalloused but idle. The intricate gears of her mind ticking silently at no one, thoughts pinging the closed windows like a trapped bee. And now, alone in their daughter's room, surrounded by the relics of their daughter's life, no lavender, only dust, in the air. It has been so long since he thought of his wife as a creature of want.

Later — and for the rest of his life — James will struggle to piece words to this feeling, and he will never quite manage to say, even just to himself, what he really means. At this moment he can think only one thing: how was it possible, he wonders, to have been so wrong.

Back in Middlewood, Nath does not know how long he lies there, sprawled across the front seat. All he knows is this: someone opens the car door. Someone calls his name. Then a hand grips his shoulder, warm and gentle and strong, and it doesn't let go.

To Nath, fighting through a deep and groggy stupor, the voice sounds like his father's, though his father has never spoken his name so softly, or touched him with such tenderness. In the moment before he opens his eyes, it *is* his father, and even when the world comes into focus to reveal hazy sunshine, a police cruiser, Officer Fiske crouching beside him in the open car door, it is still true. It is Officer Fiske who peels the empty whiskey bottle from his fingers and helps him lift his head, but in his heart it is his father who says, with such kindness that Nath begins to cry, "Son, it's time to go home."

ELEVEN

In April, home was the last place Nath
wanted to be. All month — weeks before
his visit to campus — he stacked books and
clothes in a growing pile. Every evening
before bed, he slipped the letter from
beneath his pillow and reread it, savoring
the details: a junior from Albany, Andrew
Bynner, an *astrophysics major,* would escort
him around campus, engage him in intel-
lectual and practical discussions over meals
in the dining hall, and host him for the long
weekend. Friday to Monday, he thought,
looking at his plane tickets; ninety-six hours.
By the time he took his suitcase down, after
Lydia's birthday dinner, he had already
sorted the things he'd take with him from
those he'd leave behind.

Even with her door closed, Lydia could
hear it: the click-click of the suitcase latches
opening, then a thud as the lid hit the floor.
Their family never traveled. Once, when

Hannah was still a baby, they'd visited Gettysburg and Philadelphia. Their father had plotted out the whole trip in the road atlas, a chain of places so steeped in Americana that it oozed out everywhere: in the names of the gas stations — Valley Forge Diesel — and in the diner specials when they stopped for lunch — *Gettystown Shrimp, William Penn's Pork Tenderloin.* Then, at every restaurant, the waitresses had stared at her father, then at her mother, then at her and Nath and Hannah, and she knew, even as a child, that they'd never come back. Since then, their father had taught summer classes every year, as if — she rightly suspected — to avoid raising the question of family vacations.

In Nath's room, a drawer shut with a bang. Lydia leaned back on her bed and propped her heels on the postcard of Einstein. In her mouth, the sick-sweet taste of frosting still lingered; in her stomach, the birthday cake roiled. At the end of summer, she thought, Nath would pack not just the one suitcase but a trunk and a stack of boxes, all his books and all his clothes, everything he owned. The telescope would disappear from the corner; the stacks of aeronautics magazines would vanish from the closet. A band of dust would border the bare shelves, clean wood at the back where the books had once stood. Every drawer, when she opened it, would be empty. Even the sheets on his bed would be gone.

Nath pushed the door open. "Which one's better?"

He held up two shirts, a hanger in each hand, so they flanked his face like curtains. On his left, a plain blue, his best dress shirt, the one he had worn to his junior award ceremony last spring. On the right, a paisley she'd never seen before, a price tag still dangling from the cuff.

"Where'd you get that?"

"Bought it," Nath said with a grin. All his life, whenever he needed new clothes, their mother dragged him to Decker's Department Store, and he agreed to anything she picked out in order to go home faster. Last week, counting over his ninety-six hours, he had driven himself to the mall for the first time and bought this shirt, plucking the bright pattern from the rack. It had felt like buying a new skin, and now his sister sensed this, too.

"A little fancy for going to class." Lydia did not right herself. "Or is that how they expect you to dress at Harvard?"

Nath lowered the hangers. "There's a mixer for visiting students. And my host student wrote me — he and his roommates are throwing a party that weekend. To celebrate the end of term." He held the patterned shirt against him, tucking collar beneath chin. "Maybe I'd better try it on."

He disappeared into the bathroom, and Lydia heard the scrape of hanger on shower rod. A mixer: Music, dancing, beer. Flirting. Phone numbers and addresses scribbled on scraps of paper. *Write me. Call me. We'll get together.* Slowly her feet slid down to rest on her pillow. A mixer. Where new students got whirled together and blended up and turned into something new.

Nath reappeared in the doorway, fastening the top button of the paisley shirt. "What do you think?"

Lydia bit her lip. The blue pattern against the white suited him; it made him look thinner, taller, tanner. Though the buttons were plastic, they gleamed like pearl. Already Nath looked like a different person, someone she'd known once a long time ago. Already she missed him.

"The other one's better," she said. "You're going to college, not Studio 54." But she knew Nath had already made up his mind.

Late that night, just before midnight, she tiptoed into Nath's room. She had wanted to tell him all evening about their father and

Louisa, about what she'd seen in the car that afternoon, what she *knew* was going on. Nath had been too preoccupied, and pinning down his attention had been like catching smoke in her hands. This was her last chance. He would be leaving in the morning.

In the dim room, only the small desk lamp was on, and Nath was in his old striped pajamas, kneeling at the windowsill. For a moment Lydia thought he was praying, and, embarrassed at catching him in such a private moment — like seeing him naked — she began to close the door. Then, at the sound of her footsteps, Nath turned, his smile as incandescent as the moon just beginning to swell over the horizon, and she realized she'd been wrong. The window was open. He had not been praying, but dreaming — which, she would realize later, came to almost the same thing.

"Nath," she began. The rush of things she wanted to say churned in her head: *I saw. I think. I need.* Such a large thing to break into tiny granules of words. Nath didn't seem to notice.

"Look at that," he whispered, with such awe that Lydia sank to her knees beside him and peered out. Above them, the sky rolled out a deep black, like a pool of ink, littered with stars. They were nothing like the stars in her science books, blurred and globby as drops of spit. They were razor-sharp, each one precise as a period, punctuating the sky with light. Tipping her head back, she could not see the houses or the lake or the lamps on the street. All she could see was the sky, so huge and dark it could crush her. It was like being on another planet. No — like floating in space, alone. She searched for the constellations she had seen on Nath's posters: Orion, Cassiopeia, the Big Dipper. The diagrams seemed childish now, with their straight lines and primary colors and stick-figure shapes. Here the stars dazzled her eyes like sequins. *This is what infinity looks like,* she thought. Their clarity overwhelmed her, like pinpricks at her heart.

"Isn't that amazing," Nath's voice said softly, out of the darkness. Already he sounded light-years away.

"Yeah," Lydia heard her own voice say, barely a whisper. "Amazing."

The next morning, as Nath tucked his toothbrush into its case, Lydia hovered in the doorway. In ten minutes, their father would drive him to the airport in Cleveland, where TWA would carry him to New York, then Boston. It was four thirty A.M.

"Promise you'll call and tell me how things are going."

"Sure," Nath said. He stretched the elastic straps over his folded clothes in a neat X and clapped the suitcase shut.

"You promise?"

"I promise." Nath shut the latches with one finger, then hoisted the suitcase by the handle. "Dad's waiting. I'll see you Monday."

And just like that, he was gone.

Much later, when Lydia came downstairs for breakfast, she could almost pretend that nothing had changed. Her homework lay beside her breakfast bowl with four little ticks in the margin; across the table, Hannah picked pebbles of cereal from her bowl. Their mother sipped oolong and leafed through the newspaper. Only one thing was different: Nath's place was empty. As if he had never been there.

"There you are," Marilyn said. "Better hurry and fix this, sweetheart, or you won't have time to eat before the bus."

Lydia, who felt as if she were floating, made her way to the table. Marilyn, meanwhile, skimmed the paper — Carter's approval rating 65 percent, Mondale settling into role of "Senior Adviser," asbestos banned, another shooting in New York —

before her eyes came to rest on a small human-interest story in the corner of the page. *Los Angeles Doctor Revives Man in Coma for Six Years.* Amazing, she thought. She smiled up at her daughter, who stood clinging to the back of her chair as if, without it, she might drift away.

Nath did not call that night, when Lydia shrank and shriveled beneath her parents' undeflected attention. *I got a course catalog from the college — do you want to take statistics this summer? Anyone ask you to prom yet? Well, I'm sure someone will soon.* He did not call Saturday, when Lydia cried herself to sleep, or on Sunday, when she awoke with eyes still scalding. So this is what it will be like, she thought to herself. As if I never had a brother at all.

With Nath gone, Hannah followed Lydia like a puppy, scampering to her door each morning before Lydia's clock radio had even gone off, her voice breathless, just short of a pant. *Guess what? Lydia, guess what?* It was never guessable and never important: it was raining; there were pancakes for breakfast; there was a blue jay in the spruce tree. Each day, all day, she trailed Lydia suggesting things they could do — *We could play Life, we could watch the*

335

Friday Night Movie, *we could make Jiffy Pop.* All her life, Hannah had hovered at a distance from her brother and sister, and Lydia and Nath had tacitly tolerated their small, awkward moon. Now Lydia noticed a thousand little things about her sister: the way she twitched her nose once-twice, fast as a rabbit, when she was talking; the habit she had of standing on her toes, as if she had on invisible high heels. And then, Sunday afternoon, as Hannah climbed into the wedges Lydia had kicked off, she delivered her latest idea — *We could go play by the lake. Lydia, let's go play by the lake* — and Lydia noticed something else, shiny and silver beneath Hannah's shirt.

"What's that?"

Hannah tried to turn away, but Lydia jerked her collar down to reveal what she'd already half glimpsed: a lithe silver chain, a slender silver heart. Her locket. She hooked it with one finger, and Hannah teetered, staggering out of Lydia's shoes with a thump.

"What are you doing with that?"

Hannah glanced at the doorway, as if the correct answer might be painted on the wall. Six days ago she had found the little velvet box beneath Lydia's bed. "I didn't think you wanted it," she whispered. Lydia wasn't listening. *Every time you look at this,* she heard her father say, *just remember what really matters.* Being sociable. Being popular. Blending in. *You don't feel like smiling? Then what? Force yourself to smile. Don't criticize, condemn, or complain.* Hannah, so pleased in that little silver snare, looked like her younger self — timid, gawky, shoulders just beginning to stoop under the weight of something that seemed so thin and silver and light.

With a loud crack, her hand struck Hannah's cheek, knocking her back, snapping her head to the side. Then she looped her whole hand through the chain and twisted, hard, jerking her forward like a dog on a choke collar. *I'm sorry,* Hannah began, but nothing emerged except a soft gasp. Lydia twisted harder. Then the necklace snapped, and both sisters found they could breathe again.

"You don't want that," Lydia said, the gentleness in her voice surprising Hannah, surprising Lydia herself. "Listen to me. You think you do. You don't." She bunched the necklace in her fist. "Promise me you'll never put this on again. Ever."

Hannah shook her head, eyes wide. Lydia touched her sister's throat, her thumb smoothing the tiny thread of blood where the chain had sliced into the skin.

"Don't ever smile if you don't want to," she said, and Hannah, half-blinded by the spotlight of Lydia's whole attention, nodded. "Remember that."

Hannah kept her word: later that night, and for years to come, she would look back on this moment, each time touching her throat, where the red mark of the chain had long since faded away. Lydia had looked more anxious than angry, the necklace dangling from her fingers like a dead snake; she had sounded almost sad, as if she had done something wrong, not Hannah. The necklace was, in fact, the last thing Hannah would ever steal. But this moment, this last talk with her sister, would puzzle her for a long time.

That evening, in the safety of her room, Lydia pulled out the piece of loose-leaf on which Nath had scrawled his host student's number. After dinner — when her father retreated to his study and her mother settled into the living room — she unfolded it and picked up the telephone on the landing. The phone rang six times before someone answered and, in the background, she could hear the raucous sounds of a party just getting under way. "Who?" the voice on the other end said, twice, and at last Lydia gave up whispering and snapped, "Nathan Lee. The visiting student. *Nathan Lee.*" Minutes ticked by, each ratcheting up the long-distance charge — though by the time the bill came, James would be too devastated to notice. Downstairs, Marilyn clicked the television dial around and around: *Rhoda. Six Million Dollar Man. Quincy. Rhoda* again. Then, finally, Nath came on the line.

"Nath," Lydia said. "It's me." To her surprise, tears welled in her eyes just at the sound of his voice — though his voice was deeper and blunter than usual, as if he had a cold. In fact, Nath was three-quarters through the first beer of his life, and the room was beginning to take on a warmish glow. Now his sister's voice — flattened by long distance — sliced through that glow like a blunt knife.

"What's the matter?"

"You didn't call."

"What?"

"You promised you'd call." Lydia wiped her eyes with the back of one wrist.

"That's why you're calling?"

"No, listen, Nath. I need to tell you something." Lydia paused, puzzling over how to explain. In the background, a burst of laughter swelled like a wave crashing ashore.

Nath sighed. "What happened? Did Mom nag you about your homework?" He tipped the bottle to his lips and found the beer had gone warm, and the stale liquid shriveled his tongue. "Wait, let me guess. Mom bought you a special present, but it was just a *book*. Dad bought you a new dress — no, a diamond necklace — and he expects you to *wear* it. Last night at dinner you had to talk and talk and *talk* and all their attention was on you. Am I getting warmer?"

Stunned, Lydia fell silent. All their lives Nath had understood, better than anyone, the lexicon of their family, the things they could never truly explain to outsiders: that a book or a dress meant more than something to read or something to wear; that attention came with expectations that — like snow — drifted and settled and crushed you with their weight. All the words were right, but in this new Nath's voice, they sounded trivial and brittle and hollow. The way anyone else might have heard them. Already her brother had become a stranger.

"I gotta go," he said.

"Wait. Wait, Nath. Listen."

"God, I don't have time for this." In a flash of bitterness, he added, "Why don't you go take your *problems* to Jack?"

He did not know then how those words

would haunt him. After he slammed the receiver back onto the cradle, a twinge of guilt, like a small sharp bubble, bored its way through his chest. But from far away, with the heat and noise of the party cocooning him, his perspective had shifted. Everything that loomed so large close up — school, their parents, their lives — all you had to do was step away, and they shrank to nothing. You could stop taking their phone calls, tear up their letters, pretend they'd never existed. Start over as a new person with a new life. Just a problem of geography, he thought, with the confidence of someone who had never yet tried to free himself of family. Soon enough Lydia, too, would head off to school. Soon enough she, too, would cut herself free. He gulped down the rest of his beer and went to get another.

At home, alone on the landing, Lydia cradled the handset in her hands for a long time after the click. The tears that had choked off her voice dried away. A slow, burning anger at Nath began to smolder inside her, his parting words ringing in her ears. *I don't have time for this.* He had turned into a different person, a person who didn't care that she needed him. A person who said things to hurt her. She felt herself becoming a different person, too: a person who would slap her sister. Who would hurt Nath as much as he had hurt her. *Go take your problems to Jack.*

Monday morning she put on her prettiest dress, the halter-neck with the tiny red flowers, which her father had bought her in the fall. *Something new for the new school year,* he had said. They had been shopping for school supplies and he had spotted it on a mannequin in the store's window display. James liked to buy Lydia dresses off the mannequin; he was sure it meant everyone was wearing them. *The latest thing, right? Every girl needs a dress for a special occasion.* Lydia, who aimed for unobtrusive — a hooded sweater and corduroys; a plain blouse and bell-bottoms — knew it was a date dress, and she did not date. She had kept it in the back of her closet for months, but today she pulled it from the hanger. She parted her hair carefully, right down the center, and clipped one side back with a red barrette. With the tip of her lipstick she traced the curves of her mouth.

"Don't you look nice," James said at breakfast. "Just as pretty as Susan Dey." Lydia smiled and said nothing, not when Marilyn said, "Lydia, don't be too late after school, Nath will be home for dinner," not

342

when James touched one finger to her dimple — that old joke again — and said, "All the boys will be after you now." Across the table, Hannah studied her sister's dress and lipsticked smile, rubbing one finger against the rusty scab, fine as a spiderweb, that ringed her neck. *Don't,* she wanted to say, though she didn't know: *don't* what? She knew only that something was about to happen, and that nothing she could say or do would prevent it. When Lydia had gone, she seized her spoon and mashed the soggy cereal in her bowl to a pulp.

Hannah was right. That afternoon, at Lydia's suggestion, Jack drove up to the Point, overlooking the town, and they parked in the shade. On a Friday night, half a dozen cars would cluster there, windows slowly fogging, until a police car scattered them away. Now — in the bright light of a Monday afternoon — there was no one else around.

"So when's Nath getting back?"

"Tonight, I think." In fact, Lydia knew, Nath would land at Hopkins Airport in Cleveland at five nineteen. He and their father would be home at six thirty. She peeked through the window to where First Federal's clock rose, just visible in the center of town. Five minutes past four.

"Must be weird not having him around."

Lydia laughed, a small, bitter laugh. "Four days wasn't long enough for him, I bet. He can't wait to leave for good."

"It's not like you'll never see him again. I mean, he'll come back. At Christmas. And summers. Right?" Jack raised an eyebrow.

"Maybe. Or maybe he'll stay out there forever. Who cares." Lydia swallowed, steadying her voice. "I've got my own life." Through the rolled-down window, the new leaves of the maples rustled. A single helicopter, leftover from fall, broke free and spiraled to the ground. Every cell in her body was trembling, but when she looked down at her hands, they lay calm and quiet in her lap.

She opened the glove compartment and fished out the box of condoms. There were still two inside, just as there had been months ago.

Jack looked startled. "What are you doing?"

"It's okay. Don't worry. I won't regret anything." He was so close she could smell the sweet saltiness of his skin. "You know, you're not like people think," she said, touching one hand to his thigh. "Everybody thinks, with all those girls, you don't care about anything. But that's not true. That's not really who you are, is it?" Her eyes met his, blue on blue. "I know you."

And while Jack stared, Lydia took a deep breath, as if she were diving underwater, and kissed him.

She had never kissed anyone before, and it was — though she didn't know it — a sweet kiss, a chaste kiss, a little-girl kiss. Beneath her lips, his were warm and dry and still. Beneath the smoke, Jack smelled as if he had just been out in the woods, leafy and green. He smelled the way velvet felt, something you wanted to run your hands over and then press to your face. In that moment Lydia's mind fast-forwarded, the way movies did. Past them clambering into the backseat, tumbling over one another, their hands too slow for their desires. Past untying the knot at the nape of her neck, past the peeling away of clothing, past Jack's body hovering over hers. All the things she had never experienced and, in truth, could barely imagine. By the time Nath came home, she thought, she would be transformed. That evening, when Nath told her everything new that he had seen at Harvard, everything about the new and fabulous life he was already beginning, she would have something new to tell him, too.

And then, very gently, Jack pulled away.

"You're sweet," he said.

He gazed down at her, but — even Lydia understood this instinctively — not like a lover: tenderly, the way adults look at children who have fallen and hurt themselves. Inside, she shriveled. She looked down at her lap, letting her hair screen her burning face, and a bitter taste bloomed in her mouth.

"Don't tell me you've grown morals all of a sudden," she said sharply. "Or am I just not good enough for you?"

"Lydia," Jack sighed, his voice flannel-soft. "It's not you."

"Then what?"

A long pause, so long she thought Jack had forgotten to answer. When he spoke at last, he turned toward the window, as if what he really meant were outside, beyond the maple trees, beyond the lake and everything beneath them. "Nath."

"Nath?" Lydia rolled her eyes. "Don't be afraid of Nath. Nath doesn't matter."

"He matters," Jack said, still looking out the window. "He matters to me."

It took Lydia a minute to process this, and she stared, as if Jack's face had changed shape, or his hair had changed color. Jack rubbed his thumb against the base of his ring finger, and she knew that he was telling the truth, that this had been the truth for a long, long time.

"But —" Lydia paused. *Nath?* "You're always — I mean, everyone knows —" Without meaning to, she glanced at the backseat, at the faded Navajo blanket crumpled there.

Jack smiled a wry smile. "How did you put it? Everybody thinks, with all those girls — but that's not who you are." He glanced at her sideways. Through the open window, a breeze ruffled his sandy curls. "No one would ever suspect."

Snatches of conversation floated back to Lydia now, in a different tone. *Where's your brother? What's Nath going to say?* And: *Are you going to tell your brother we've been hanging out, and I'm not such a bad guy?* What had she said? *He'd never believe me.* The half-empty box of condoms gaped up at her, and she crushed it in her fist. *I know you,* she heard herself say again, and cringed. How could I have been so stupid, she thought. To have gotten him so wrong. To have gotten everything so wrong.

"I gotta go." Lydia snatched her bookbag from the floor of the car.

"I'm sorry."

"Sorry? For what? There's nothing to be sorry about." Lydia slung the bag over her

347

shoulder. "Actually, I'm sorry for you. In love with someone who hates you."

She glared at Jack: one sharp wince, as if she'd splashed water in his eyes. Then Jack's face grew wary and pinched and closed, like it was with other people, like it had been the first day they'd met. He grinned, but it looked more like a grimace.

"At least I don't let other people tell me what I want," he said, and she flinched at the contempt in his voice. She had not heard it in so many months. "At least I know who I am. What I want." His eyes narrowed. "What about you, Miss Lee? What do *you* want?"

Of course I know what I want, she thought, but when she opened her mouth she found it empty. In her mind words ricocheted like glass marbles — *doctor, popular, happy* — and scattered into silence.

Jack snorted. "At least I don't let other people tell me what to do all the time. At least I'm not afraid."

Lydia swallowed. Under his eyes her skin felt flayed away. She wanted to hit Jack, but that would not be painful enough. And then she knew what would hurt him most.

"I bet Nath would love to hear about all this," she said. "I bet everyone at school would. Don't you think so?"

Before her eyes, Jack deflated like a pricked balloon.

"Look — Lydia —" he began, but she had already shoved the car door open and slammed it behind her. With each step, her bookbag thumped against her back, but she kept running, all the way down to the main road and toward home, not stopping even when a stitch knotted her side. At the sound of every car, she wheeled around, expecting to see Jack, but the VW was nowhere in sight. She wondered if he was still parked up there on the Point, that hunted look still in his eyes.

When she passed the lake and reached her own street, slowing to catch her breath at last, everything looked unfamiliar: strangely sharp, all the colors too bright, like an over-tuned TV set. Green lawns were a little too blue, Mrs. Allen's white gables a little too dazzling, the skin of her own arms a little too yellow. Everything felt just a bit dis-torted, and Lydia squinted, trying to squash it back into familiar shape. When she reached her own house, it took her a mo-ment to realize that the woman sweeping the porch was her mother.

Marilyn, spotting her daughter, held out her arms for a kiss. Only then did Lydia discover the box of condoms still clutched in her hand, and she shoved it into her bookbag, inside the lining.

"You feel warm," Marilyn said. She picked up the broom again. "I'm almost finished. Then we can start reviewing for your exams." Tiny green buds, fallen from the trees, crushed themselves beneath the bristles.

For a moment Lydia's voice froze, and when it finally emerged, it was so jagged neither she nor her mother recognized it. "I told you," she snapped. "I don't need your help."

By tomorrow, Marilyn would forget this moment: Lydia's shout, the shattered edges in her tone. It would disappear forever from her memory of Lydia, the way memories of a lost loved one always smooth and simplify themselves, shedding complexities like scales. For now, startled by her daughter's unusual tone, she attributed it to fatigue, to the late afternoon.

"Not much time left," she called as Lydia pulled the front door open. "You know, it's already May."

Later, when they look back on this last evening, the family will remember almost nothing. So many things will be pared away by the sadness to come. Nath, flushed with excitement, chattered through dinner, but none of them — including him — will remember this unusual volubility, or a single word he said. They will not remember the early-evening sunlight splashing across the tablecloth like melted butter, or Marilyn saying, *The lilacs are starting to bloom.* They will not remember James smiling at the mention of Charlie's Kitchen, thinking of long-ago lunches with Marilyn, or Hannah asking, *Do they have the same stars in Boston?* and Nath answering, *Yes, of course they do.* All of that will be gone by morning. Instead, they will dissect this last evening for years to come. What had they missed that they should have seen? What small gesture, forgotten, might have changed everything? They will pick it down to the bones, wondering how this had all gone so wrong, and they will never be sure.

As for Lydia: all evening, she asked herself the same question. She did not notice her father's nostalgia, or her brother's illuminated face. All through dinner, and after dinner, after she had said goodnight, that one question churned through her mind. How had this all gone so wrong? Alone, record player humming in the lamplight, she dug back through her memory: Before Jack's face that afternoon, defiant and tender and hunted all at once. Before Jack.

Before the failed physics test, before biology, before the ribbons and books and the real stethoscope. Where had things gone askew?

As her clock flipped from 1:59 to 2:00 with a gentle click, it came to her, falling into place with the same tiny sound. The record had long since spun to a halt, and the darkness outside made the silence deeper, like the muffled hush of a library. She knew at last where everything had gone wrong. And she knew where she had to go.

The wood of the dock was just as smooth as she remembered it. Lydia sat down at the end, as she had so long ago, feet dangling over the edge, where the rowboat knocked softly against the pier. All this time, she had never dared come so close again. Tonight, in the dark, she felt no fear, and she noted this with a calm sense of wonder. Jack was right: she had been afraid so long, she had forgotten what it was like not to be — afraid that, one day, her mother would disappear again, that her father would crumble, that their whole family would collapse once more. Ever since that summer without her mother, their family had felt precarious, as if they were teetering on a cliff. Before that she hadn't realized how fragile happiness was, how if you were careless, you could knock it over and shatter it. Anything her mother wanted, she had promised. As long as she would stay. She had been so afraid.

So every time her mother said *Do you want — ?* she had said yes. She knew what her parents had longed for, without them saying a word, and she had wanted them happy. She had kept her promise. And her mother had stayed. Read this book. *Yes.* Want this. Love this. *Yes.* Once, at the college museum, while Nath had pouted about missing the star show, she had spotted a nugget of amber with a fly trapped inside. "That's four million years old," Marilyn whispered, wrapping her arms around her daughter from behind. Lydia had stared until Nath, at last, had dragged them both away. Now she thought of the fly landing daintily in the pool of resin. Perhaps it had mistaken it for honey. Perhaps it hadn't seen the puddle at all. By the time it had realized its mistake, it was too late. It had flailed, and then it had sunk, and then it had drowned.

Ever since that summer, she had been so afraid — of losing her mother, of losing her father. And, after a while, the biggest fear of all: of losing Nath, the only one who understood the strange and brittle balance in their family. Who knew all that had happened. Who had always kept her afloat.

That long-ago day, sitting in this very spot on the dock, she had already begun to feel it: how hard it would be to inherit their parents' dreams. How suffocating to be so loved. She had felt Nath's hands on her shoulders and been almost grateful to fall forward, to let herself sink. Then, when her head had plunged beneath the surface, the water was like a slap. She had tried to scream and coldness slid down her throat, choking her. She'd stretched out her toes looking for ground and there wasn't any. Nothing when she reached out her arms. Only wetness and cold.

Then: warmth. Nath's fingers, Nath's hand, Nath's arm, Nath pulling her back up and her head coming up out of the lake, water dripping out of her hair into her eyes and her eyes stinging. Kick, Nath had told her. His hands held her up, surprising her with their strength, their sureness, and she had felt warm all over. His fingers caught hers and right then she had stopped being afraid.

Kick your legs. I've got you. *Kick.*

It had been the same ever since. Don't let me sink, she had thought as she reached for his hand, and he had promised not to when he took it. This moment, Lydia thought. This is where it all went wrong.

It was not too late. There on the dock, Lydia made a new set of promises, this time to herself. She will begin again. She will tell her mother: enough. She will take down the posters and put away the books. If she fails physics, if she never becomes a doctor, it will be all right. She will tell her mother that. And she will tell her mother, too: it's not too late. For anything. She will give her father back his necklace and his book. She will stop holding the silent phone to her ear; she will stop pretending to be someone she is not. From now on, she will do what *she* wants. Feet planted firmly on nothing, Lydia — so long enthralled by the dreams of others — could not yet imagine what that might be, but suddenly the universe glittered with possibilities. She will change everything. She will tell Jack she's sorry, that she'll never tell his secret. If he can be brave, so sure of who he is and what he wants, perhaps she can, too. She'll tell him that she understands.

And Nath. She will tell him that it's all right for him to leave. That she will be fine. That he's not responsible for her anymore, that he doesn't need to worry. And then she will let him go.

And as she made this last promise, Lydia understood what to do. How to start everything over again, from the beginning, so she would never again be afraid to be alone. What she must do to seal her promises, to make them real. Gently she lowered herself into the rowboat and loosed the rope. As she pushed away from the dock, she expected a surge of panic. It didn't come. Even once she had rowed, stroke by clumsy stroke, out onto the lake — far enough that the lamppost was just a dot, too small to contaminate the darkness around her — she felt strangely calm and confident. Above her the moon was coin-round, sharp and perfect. Beneath her the boat rocked so gently that she could hardly feel its motion. Looking up at the sky, she felt as if she were floating in space, completely untethered. She could not believe that anything was impossible.

In the distance, the light from the dock shone like a star. If she squinted, she could just make out the dim shape of the dock itself, the pale line of boards against the darker night. When she got a little closer, she thought, she would be able to see it perfectly: the boards worn smooth by generations of bare feet, the posts that held them up just above the surface of the water. Carefully, she got to her feet, spreading her arms as the boat swayed. It was not so far. She could do this, she was certain. All she had to do was kick. She would kick her way to the dock and reach up to the planks and pull herself up out of the water. Tomorrow morning, she would ask Nath about Harvard. What it was like there. She would ask him about the people he met, the classes he would take. She would tell him he'd have a wonderful time.

She looked down at the lake, which in the dark looked like nothing, just blackness, a great void spreading beneath her. It will be all right, she told herself, and she stepped out of the boat into the water.

TWELVE

All the way home, James thinks to himself: *It is not too late. It is not too late.* With each mile marker, he repeats it until he is back in Middlewood, the college and then the lake whipping by. When at last he pulls into their driveway, the garage door is open, and Marilyn's car nowhere in sight. Each breath sways him, no matter how hard he tries to keep upright. All these years he has remembered only: *She ran away.* He has taken this for granted: *She came back.* And: *She stayed.* As he reaches for the front doorknob, his legs wobble. It is not too late, he assures himself, but inside, he quavers. He cannot blame her if she has gone away again, this time for good.

In the front hall, a heavy silence greets him, like that of a funeral. Then he steps into the living room and sees a small figure huddled on the floor. Hannah. Curled in a ball, hugging herself with both arms. Eyes a watery red. He remembers suddenly a long-ago afternoon, two motherless children on a cold doorstep.

"Hannah?" he whispers, even as he feels himself collapsing, like an old building grown too weak to stand. His bag drops from his fingers to the floor. It's as if he's breathing through a straw. "Where's your mother?"

Hannah looks up. "Upstairs. Sleeping." Then — and this is what gives James his breath again — "I told her you would come home." Not smugly, not triumphantly. Just a fact, round and simple as a bead.

James sinks to the carpet beside his small daughter, silenced by gratitude, and Hannah considers whether to say more. For there is more, much more: how she and her mother had curled up together on Lydia's bed and cried and cried all afternoon, holding each other so close that their tears mixed, until her mother had fallen asleep. And how, half an hour ago, her brother had arrived home in a police car, rumpled and groggy and stinking to high heaven but strangely serene, and had gone straight up to his room and into bed. Hannah, peeking from behind the curtain, had seen Officer Fiske at the wheel, and late that night, Marilyn's car will quietly reappear in the driveway, washed, keys set neatly on the driver's seat. It can wait, she decides. She is used to keeping people's secrets, and there is something more pressing to tell her father.

She tugs at his arm, pointing upward, and James is surprised by how small her hands are, and how strong. "Look."

At first, so overcome with relief, so accustomed to ignoring his youngest, he sees nothing. It is not too late, he thinks, glancing up at the ceiling, clean and bright as a new sheet of paper in the late-afternoon sun. Not yet the end.

"Look," Hannah insists again, tipping his head with a peremptory hand. She has never dared to be so bossy, and James, startled, looks carefully and sees it at last: a white footprint against the off-white, as if someone has stepped in paint and then onto the ceiling, leaving one faint but perfect track. He has never noticed it before. Hannah catches his eye and the look on her face is serious and proud, as if she's discovered a new planet. It's ridiculous, really, a footprint on the ceiling. Unexplainable and pointless and magical.

Hannah giggles, and to James it sounds like the tinkling of a bell. A good sound. He laughs too, for the first time in weeks, and Hannah, suddenly bold, nestles close to her father. It feels familiar, the way she melts into him. It reminds him of something he's forgotten.

"You know what I'd do with your sister sometimes?" he says slowly. "When she was small, really small, even smaller than you. You know what I'd do?" He lets Hannah climb onto his back. Then he stands and turns side to side, feeling her weight shift against him. "Where's Lydia?" he says. "Where's Lydia?"

He'd say this, over and over, while she nestled her face in his hair and giggled. He could feel her hot little breath on his scalp, on the back of his ears. He'd wander the living room, peering behind furniture and around doorways. "I can hear her," he'd say. "I can see her foot." He'd squeeze her ankle, clutched tight in his hand. "Where is she? Where's Lydia? Where could she be?" He would twist his head and she'd duck, squealing, while he pretended not to notice her hair dangling over his shoulder. "There she is! There's Lydia!" He'd spin faster and faster, Lydia clinging tighter and tighter, until he collapsed on the rug, letting her roll, laughing, off his back. She never got tired of it. Found and lost and found again, lost in plain sight, pressed to his back, her feet clasped in his hands. What made something precious? Losing it and finding it. All those times he'd pretended to lose her. He sinks down on the carpet, dizzy with loss.

Then he feels small arms curling round his neck, the warmth of a small body leaning against him.

"Daddy?" Hannah whispers. "Will you do that again?"

And he feels himself rising, pushing himself back up to his knees.

There is so much more to do, so much yet to be mended. But for now, he thinks only of this, his daughter, here in his arms. He had forgotten what it was like to hold a child — to hold anyone — like that. How their weight sank into you, how they clung instinctively. How they trusted you. It is a long time before he is ready to let her go.

And when Marilyn wakes and comes downstairs, just as the light is fading, this is what she finds: her husband cradling their youngest in a circle of lamplight, a tender look of calm on his face.

"You're home," Marilyn says. All of them know it is a question.

"I'm home," James says, and Hannah rises on tiptoes, edging toward the door. She can feel the room is poised on the edge — of what, she's not sure, but she does not want to destroy this beautiful, sensitive balance. Accustomed to being overlooked, she sidles toward her mother, ready to slip by unnoticed. Then Marilyn touches a gentle hand to her shoulder, and Hannah's heels land on the floor with a surprised thump.

"It's all right," Marilyn says. "Your father and I just need to talk." Then — and Hannah flushes with delight — she kisses her on the head, right where the hair parts, and says, "We'll see you in the morning."

Halfway up the steps, Hannah pauses. From downstairs, she hears only a low murmur of voices, but for once she does not creep back down to listen. *We'll see you in the morning,* her mother had said, and she takes this as a promise. She tiptoes across the landing — past Nath's room, where behind the closed door her brother lies in a dreamless sleep, the remnants of the whiskey slowly steaming from his pores; past Lydia's room, which looks, in the dark, like nothing has changed, though nothing could be further from the truth; all the way up to her own room, where through the windows the lawn outside is just beginning to turn from inky blue to black. Her glow-in-the-dark clock reads just past eight, but it feels later, like the middle of the night, the darkness quiet and thick as a down comforter. She wraps that feeling around her. From up here, she can't hear her parents talking. But it's enough to know that they're there.

Downstairs, Marilyn lingers in the doorway, one hand on the jamb. James tries to swallow, but something hard and sharp lodges in his throat, like a fishbone. Once he had been able to read his wife's mood even from her back. By the tilt of her shoulders, by the shifting of her weight from left foot to right, he would have known what she was thinking. But it's been a long time since he looked at her carefully, and now, even face-to-face, all he can see are the faint wrinkles at the corners of her eyes, the faint wrinkles where her blouse has been crushed, then straightened.

"I thought you'd gone," she says at last.

When James's voice squeezes around the sharp thing in his throat, it comes out thin and scratched. "I thought you had."

And for the moment, this is everything they need to say.

Some things they will never discuss: James will never talk to Louisa again, and he will be ashamed of this for as long as he lives. Later, slowly, they will piece together other things that have never been said. He will show her the coroner's report; she will press the cookbook into his hands. How long it will be before he speaks to his son without flint in his voice; how long it will be before Nath no longer flinches when his father speaks. For the rest of the summer, and for years after that, they will grope for the words that say what they mean: to Nath, to Hannah, to each other. There is so much they need to say.

In this moment of silence, something touches James's hand, so light he can barely feel it. A moth, he thinks. The sleeve of his shirt. But when he looks down, he sees Marilyn's fingers curled over his, the merest curve as they squeeze. He has almost forgotten what it felt like, to touch her. To be forgiven even just this much. He bows his head and rests it on the back of her hand, overwhelmed with gratitude at having one more day.

In bed, they touch each other gently, as if it's the first time they've ever been together: his hand sliding carefully across the small of her back, her fingers careful and deliberate as she undoes the buttons of his shirt. Their bodies are older now; he can feel his shoulders sagging, he can see the silver scars from childbirth crisscrossing just below her waistline. In the dark they are careful of each other, as if they know they are fragile, as if they know they can break.

In the night, Marilyn wakes and feels her husband's warmth beside her, smells the sweet scent of him, like toast, mellowed and organic and bittersweet. How lovely it would be to stay curled here against him, to feel his chest rising and falling against her, as if it were her own breath. Right now, though, there is something else she must do.

At the doorway to Lydia's room, she pauses with her hand on the knob and rests her head against the frame, remembering that last evening together: how a glint of light had caught Lydia's water glass and she'd looked at her daughter across the table and smiled. Spinning out her daughter's future, brimming with confidence, she'd never imagined even for a second that it might not happen. That she might be wrong about anything.

That evening, that sureness, feels ancient now, like something grown small with the distance of years. Something she'd experienced before her children, before marrying, while she was still a child herself. She understands. There is nowhere to go but on. Still, part of her longs to go back for one instant — not to change anything, not even to speak to Lydia, not to tell her anything at all. Just to open the door and see her daughter there, asleep, one more time, and know all was well.

And when at last she opens the door, this is what she sees. The shape of her daughter there in the bed, one long lock of hair stretched across the pillow. If she looks hard, she can even see the rise and fall of the flowered comforter with each breath. She knows she's been granted a vision, and she tries not to blink, to absorb this moment, this last beautiful image of her daughter sleeping.

Someday, when she's ready, she'll pull the curtains, gather the clothing from the bureau, stack the books from the floor and pack them away. She'll wash the sheets, open desk drawers, empty the pockets of Lydia's jeans. When she does, she'll find only fragments of her daughter's life: coins, unsent postcards, pages torn from magazines. She'll pause over a peppermint, still twisted in cellophane, and wonder if it's significant, if it had meant something to Lydia, if it was just overlooked and discarded. She knows she'll find no answers. For now, she watches the figure in the bed, and her eyes fill with tears. It's enough.

■ ■ ■ ■

When Hannah comes downstairs, just as the sun is rising, she counts carefully: two cars in the driveway. Two rings of keys on the hall table. Five sets of shoes — one Lydia's — by the door. Though this last causes a sting, just between the collarbones, these sums bring her comfort. Now, peeking through the front window, she sees the Wolffs' door open and Jack and his dog emerge. Things will never be the same again; she knows this. But the sight of Jack and his dog, heading for the lake, brings her comfort, too. As if the universe is slowly returning to normal.

For Nath, though, at his window upstairs, the opposite is true. Awaking from his deep and drunken sleep, the whiskey purged from his body, everything seems new: the outlines of his furniture, the sunbeams slicing across the carpet, his hands before his face. Even the pain in his stomach — he hasn't eaten since yesterday's breakfast, and that, like the whiskey, is long gone — feels bright and clean and sharp. And now, across the lawn, he spots what he's sought every day for so long. Jack.

He does not bother to change his clothes,

or to grab his keys, or to think at all. He simply pulls on his tennis shoes and barrels down the stairs. The universe has given him this chance, and he refuses to squander it. As he yanks open the front door, Hannah is merely a startled blur in the front hall. For her part, she does not even bother to put on shoes. Barefoot, she darts after him, the asphalt still cool and damp against her feet.

"Nath," she calls. "Nath, it's not his fault." Nath doesn't stop. He's not running, just marching with a fierce and angry stride toward the corner, where Jack has just disappeared. He looks like the cowboys in their father's movies, determined and tense-jawed and unshakable in the middle of the deserted street. "Nath." Hannah grabs his arm, but he keeps walking, unmoved, and she scurries to keep up. They're at the corner now, and both of them see Jack at the same moment, sitting on the dock, arms wrapped around his knees, the dog lying beside him. Nath pauses to let a car go by and Hannah tugs his hand, hard.

"Please," she says. "Please." The car passes and Nath hesitates, but he's been waiting for answers so long. Now or never, he thinks, and he jerks himself free and crosses the street.

If Jack hears them coming, he doesn't

show it. He stays there, looking out over the water, until Nath is standing right over him.

"Did you think I wouldn't see you?" Nath says. Jack doesn't reply. Slowly, he gets to his feet, facing Nath with his hands tucked in the back pockets of his jeans. As if, Nath thinks, he's not even worth fighting. "You can't hide forever."

"I know it," Jack says. At his feet, the dog utters a low, moaning whine.

"Nath," Hannah whispers. "Let's go home. Please."

Nath ignores her. "I hope you were thinking about how sorry you are," he says.

"I am so sorry," Jack says. "About what happened to Lydia." A faint tremor shakes his voice. "About everything." Jack's dog backs away, huddling against Hannah's legs, and she's sure now that Nath's hands will unclench, that he'll turn around and leave Jack alone and walk away. Except he doesn't. For a second he seems confused — then being confused makes him angrier.

"Do you think that changes anything? It doesn't." The knuckles of his fists have gone white. "Tell me the truth. Now. I want to know. What happened between you two. What made her go out on that lake that night."

Jack half shakes his head, as if he doesn't

understand the question. "I thought Lydia told you —" His arm twitches, as if he's about to take Nath by the shoulder, or the hand. "I should have told you myself," he says. "I should have said, a long time ago —"

Nath takes a half-step closer. He is so close now, so close to understanding, that it makes him dizzy. "What?" he says, almost whispering, so quiet now that Hannah can hardly hear him. "That it's your fault?"

In the second before Jack's head moves, she understands what's going to happen: Nath needs a target, somewhere to point his anger and guilt, or he'll crumble. Jack knows this; she can see it in his face, in the way he squares his shoulders, bracing himself. Nath leans closer, and for the first time in a long time, he looks Jack right in the eye, brown on blue. Demanding. Begging. *Tell me. Please.* And Jack nods his head. *Yes.*

Then his fist smashes into Jack and Jack doubles over. Nath has never hit anyone before, and he'd thought it would feel good — powerful — his arm uncoiling like a piston. It doesn't. It feels like punching a piece of meat, something dense and heavy, something that does not resist. It makes him feel a little sick. And he'd expected a *pow,*

371

like in the movies, but there's hardly any noise at all. Just a thump, like a heavy bag falling to the floor, a faint little gasp, and that makes him feel sick, too. Nath readies himself, waiting, but Jack doesn't hit back. He straightens up, slowly, one hand on his stomach, his eyes watching Nath. He doesn't even make a fist, and this makes Nath feel sickest of all.

He had thought that when he found Jack, when his fist hit Jack's smug face, he'd feel better. That everything would change, that the hard glob of anger that has grown inside him would crumble like sand. But nothing happens. He can still feel it there, a lump of concrete inside, scraping him raw from the inside out. And Jack's face isn't smug, either. He'd expected at least defensiveness, maybe fear, but in Jack's eyes he sees nothing of that. Instead Jack looks at him almost tenderly, as if he's sorry for him. As if he wants to reach out and put his arms around him.

"Come on," Nath shouts. "Are you too ashamed to hit back?"

He grabs Jack by the shoulder and swings again and Hannah looks away just before his fist meets Jack's face. This time, a trickle of red drips from Jack's nose. He doesn't wipe it away, just lets it drip, from nostril to lip to chin.

"Stop it," she screams, and only when she hears her own voice does she realize she's crying, that her cheeks and her neck and even the collar of her T-shirt are sticky with tears. Nath and Jack hear it too. They both stare, Nath's fist still cocked, Jack's face and that tender look now turned on her. "Stop," she screams again, stomach churning, and she rushes between them, trying to shield Jack, battering her brother with her palms, shoving him away.

And Nath doesn't resist. He lets her push him, feels himself teetering, feet slipping on the worn-smooth wood, lets himself fall off the dock and into the water.

So this is what it's like, he thinks as the water closes over his head. He doesn't fight it. He holds his breath, stills his arms and legs, keeps his eyes open as he plummets. This is what it looks like. He imagines Lydia sinking, the sunlight above the water growing dimmer as he sinks farther, too. Soon he'll be at the bottom, legs and arms and the small of his back pressed to the sandy lake floor. He'll stay there until he can't hold his breath any longer, until the water rushes in to snuff out his mind like a candle. His eyes sting, but he forces them open.

This is what it's like, he tells himself. Notice this. Notice everything. Remember it.

But he's too familiar with the water. His body already knows what to do, the way it knows to duck at the corner of the staircase at home, where the ceiling is low. His muscles stretch and flail. On its own, his body rights itself, his arms claw at the water. His legs kick until his head breaks the surface and he coughs out a mouthful of silt, breathes cool air into his lungs. It's too late. He's already learned how not to drown.

He floats faceup, eyes closed, letting the water hold his weary limbs. He can't know what it was like, not the first time, not the last. He can guess, but he won't ever know, not really. What it was like, what she was thinking, everything she'd never told him. Whether she thought he'd failed her, or whether she wanted him to let her go. This, more than anything, makes him feel that she is gone.

"Nath?" Hannah calls, and then she's peering over the side of the dock, her face small and pale. Then another head appears — Jack's — and a hand stretches down toward him. He knows it's Jack's, and that when he gets there, he'll take it anyway.

And after he takes it, what will happen? He'll struggle home, dripping wet, muddy, knuckles raw from Jack's teeth. Beside him, Jack will be bruised and swollen, the front of his shirt a Rorschach of dark brown. Hannah will obviously have been crying; it will show in the streaks under her eyes, in the damp thwack of lashes against her cheek. Despite this, they will be strangely aglow, all of them, as if they've been scoured. It will take a long time to sort things out. Today they will have to deal with their parents, Jack's mother, too, all the questions: *Why were you fighting? What happened?* It will take a long time, because they won't be able to explain, and parents, they know, need explanations. They will change into dry clothing, Jack wearing one of Nath's old T-shirts. They will dab mercurochrome on Jack's cheek, on Nath's knuckles, making them look bloodier, like their wounds are reopened, even though in reality they are beginning to close.

And tomorrow, next month, next year? It will take a long time. Years from now, they will still be arranging the pieces they know, puzzling over her features, redrawing her outlines in their minds. Sure that they've got her right this time, positive in this moment that they understand her completely, at last. They will think of her often: when Marilyn opens the curtains in Lydia's room, opens the closet, and begins to take the clothing from the shelves. When their father, one day, enters a party and for the first time does not glance, quickly, at all the blond heads in the room. When Hannah begins to stand a little straighter, when she begins to speak a bit clearer, when one day she flicks her hair behind her ear in a familiar gesture and wonders, for a moment, where she got it. And Nath. When at school people ask if he has siblings: *two sisters, but one died;* when, one day, he looks at the small bump that will always mar the bridge of Jack's nose and wants to trace it, gently, with his finger. When, a long, long time later, he stares down at the silent blue marble of the earth and thinks of his sister, as he will at every important moment of his life. He doesn't know this yet, but he senses it deep down in his core. So much will happen, he thinks, that I would want to tell you.

For now, when he opens his eyes at last, he focuses on the dock, on Jack's hand, on Hannah. From where he floats, her upside-down face is right-side up, and he dog-paddles toward her. He doesn't want to dive underwater and lose sight of her face.

AUTHOR'S NOTE

I've taken a few minor historical liberties: the cover of *How to Win Friends and Influence People* that I describe in the novel is an amalgamation of several different editions' covers, though the text is all real. Likewise, the quotes from *Betty Crocker's Cookbook* are from my mother's own 1968 edition, although Marilyn's mother would have used an earlier edition.

ACKNOWLEDGMENTS

Enormous thanks to my agent, Julie Barer, who waited patiently for this novel for six years and who always had more faith in it (and me) than I did. I thank my lucky stars for her. William Boggess, Anna Wiener, Gemma Purdy, and Anna Knutson Geller at Barer Literary have been a delight to work with, and I couldn't have been in better hands.

My editors at The Penguin Press, Andrea Walker and Ginny Smith Younce, helped make this book immeasurably better and guided me every step of the way. Sofia Groopman brightened my day literally every time we emailed. Jane Cavolina, my copyeditor; Lisa Thornbloom, my proofreader; and Barbara Campo and the production team straightened out my myriad inconsistencies and were exceptionally patient about my use of italics. My publicist, Juliana Kiyan, has been a dynamic and tireless advocate, and I'm deeply grateful to Ann Godoff, Scott Moyers, Tracy Locke, Sarah Hutson, Brittany Boughter, and everyone else at The Penguin Press and Penguin Random House for bringing this book into the world with such enthusiasm and love.

People often insist that writing can't be taught, but I learned a tremendous amount — about both writing and the writing life — from my teachers. Patricia Powell helped me take my work seriously in my first real writing workshop. Wendy Hyman first suggested the idea of an MFA, and I will forever be in her debt for that. Eliezra Schaffzin offered crucial early encouragement and support, and my incredibly generous professors at Michigan — Peter Ho Davies, Nicholas Delbanco, Matthew Klam, Eileen Pollack, and Nancy Reisman — continue to be a source of wisdom and guidance.

I owe a huge debt to my informal teachers — my writer friends — as well. I'm especially grateful to my fellow Michigan MFAers, especially Uwem Akpan, Jasper Caarls, Ariel Djanikian, Jenni Ferrari-Adler, Joe Kilduff, Danielle Lazarin, Taem Lim, Peter Mayshle, Phoebe Nobles, Marissa Perry, Preeta Samarasan, Brittani Sonnenberg, and Jesmyn Ward. Ayelet Amittay,

Christina McCarroll, Anne Stameshkin, and Elizabeth Staudt deserve double — triple, quadruple — thanks for reading early drafts of this novel over the years and cheering me on. Jes Haberli is not only a trusted sounding board but a much-needed voice of sanity.

Writing is a lonely business, and I'm immensely grateful for the communities that have offered me fellowship along the way. The staff of *Fiction Writers Review* reminded me, always, that *fiction matters,* and the Bread Loaf Writers' Conference introduced me to many friends and literary idols, including the Voltrons. In Boston, Grub Street adopted me into its warm and welcoming writing family — extra helpings of thanks to Christopher Castellani for bringing me into the fold. My writers' group, the Chunky Monkeys (Chip Cheek, Jennifer De Leon, Calvin Hennick, Sonya Larson, Alexandria Marzano-Lesnevich, Whitney Scharer, Adam Stumacher, Grace Talusan, and Becky Tuch) provides boundless encouragement and merciless critiques. And whenever I get stuck, Darwin's Ltd. in Cambridge magically gets me going again with hot tea, the best sandwiches in town, and (somehow) always exactly the right music on the stereo.

Finally, my heartfelt thanks to my friends and family, who have shaped me in innumerable ways. Katie Campbell, Samantha Chin, and Annie Xu have been cheerleaders and confidantes for more than two decades. Many more friends have been there for me along the way than I can list here; you know who you are — thank you. Carol, Steve, and Melissa Fox graciously welcomed me into their word-loving home more than a decade ago. And my family has been an continual source of support, even when they weren't *totally* sure what to make of this writing thing; thank you to my parents, Daniel and Lily Ng, and my sister, Yvonne Ng, for letting me (and helping me) find my way. My husband, Matthew Fox, not only encouraged me at every step, he took on endless responsibilities to make it possible for me to write. Without him, this book would not have been possible. And last but not least, thank you to my son, who graciously puts up with his daydreaming mother, constantly makes me laugh, and helps keep everything in perspective: you will always be my proudest accomplishment.